LEAVING BENNET BEHIND
volume 3

Pursued

CW01425963

SARAH JOHNSON

Cover Design by: Peculiar World Designs
Section Dividers by: vectorbeast

ISBN-10: 1511756047
ISBN-13: 978-1511756044

DEDICATION

To my husband of sixteen years, Paul. You are truly my own Mr Darcy. Without your love and support I would have never found the courage to complete this journey. *Thank you!*

TABLE OF CONTENTS

ACKNOWLEDGMENTS

While I would love to personally thank each person who has read the original version of this story online, I know such a task is not possible. Every comment written, and every nudge I received was what gave me the courage to eventually pursue publishing this story. So to all my readers – *Thank you!*

There are six ladies I would like to acknowledge by name, the first being Brenda. In her quest to draw new authors out of the woodwork she began a writing challenge on her forum. It was with her encouragement that I first put pen to paper – or rather, hit that first keystroke – thus beginning this journey. She has been behind me from the start and has reassured me every step of the way. I cannot effectively express how much I appreciate her friendship and guidance. *Thank you, Brenda!*

Two others who deserve my personal gratitude would be my original editing team – Linnea and Anita. Both of these ladies were willing to take on the enormous task of helping a new writer, and for their time and patience I am truly grateful. When they signed on none of us knew where this story would even lead, and yet they have stuck with me through it all, giving me wonderful feedback and ideas along the way. They have both become so integral to this story that I know it would not be the same without their help. So to both of them I must give a heartfelt – *Thank You!*

Also there are three who have taken on the task of helping me with athe editing for turning this story into a series. I enjoy hearing all their input, and look forward to finishing the three books to come with them. So to Rose, Kathy, and Zoe – *Thank You!*

CHAPTER I

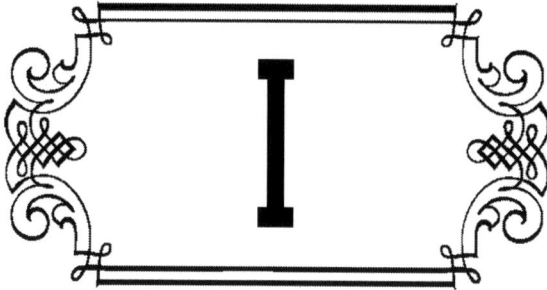

Friday, April 3, 1812

Mary had to admit, Georgiana's carriage was well-sprung. More so than any in which she had ever ridden, especially her father's that bounced all around. She was fortunate enough to be in such luxury for the trip, unlike the rest of her family who now traveled directly behind them. They would stay with the Gardiners for only a week, but Mary was to stay at Darcy House the entire Season, and Elizabeth and her husband talked of her going to Pemberley with them as well. It was an experience she would not soon forget.

She looked over to her friend who lay in the bed fashioned for her comfort while traveling. Georgiana was fast asleep, the velvet, fur-lined blanket she adored, with the Darcy crest embroidered in the center, was tucked in around her and pulled up to her chin, keeping her warm. It was a peaceful sight.

Mary's eyes moved to the two who sat across from her. Elizabeth was leaning against her husband who had his arm wrapped around her shoulders. She, too, was asleep, her hand resting gently on her expanding mid-section. Mary smiled when she thought of the couple having their first baby in the autumn.

Oh, what a memorable evening when the news of their expanding family was revealed to all! It was suspected by their friends and family for many weeks leading up to the announcement, but no one would dare ask until the couple was ready to tell their secret. Everyone knew they only awaited the arrival of the newly wedded Bingleys to complete those Elizabeth wished to be present for their announcement. It was no surprise, but felicitations were heard all around and a flourish of emotion from Mrs Bennet reminded them all quickly just how loved the baby would be. What was a surprise that evening was when her mother revealed the contents of a letter from the Gardiners in which it was said they too would be having another child around the same time as Elizabeth and Darcy. Mary chuckled to herself when her next thought was that Jane and Bingley may have a similar announcement by summer.

Darcy looked up from his book, his face questioning Mary, though he did not speak. When he saw her looking towards where Elizabeth's hand rested, he too smiled, then he pulled his wife a little closer, drew the rug up over her shoulder from where it had fallen, and went back to reading his book in silence.

Mary was too excited to rest, so she pulled her journal from her bag and flipped through all the entries she had made since her last birthday when she received it. She would need a new one soon—she thought this one might last until her birthday again in June, but maybe not. She had pin money saved up for her Season in London though, so she would just have to purchase one if she ran out of pages.

Her thumb stopped on one entry, and her eyes scanned the words.

October 1, 1811

Mama is overjoyed with a new addition to the neighborhood. It is said a single gentleman of some wealth has taken on Netherfield Park, and Mama is determined he will be smitten with Jane. Who wouldn't be though? She is the sweetest person, and only an ogre would not be taken with her beauty. I just hope he is as amiable as Mama wishes him to be.

As it turned out, the single gentleman *was* smitten with her—so much so that they were now married. She turned back a few pages to an entry a few weeks before.

> September 18, 1811
>
> What a birthday Kitty has had this year! Papa's
> hound had her puppies today. Just how many pups
> can one dog have? I have never seen such a large
> litter before—eleven! I wonder if it is a record.
> Papa says they will be the talk of hunting season…

She smiled. Just as her father predicted, they were the talk of gatherings for many months, causing quite the quarrel among some of the gentlemen when they were old enough to be sold. She again flipped through the pages.

> October 31, 1811
>
> Today was the first day of Lizzy's engagement to
> Mr Darcy. Not to be outdone however, Mr Bingley
> asked to court Jane. These two brave gentlemen
> will, I fear, soon find out of what mettle they are
> made. Mama was full of anxiety after they left this
> morning.
>
> I wonder—will I ever marry?

Mary knew exactly what this entry contained. She had flipped back to it and read her list of requirements in a mate many times since that night when it was penned. Her finger drew down to the bottom of the page.

> …what if I decide I do want to marry and yet no
> gentleman will have me? I know what torment
> Charlotte Lucas receives from the neighborhood for
> not marrying by her age…

Sarah Johnson

She could not help but chuckle at how it had all changed for Charlotte, and so quickly. Just yesterday she was married, and to an earl at that! Having stayed at Netherfield the last month where the earl was also a visitor, Mary watched as the romance between the two was unfolded, and she could not help but feel a pang at hoping she too would have that one day as well. Naturally her next thoughts turned to Lord Primrose, and her body reacted as it always did—her heart began to beat more rapidly and her palms began to sweat.

She shook her head slightly, determined to not think of him at this moment. Her eyes returned to her journal, but she could not stop herself from turning just a couple of pages back and reading the familiar messy entry, her first about *him*.

October 30, 1811

How could I have known what a tale I would have when I awoke this morning? If only we did not need more flowers for the tables tonight, but we did, so I decided to search for them on my own. What a disaster! I slid down a muddy embankment, nearly falling into the river, and lost my spectacles! Papa has joked often that without them I could not see a tree standing in front of me, but I learned today it is the absolute truth. As I sat on the side of the road, covered in mud and anxious as to how I was to return home, I was sent a savior—*Alexander Fitzwilliam.*

Unfortunately I had to ride on his horse, but he did offer to accompany me when he saw how frightened I am of the beasts. I can feel my cheeks flushing even now as I recall the terrifying moment when the horse moved unexpectedly and I, in turn, buried my face into the gentleman's chest. Oh, what mortification I felt! How could I act so wantonly? This gentleman only meant to help me home; I am certain he did not wish to be accosted by me in a moment of fright.

4

If I am to be truthful though, and I know I must
be, even if only here within these private pages
of my journal, the moment was one I shall never
forget. He drew his arms around me in an embrace
I could only call magical, and I began to calm as his
soothing voice washed over me. I have never felt
such emotions welling within me before. It felt as
if I belonged there his embrace. Even just writing
those words I can once again feel the warmth of his
presence around me and his eyes piercing into my
soul. I was so close I could see small flecks of gold
in his bright green eyes. I now sit in my chambers,
having washed the mud away, and I cannot but
wonder who this gentleman is. I have never seen
him before, nor heard his name in conversation
with others, and have no idea if I will ever see him
again.

Mary's heart pounded in her ears, and she knew her cheeks were aflame,
but she could not stop reading. She glanced up to see that no one was
looking at her, then continued on with the entry she made just a few hours
later.

He is a viscount! <u>A VISCOUNT</u>! And even
worse than that, he is Mr Darcy's cousin! I felt
such mortification as never before when he was
introduced to me tonight at the dinner party. He
even returned my spectacles! Knowing how much
mud was on me when I returned home, I am certain
he ruined his clothes today just searching for them.
Why would he do that for me, a stranger?

Even worse than the headache I had from not
having my spectacles for so long today was the ache
that rose within me at hearing him tell his cousin
about meeting me. *"She had no bonnet, and her dress
was at least six inches deep in mud. How she could have
thought to be out like that is beyond me. She looked almost
wild..."*

Mary saw the tear streaked ink of the sentence that cut so deeply into her heart, and she felt her eyes begin to fill with tears even now. She must refrain from reading about him any longer, so instead she put her journal back into her bag and turned, curling into the corner of the carriage and drawing the rug on her lap up over her arms. As she dried her eyes she hoped Darcy did not see her tears, for she knew if he did he would question his wife later and Elizabeth would then ask her about it. This aching in her soul was not something she could discuss with anyone. Even after all these months, and many interactions since, she felt the stab of pain as those words he spoke that night echoed within her.

She was determined to not let it affect her any longer. She was to have her second Season, her first in London, and she would enjoy all the diversions without a second thought to what the viscount thought of her. Even if he was to be around quite often, she could learn to ignore the reactions her body had to him. Perhaps she would even find the person who she would marry while she was in Town?

***

Saturday, April 4, 1812

Lady Rosebery entered the breakfast room and saw her eldest son sitting at the table pushing the food around his plate with his fork. She walked over to him and leaned down to kiss his cheek, "I pray you have had a pleasant birthday so far?"

He looked up at her absently, "Oh, good morning Mother, and thank you."

She sat in her seat and nodded to the footman as she placed the serviette in her lap. The plate before her held her usual–a piece of delicate French bread. A cup of steaming chocolate was placed before her to accompany the soft confection. She cut into the tender bread and took a bite, noticing her son was still not eating.

"Is something wrong, Alex?" she asked. "Did the cook not live up to his usual high standard today?"

"Wha…?" Alex said distractedly, "What was that Mother?"

"Is the meal to your satisfaction?" she replied.

Looking at the mess he had made of the food on his plate, he put his fork down. "It is adequate–I am just not hungry, I guess."

She looked to the doorway where her husband stood observing their son. His gaze met hers with a knowing look and he entered the room. "It is hard to believe we are old enough to have a son in his thirties," the earl said, patting Alex on the back.

Alex chuckled, "You make it sound as if I am *very* old, not *just* turning thirty today."

Hugh sat beside his wife and reached for her hand, drawing it to his lips for a simple kiss. "I remember just what I was doing on this day thirty years ago." Letting go of her hand and nodding to the footman who set his plate on the table before him, he looked towards Alex. "My best friend, George Darcy, later that year to marry my dear sister, Anne, had the unfortunate job of keeping me from your mother's bedside. We nearly came to blows twice, and yet he still stayed beside me until they came out to say you were born. It was a long night, but the morning brought a fresh hope of what our future held."

Alex smiled and thought to himself, *I wonder if my long night will be coming to an end soon and bringing a fresh hope for my own future?*

Lady Rosebery, having finished, stood, interrupting his thoughts. "I am to accompany Mrs Darcy, Mrs Bingley, and Miss Bennet to the shops today for some last minute additions to their ball gowns." Once again kissing her son's cheek and smiling at him, she said, "I will see you later."

<hr/>

"Look at these," Elizabeth said to Mary as she held up a pair of lilac colored, satin, ball length gloves. "Do you think they will match your gown?"

Pulling out the swatch of material from her reticule, Mary held it up to the light shining in from the window. "Hmmmm... I am not sure." Turning, she asked, "What do you think Lady Rosebery?"

She took the gloves and material, comparing them carefully. "Is this the under layer of your gown?" she asked.

"Yes," Mary replied. "The lilac is layered beneath a sheath of light cream lace, and darker purple flowers are embroidered along the sleeves and bodice, with a six inch border of the darker purple on the bottom of the skirt."

Lady Rosebery chose, instead, a pair of cream gloves from the table, "Perhaps it would be best to accent the lace color instead of trying to match the gown itself."

Looking at the satin gloves, Mary smiled, "I think I like that color best. Thank you."

Helen handed her the gloves, "I have enjoyed shopping with you ladies today. It is a shame I never had a daughter with whom I could enjoy such activities."

Jane smiled and looked at the others gathered around them waiting, "We have enjoyed having your company as well, my lady." Addressing Mary, she said, "I believe we have all we came to find. Are you ready now, Mary?"

"I have one more item on my list."

"If you all wish to leave, I can remain with Miss Bennet and return her to Darcy House when her purchases are completed," Helen offered.

"Are you certain? You do not mind?" Elizabeth asked.

"No, my dear, I do not mind at all." she wound her arm through Mary's, "Why, Miss Bennet is a lovely young lady and I quite enjoy her company."

Elizabeth said, "I *am* sorry we cannot stay any longer, but Jane and I are to practice our curtsies and I promised William I would not overtax myself today, especially with tonight's dinner."

"Are you able to perform your curtsy adequately?"

Elizabeth looked at her older sister. "Jane has been able to improve upon my woefully inadequate skills quite well, but if I am to not embarrass my husband, I must keep practicing, especially with my balance being off right now," she indicated her expanding abdomen.

"Who are your sponsors?" Lady Rosebery asked.

"My husband's great aunt is sponsoring me," Elizabeth replied.

Helen chuckled, "Dear Mrs. Darcy... she helped several of my friends' daughters prepare for their presentations as well. With her guidance, I believe you will do very well." She turned to Jane, "And who is sponsoring you, Mrs Bingley?"

Jane replied, "My sponsor was to be Mrs Hurst, but with the recent addition of Amelia to their family, they will not be in Town this year. So, instead, Mrs Preston has taken on the task."

"Oh how marvelous! I think you are both in very capable hands." She nodded her head and smiled, "You two may leave your sister in *my* capable hands, as we finish our shopping, and then maybe we will have a bit of tea. I will have her home in time to dress for supper... or, if you prefer," she said, looking at Mary, "we can have your clothes sent to my house and you can dress there?"

Blushing at such attention, Mary replied, "I would like that, my lady."

"It is settled then," Helen said. "We will see you all tonight at my house for our special supper, and, if you see my son, remember not to mention the surprise to him. Will you need my carriage?"

"My husband is to send one for us; in fact I see our footman at the door now," Elizabeth said, looking over Jane's shoulder towards the door. Elizabeth assured Mary she would have her things sent over to the Fitzwilliam's house, then she and Jane bid them farewell and left.

Helen turned to Mary, "What is it you still need?"

"Shoe roses, my lady."

Helen had a determined look in her eye, "I know just the place on Piccadilly, and they may even have something to match the dark purple in your dress. Come," she said as she led the younger girl to her waiting carriage.

While they were looking at the ribbons made into delicate roses, trying to decide which would look best, Mary asked the countess, "May I ask you a question?"

"Of course, my dear."

Choosing one pair of flowers and setting the others back down, she replied, "I do not know what the custom in Town is, as this is my first Season here, but in the country I would not dare show up at a birthday supper without something small to give to the person we were celebrating."

Squeezing her hand in a motherly fashion, Helen answered, "It is not necessary for you to bring a gift, but if you feel you must, then something small would do."

"I would feel awkward not having *something*."

"Then maybe we can find just the right thing," Helen led her over to a display of men's handkerchiefs and fob ribbons.

Mary's eye was drawn to one handkerchief in particular. It had tiny blue and yellow primroses embroidered along the edge of two opposite corners, with a larger primrose on one corner. Picking it up, she fingered the flowers, remembering the handkerchief the viscount wrapped her spectacles in the day they met, "Do you think he would like this?"

Looking at the handkerchief, then at the girls face, Helen answered, "I think it is the perfect gift."

"I will buy this and these" Mary said to the sales person, handing over the handkerchief and shoe roses. She pulled a coin from her reticule, and the two women were soon on their way back to Lady Rosebery's house for tea.

Sarah Johnson

CHAPTER

II

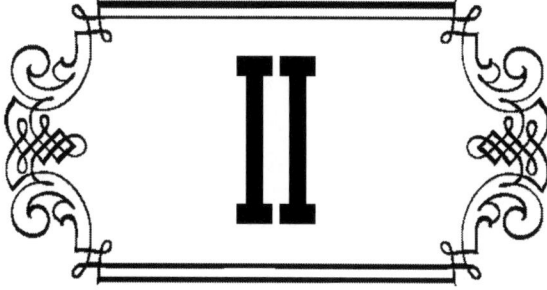

They sat in Lady Rosebery's private sitting room, tea tray laid out on the table between them, when Alex passed the door. Hearing his mother talking to someone inside, he knocked.

"Enter," Helen called out.

When he opened the door he did not expect to see Mary, and his surprise showed.

"Would you like to join us for tea?" his mother asked.

Looking to Mary's face to see how she felt about such an invitation, he smiled when she did not seem displeased at his presence. "I do not wish to inconvenience you or your guest…"

"Nonsense, there is plenty here," Helen's hand sweeping over the vast array of treats and sandwiches on the tray.

"Are you certain you do not mind?" he asked, looking directly at Mary.

She glanced down at her hands folded in her lap, timidly answering, "I do not mind, my lord."

Alex sat on the sofa across from the two chairs in which the ladies sat. Mary accepted the tea Helen offered her, then she blushed when she realized *he* was watching her every move. *Why does he stare at me? I know he is not drawn to my looks, as he called me 'almost wild looking' nearly upon our first meeting, but I cannot imagine what he is looking at when he stares as me so.*

They were interrupted when Mrs Gibson, the housekeeper, came to request Lady Rosebery's assistance with a detail for supper. Looking to her son, she asked, "You do not mind entertaining my guest for a minute, do you?"

He bowed his head, "Of course not, Mother."

"I will return momentarily," she assured Mary as she joined the housekeeper in the hall. They talked for a minute then the two walked off towards the kitchens to take care of a problem that had arisen.

Alex cleared his throat, setting his cup down, "I am sorry I was unable to speak with you when I was in Meryton a few days ago."

Mary looked down at her tea. She slowly stirred it, hoping it would settle her stomach, "I presumed you were too busy to stay for long."

"Yes, as a matter of fact, I was. A… *business venture* of sorts, I suppose you could call it… has kept my attention these last few weeks, and an unexpected problem drew me back to Town earlier than I had planned." Looking at her, he said, "I meant to take my leave of you, but the express I received spoke of an urgency which dictated my leaving early yesterday morning. I had every intention of staying long enough to accompany you all to Town yesterday afternoon."

"You did?" she asked tentatively.

Quietly, he answered, "Yes, I did." Looking at the door and not hearing anyone coming yet, he continued, "In fact, I was looking forward to speaking with you about something, but did not have the chance."

Nervously, she said, "I cannot imagine what you could want with me, my lord."

Noticing her return to formality, he knew he would have to be careful how he worded this request. "I… well, you see, because of the ball on Monday being in honour of my birthday, I am expected to lead off the dancing. I enjoyed our last dance, and meant to ask if you were already promised for the first set?"

Mary looked at him, shocked at what she heard. This was now the third time he asked for her hand in the opening dance at a ball, this time being as the lead couple. She felt her head spin and everything around her seemed to slow down. "*But, you said my looks were wild,*" she mumbled under her breath, not sure what she felt at such a question.

His mother's entrance back into the room stopped their conversation. Clearing his throat, he picked up his tea and took a sip, making a face at the flavor. "This blend of tea is a bit too bitter for my tastes, Mother."

"Perhaps you should add a little honey to it," Lady Rosebery said, indicating the server for Mary to pass to her son.

Her hands shook as she picked up the dish and held it out to him, his fingers brushing hers when he took it. Alex carefully added a little into his tea then held it out to her again. Helen saw Mary's shaking hands and helped her set it back down on the tray.

"Are you well, Miss Bennet?" she asked.

Looking at her host, she took a deep breath, and responded, "Y-y-yes, I will be… well."

"Maybe you need some air?" Helen asked.

"Yes," she answered, "I think that would help."

Alex knew he needed to finish their conversation and took this opening to do just that. "May I escort you outside to the garden, Miss Bennet?"

Mary was just about to refuse when she looked at him. His eyes pleaded with her, and although she did not know why, she accepted his offer.

Helen saw the look on her son's face also, but chose not to say anything. She would have to watch him a little while longer to be certain, but she thought she saw a regard in his eyes for this quiet girl who sat beside her.

Alex stood, putting out his arm out towards Mary. She accepted, though she kept her distance. Alex then turned to his mother, "Would you care to join us?"

With a keen eye, she replied, "If you do not mind, I have a few things I must see to this afternoon."

Alex smiled slightly, and Mary nodded her assent. "We will return in a short while."

The silence between the two was growing more strained with each step they took, until finally Alex said, "Miss Bennet, I do not mean to cause you such distress, but you did not answer my request earlier." He smiled as he added, "I dare not assume I have your hand for the set, as we both know where that has led us in the past."

Sitting on the bench he indicated, Mary quietly replied, "I do not know how to respond, my lord. You puzzle me greatly."

He was intrigued at her statement, "How so?"

Mary looked down at the ground. "I just do not know your intent, my lord."

Alex knew he must take things slowly or he would frighten her. "My intent is simply to dance with you again, madam." She looked up at him, but did not answer, so he sat beside her, "As I have yet to garner the response for which I greatly hoped, I will ask you again—may I have your hand for the first set at the ball, Miss Bennet?"

"I am sorry—but I must deny you, my lord," she responded sharply.

"Are you already promised for the first? If so I will ask for another," he said dejectedly.

"No... I just... I cannot... no," she said nervously before she stood and ran from the garden through the side gate.

"Miss Bennet," he called after her, his eyes following her form as she passed between the two houses, crossed the street, narrowly escaping a mishap with a horse, and entered the park across the street.

"What did you do to the poor girl," he heard Fitz ask.

"I just asked if she would join me for the first set at the ball," Alex answered. "I did not mean to frighten her, but she refused and ran off."

Fitz nodded, "I told you this would be difficult."

"More than you know," Alex said, then turned towards the door. "Excuse me; I must go after her," he stated.

He immediately felt a firm hand on his shoulder. His brother's eyes caught his as he said, "No, let me. There is no telling where she will run to if she is frightened yet again."

Alex nodded in understanding, "Yes, of course you are correct."

Mary was sitting on the bench facing the pond when she felt something drape around her shoulders. Looking up, she saw the kind face of the colonel looking down at her. "I did not want you to become too chilled," he said of the cape that now lay around her shoulders. Indicating the bench on which she sat, he asked, "May I join you?"

"Yes, of course," Mary quietly answered as she slid down to one end and pulled the cape around her arms.

The two sat in silence for a few minutes before Fitz replied, "I always said I wanted a sister."

"I always wished for an older brother."

"As a younger brother myself, I must ask, why an *older* brother; why not a *younger* brother?"

"I have always wanted someone who could look after me, show me what to do and how to handle situations with which I am not very familiar. Someone to whom I would not have to say anything, they would just know what I needed."

"You do not have that in any of your sisters?" he asked.

Mary looked back to the pond, "No; I love my sisters dearly, but they do not understand me very well at all."

"If you would allow me the freedom, I would like to offer you some advice that I am certain an *older brother* would say to you," Fitz said.

Mary responded quietly, "What is that Colonel?"

"You cannot truly know someone's intent if you are unwilling to give them a chance."

"But what if I am uncertain if the person truly deserves a chance?"

Fitz looked out to the ducks swimming around and responded quietly, "How do you know he does not if you have not given him the opportunity to show you his character?"

"I have heard of his character from others, and it is not someone with whom I care to be associated," Mary said firmly.

"Do not believe all you hear unless it comes from a reputable source.

Gossip is what the Ton thrives upon, and from what I have found, rarely does it contain more than just a thread of the truth. If you truly want answers, then you must go directly to the source and ask, unless of course you are worried of the answer you will receive."

"I do not know what frightened me in the garden, but I knew I had to get away," Mary replied.

"Please give him a chance, Miss Bennet. I have a good idea of what you have heard through the rumor mills, and I can assure you my brother's character is not what they would have you believe." Fitz stood and stepped in front of her. "I will also caution you not to leave the house without an escort. This is not the country where you are safe to wander about. Please allow me to escort you back, either to Rosebery House or Darcy House."

"I am sorry, sir; I did not realize…" Mary started to say.

"I do not mean to be harsh, but please take this rebuke to heart—the streets of London are not safe for a young lady to traverse without an escort. I would not have you hurt when you are here to enjoy the Season." At her nod of acceptance, he put out his arm and continued, "Now, do you wish to return immediately, or would a stroll around this pond do you some good?"

"I think I will just return to Darcy House, sir," she answered, standing and placing her arm through his. "Oh, but my trunk has already been sent to Rosebery House, and your mother expects me there this afternoon…"

"It is no trouble to have it returned, if that is what you desire," he quipped, "it is but three houses down, and the footman can make quick work of it."

"Thank you; you have given me a lot to think about before tonight when I will see your brother again."

"Speaking on my own behalf, I hope you determine that dancing a set with him would be a good start to learning who he truly is."

"Your own behalf, sir? I do not understand," Mary replied.

"My brother can be quite brooding at times," Fitz replied. "In fact, he has been distracted since coming back from Hertfordshire last year. I am certain it has to do with *someone* who has caught his attention while he was there."

Shock evident in her voice, Mary replied, "Me? Oh Colonel, I can assure you, you are wrong."

"Am I?"

"Your brother thinks me to be *'almost wild'*; I heard him say so himself," Mary explained.

"Then why would he ask for your hand in an opening set three times, madam?" Fitz countered.

"I do not know," Mary said; "*I truly do not know.*"

CHAPTER

III

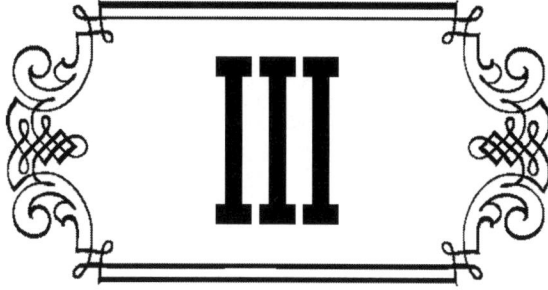

Alex sat amongst those gathered to celebrate his birthday, trying not to stare at Mary. She looked lovely this evening. Her pale yellow dress set off her dark hair and light skin. She would not meet his eyes though, so he kept his distance; she made it very clear this afternoon that she did not wish to dance with him, the first or any other set.

"Lady Catherine de Bourgh to see you, Lord and Lady Rosebery," the butler said as the grand lady came into the room, followed by a smaller, almost frail young lady behind her.

"Lady Catherine!" Helen said, standing. "We did not know you to be in Town."

"Of course I am in Town," she said, looking over those gathered around the room. "Are you not going to introduce me to your guests?"

"Yes of course," Hugh said, taking his sister's arm. "May I introduce you to Mrs Darcy and her family; Mr and Mrs Bennet and their daughters, Miss Bennet, Miss Katherine, and Miss Lydia; Mrs Bennet's brother, Mr Gardiner, and his wife; and some neighbors of theirs from Meryton, Sir

William and Lady Lucas, along with two of their children, Mr Lucas and Miss Lucas."

"Lucas—would you be any relation to Lord Ashbourne's new *wife?*" she addressed Sir William.

"Yes, Lady Ashbourne is their eldest daughter," Hugh answered. "We have all just arrived in Town yesterday from attending the wedding."

"There seem to be many stories of the couple already," Lady Catherine said.

"It was a lovely ceremony, Lady Catherine," Lady Lucas replied.

"Hmm, I am certain it will be nothing to my own daughter's wedding," she said condescendingly, turning her attention immediately to her nephews. "Do I receive no greeting from my nephews?"

"I am sorry—how lovely to see you, Aunt Catherine," Fitz said, bowing to his aunt and kissing her hand. As he turned, he winked at Anne, making her blush.

Alex accepted her outstretched hand and bowed, "Hello Aunt Catherine." Turning, he walked to Anne, lifting her hand as he bowed, "I pray your journey went well?"

"Tolerable," Anne answered him.

The butler announced supper was served, and Alex held out his arm to his cousin, following the others to the dining room. The two unexpected places were added quickly to the table, and Alex led Anne to the seat next to him with Fitz on her other side. When everyone was seated, he leaned near her and quietly asked, "Are you truly well?"

"I am a bit weak, but nothing a little rest will not cure." Touching his hand in a compassionate manner, she said, "Truly, do not worry about me."

Fitz leaned over towards the pair, "Is there anything amiss?"

"No," Alex assured him.

"Good," he said, looking at Anne. "Are you to be in Town for the Season?"

"Yes, my mother decided just two days ago. I was unable to get a note of warning to you before she insisted we come unannounced for supper. We did not know you were entertaining until we arrived."

"It is my brother's birthday," Fitz replied.

"Oh, I am so sorry—I forgot completely! Please do accept my felicitations, Alex."

"It is of no consequence, but thank you," he said, cutting into the tender piece of meat on his plate.

Lady Catherine's unexpected presence would not be rewarded by her sister-in-law, so she found herself seated between Miss Bennet and Mrs Gardiner. Looking at the older woman, she said, "*Gardiner*—I recognize that name, but cannot place it. Where is your husband's estate?"

"We do not own an estate, my lady," she answered. "My husband has a warehouse on Gracechurch Street called *Gardiner's Goods.*"

Taken aback at having been seated next to a tradesman's wife, she immediately put her nose in the air and turned to the person on her other side, "And *who* are you again?"

"I am Mrs Darcy's younger sister," Mary replied.

"Yes, I thought so; you resemble her in many ways," Lady Catherine replied. "Just how she earned the place beside my nephew I shall never understand. Her *presumptuous* nature will not make her way into the Ton easier."

"*Presumptuous*, my lady?"

"Yes, *presumptuous*," she answered harshly. "What else would you call someone who aspires to marry so far above their own situation? I cannot approve of such a match. At least my other nephew will be marrying into an old and well established family."

"Your other nephew?" Mary asked, trying not to look at the viscount.

"Yes, as I am sure you have been informed; the two were formed for each other from their cradles. It has been the family's wish for many years to join the two estates of Dalmeny and Rosings Park. Now that he is past his youth, I expect he will be coming to my door any day now to officially propose to my Anne."

Mary looked towards the three cousins sitting at the opposite end of the table and was taken aback at the familiarity the viscount seemed to have with Miss de Bourgh. "I did not know, my lady," she replied.

The remainder of the meal was spent listening to Lady Catherine's ideas about the redecorating her daughter would do at Dalmeny and which Wedgwood patterns she would choose with which to grace their table.

When time for the separation of the gentlemen from the ladies came, Mary was unsure of what she felt. After talking with the colonel, she had spent the rest of the afternoon trying to understand her own feelings for the viscount. Calmed by the colonel's assurance, she finally determined she would accept his hand for the set, only now she was completely confused yet again. *Is he expected to marry his cousin? I know the colonel would not have said what he did if he thought such a match was to be made. Does he not know of the family's expectation?*

Trying to calm her fears, Mary decided to seek what information she could glean from Miss de Bourgh. When she finally saw her sitting alone on the sofa nearest the fireplace, she decided now was the perfect opportunity to speak with her.

"Miss Bennet," Anne smiled, "I have heard quite a bit about you from my cousin."

Shocked, she inquired, "Lord Primrose?"

"No, Georgiana; we exchange letters often and she has told me much about you and your family," Anne replied.

A small smile graced her face, "Yes, she has become a dear friend."

"I do not see Miss Darcy here this evening; is she feeling well?"

"The traveling, though short, was difficult on her, so she chose to stay at home instead," Mary explained.

"I will have to visit her next week," Anne smiled.

The gentlemen joined the ladies again almost immediately, the earl insisting he must not leave his sister alone for very long, especially without knowing what her intentions were for showing up in such a manner this evening.

When the brothers entered the room, Anne's gaze naturally went to that of Fitz.

Noticing the look on her face and the direction in which she gazed, Mary said, "You seem quite taken with your cousin."

Anne blushed, "Yes; we have been trying to keep it a secret though. He is not ready to marry just yet." Turning to her, she asked, "You will not tell anyone, will you?"

"No," Mary assured her, "I will not."

"My mother cannot know right now," Anne replied quietly. "She has her own agenda for my wedding, and I do not feel strong enough to fight her on such issues. When the time is right, we will inform the family."

"Yes, your mother talked all through dinner of her opinions on your marriage," Mary said.

"I am sure she did," Anne replied. "She always does."

The two stood and began to walk towards the others in the group. Mary's head was hurting before she even came to dinner this evening, but now the pain was nearly unbearable. She excused herself from the party and asked Lady Rosebery if she would have a footman escort her home.

The older lady was worried, especially after her early departure this afternoon. She placed her hand on Mary's forehead, "Are you feeling well, my dear?"

"I just need to rest," Mary replied. "My head has been aching all day, and it is getting worse now."

"Yes, Fitz told me earlier about your return to Darcy House because you did not feel well. You go and gather your things," she said, "and I will find someone to escort you home."

Mary was just about to pull the cape around her shoulders when she felt it being taken from her hands. "Allow me," she heard the viscount say.

Turning, she replied, "My lord, I…"

"My mother said you required an escort, and I wished to escape my Aunt Catherine for a few minutes." Smiling, he joked, "Consider it a birthday favor you are doing me."

Mary took his outstretched arm as he led her outside through the garden courtyard. "If you do not mind, we have a path at the back of the garden that connects the two houses. My Uncle George had it put in years ago."

Not sure what to say, she lightly held his arm as he led her through the winding garden. Remembering the gift she bought, Mary pulled a brown package from her pocket and held it out to Alex, "I wanted to give this to you, my lord."

"For me?" he was confused.

"Because it is your birthday," she explained.

"Oh, right… my birthday; I thank you," he said as he took it and reached towards his pocket.

"Are you not going to open it?"

"Oh—yes, of course. Do you care to sit for a minute?" he asked, indicating a nearby bench. At her acceptance, he led her over and they sat. When the last of the paper was peeled away and the handkerchief within revealed, Alex smiled. "It seems we are forever exchanging handkerchiefs," he joked.

Mary chuckled, "Yes, I am forever in need of one."

Smiling, he looked up at her, as he quietly said, "*You remembered.*"

Mary was touched by his emotional response to her gift, "Primroses, just like the one in which you returned my spectacles."

Alex fingered the embroidery, "Yes, I remember that day well."

Knowing she must make things right, even if he was to marry his cousin, Mary took a deep breath, and with determination, said, "My lord, I owe you an apology for how I treated you earlier today."

He interrupted her, "No, it is I who must apologize. I did not mean to frighten you with my request. I did not mean… that is…"

"I now understand fully what you meant," Mary said, certain now he just wanted to extend his hand to his cousin's new sister. There could be nothing more in his request; after all, he was very nearly engaged.

"Alex," Fitz called through the garden. Coming upon the couple, he blushed, "Oh, excuse me Miss Bennet; I did not know you were out here also."

"I was just escorting her back to Darcy House," Alex replied.

"Aunt Catherine insists on your presence inside," Fitz said.

"Yes, of course," Alex stood. "Will you escort Miss Bennet in my stead?"

Smiling, he put out his arm, "It would be my pleasure."

When they walked away, Fitz asked, "Is everything well?"

"Yes, I just have a headache, Colonel."

"And you talked with my brother?"

"Yes," she answered.

"Am I to know the subject of this conversation?" he goaded.

"I am a very private person, Colonel." Mary replied.

"Then I will not intrude upon your privacy, Miss Bennet," he said, leading her the rest of the way in silence. When she was delivered to the door, he bowed over her hand, "I will see you Monday evening at the ball."

Mary smiled and watched him walk away. *No, he could not know about his family's expectations.*

Sunday, April 5, 1812

Lady Catherine was seething. First, to arrive and find that the entire family was gathered with those… those… interlopers! Then further, to see that her brother and sister accepted them as family, when they hardly had the time of day to give her, their true family!

Now she awoke this morning to find that her brother had come to get Anne and take her with them to Sunday services. There was clearly no intention in asking for permission, just a note from him stating they would have her home later in the day, if she was feeling well enough after such an arduous journey as Catherine insisted upon in coming to Town so unexpectedly.

If she was feeling well enough? Why, *she* was the mother! *She* was the one who need give permission for such an outing; after all, it was *her* daughter!

As she sat with a cloth draped over her eyes, hoping it would stave off the headache she could feel building already so early in the day, her mind began to replay the encounters of the evening before in graphic detail.

How she longed to permanently get rid of the whole lot of them... the Bennets were not worthy of the privilege that came with such connections as *her* family held. Why, even as much as she hated her long departed husband, at least he was a knight. Not just some lowly country gentleman. He was titled! Not as highly ranked as her own family, but the bloodlines went back many generations.

And yet here they were consorting with a family whose connection to trade was so close she could smell it. Beyond that, her *gracious* sister, whom she had never gotten on well with at all, placed her at the table next to the wife of that tradesman! What arrogance! She was Lady Catherine de Bourgh— daughter of the previous Earl of Rosebery, and wife of the late Sir Lewis de Bourgh.

Not only was she expected to sup with them, but she was also required to join them for tea afterward while the gentlemen partook of some cigars. She heard Alexander tell Anne when they returned that the cigars were from Mr Gardiner's own shop. No wonder the stench on the gentlemen was so horrendous when they returned to the ladies sides. She could not abide such a smell, and had long forbidden her husband from partaking of such societal customs. Not that he fully gave them up, but at least he kept the habit only while he was in Town. Of course, in his later years, he was in Town more than he was at Rosings.

She was determined to keep her nephews from the clutches of this family any more than what they already had in their grasp. She would see to it that Anne danced with the viscount for the first dance, assuring herself, and all those in attendance, that the family would be connected through their wedding very soon.

She would have her revenge on the Bennets. Her daughter would be married to… Alexander… no, she was to marry William—yes William! It was always planned that Anne would marry Fitzwilliam Darcy. She would do away with his wife, and Anne would be the next Mistress of Pemberley. Or was it Dalmeny she was to become Mistress over?

Anne de Bourgh, Mistress of Dalmeny. That has a nice ring to it.

The now tepid cloth was not doing any good, so she threw it across the room, calling for her maid to assist her in dressing. When she stood, she nearly fainted, the maid catching her and helping her to sit again. After resting for a few more minutes, this time with her maid's fingers rubbing circles on her temples, she finally felt well enough to dress and go downstairs to await the return of her daughter.

It was several more hours before she arrived, and after only a few short rants of the insipid nature of the Bennets, Lady Catherine was too weak to remain downstairs, so she returned to her chamber, allowing Anne to go to hers as well.

CHAPTER IV

Monday, April 6, 1812

Lydia knocked on the door, opening it in a flourish of excitement when she was bid enter.

Kitty followed her sister into Georgiana's chambers, listening to her chatter on about everything they expected to do with Georgiana tonight. After hugging Mary's neck, Kitty asked, "Are you feeling ill Mary? You look a little pale."

"I am well enough," she assured her sister. When she received a look that said she did not believe her, especially after Mary did not even leave her chambers the day before due to a headache, Mary smiled, "Truly, I am."

"Do you have a dance partner yet?" Georgiana asked Mary.

Not knowing how to answer such a question, she finally said, "I do not know if I will dance tonight."

"Not dance? Oh, if I were to attend, I would dance every set with the finest gentlemen," Lydia cried, twirling around the room in a fanciful manner.

"Unfortunately, the dictates of society being what they are, a lady can only accept or reject a partner, not ask for one herself," Kitty said to her younger sister.

"Well," Lydia shrugged, "I will have to wait a few more years anyway."

"When will you be coming out?" Georgiana asked.

"Not until I am eighteen, and I just turned sixteen last month," Lydia answered. "Kitty's coming out will be when she turns eighteen in September." Lydia twirled around once more, this time ending with a flourishing drop to the bed. "Oh how wonderful it would be to have her coming out now though! Can you imagine dancing the night away? Mama tried to convince Papa to let her dance this evening, at least once, but he would not hear of it."

"And for good reason," Mary replied.

Lydia stopped and turned toward her sister, "I shall never understand your aversion to dancing."

"It is not an aversion to dancing, Lydia. I am certain with the proper partner, a dance could be very entertaining."

Lydia wiggled her eyebrows, "And just who would this partner be?"

Mary rolled her eyes and turned to address Georgiana instead. "What about you? When will your coming out be?"

Looking down at her legs, Georgiana quietly replied, "I am not certain I will have an official coming out Season. I know not if I will even marry…"

Kitty stepped in front of Georgiana and grabbed her hand, "Now, we will not let you become disheartened, especially not today. Of course you will have your coming out, and as we have already proven at Netherfield Park, you can also dance if you so choose."

Georgiana felt a tear try to escape her eyes and Lydia pressed a handkerchief into her hand. In her excited manner, she then bounced across the room stating, "We have not a moment to lose—you must show us your ball gown! Oh, and how will you fix your hair? You should leave some curls down around your neck like Lizzy does, Mary."

"Lydia, I am happy with my current style and see no reason for changing," Mary replied.

"Oh, la, I will just speak with Claire about the vision I see in my head. I am certain she can create it with your hair tonight," Lydia beamed.

Mary sighed and sat down next to Georgiana as her two sisters went on about the dress laid out and the hair style Lydia insisted would look perfect on her.

"She is just excited," Georgiana said quietly, squeezing Mary's hand.

"Yes, I know. I am also, just not as enthusiastic about this ball as my sister is," she explained.

"Is there a particular reason, or are you just nervous?" Georgiana asked.

"Just nerves I suppose," she tried to sound convincing. "I do not really like crowds, and the Assembly in Meryton is even sometimes too much for me." Mary felt her heart begin to beat wildly as the thought of so many in attendance started to loom over her.

"You will be well, I know it," Georgiana assured her friend. "Here," she said, reaching for her jewelry box and pulling something from within. "I would like you to wear this tonight."

Mary looked at Georgiana's outstretched hand, where the fancy comb her brother had given her just before her accident lay. "Oh, Georgiana! I cannot! That is your special comb, and should be saved for your debut."

She gave a simple smile and reached for Mary's hand, placing the comb in her palm and closing Mary's fingers around it. "Tonight, wear it for me. Now, let us begin, as dressing you may take a few hours."

Darcy heard the girls in his sister's room as they giggled and talked. He knocked and heard Georgiana ask, "Who is it?"

"It is me, Georgiana," he answered.

"Just a minute, William," she said.

He heard some banging around in the room before Mary finally opened the door to him.

"Is there something you needed?" Georgiana asked her brother when he came into the room.

Looking around, he tried to figure out what all the banging had been, "I just wanted to check on you; you were making quite the commotion in here."

"I know we have completely destroyed my room, but I promise we will have it in proper order again before the night is through," she assured him.

Smiling, he replied, "I know you will, Sweetling. If any of you need anything, just let me know." As he turned to leave the room, his eye caught the comb Mary wore in her hair. His heart beat loudly in his own ears and he glanced at his sister, who gave him a wink. It was obvious it was her idea. He winked back, and left them alone once again.

Lydia began to giggle when the door finally closed, "Your brother is such a peculiar individual, Georgiana."

Smiling, Georgiana replied, "Yes, at times he is. Now let us complete our toilettes with haste!"

Alex and Fitz descended the stairs just as Lady Catherine was announced.

Kissing their cheeks in greeting, she admonished her youngest nephew, "Stand up straight, Richard—you will never catch the attention of a lady with a large dowry if you slouch." Turning, she said, "Does not Anne look well this evening?"

"Yes, beyond lovely," Fitz bowed and brought his cousin's hand to his lips, winking at her when she smiled.

Alex greeted Anne as well and was about to walk away when his aunt stopped him.

"Alexander, I was informed you have not asked for my daughter's hand for a set," she turned her nose up at him in her haughty manner.

"You are correct, Aunt Catherine, I have not yet had the opportunity to secure a set with her," Alex replied.

"You are to dance the first with her," she said firmly.

"My lady…"

"I will hear nothing more about it," she replied. "Your place is beside my daughter for the first set."

Fitz looked at his brother, "I am sorry, Aunt Catherine, but I have already requested Anne's hand for the first set."

"Do not be preposterous, Richard; she will dance the first with your brother." Lady Catherine linked her arm with Anne's and walked away, "Come Anne, we will greet the rest of the family."

Anne looked back at Fitz and mouthed, "*I am sorry.*"

With a wave of his hand, he assured her he understood. Putting up two fingers, he smiled when she nodded her assent that the second set was his.

Fitz patted his brother's shoulder, "I am sorry. If you wish, I will dance the first with Miss Bennet in your stead."

"I am not to dance with Miss Bennet," Alex replied gloomily.

"What? I thought she changed her mind and spoke with you about it the other night in the garden?" Fitz asked in shock.

"She did speak to me, and she apologized for being so harsh in her refusal, but she did not accept my request." Alex turned to walk down the hallway.

Fitz was so shocked he could not move. When he finally realized his brother had walked away, he rushed forward, blocking the hallway. "What happened?"

"I already told you what happened. I asked for her hand for the first set, she refused and ran from the garden. That evening she apologized for her harsh refusal, and that was all." Alex tried to continue on, but Fitz detained him.

"But when I escorted her home, she assured me everything was well?"

"Fitz, I am not certain what more you want me to tell you. I have said what happened, and I cannot change her answer, no matter how many times you ask." Alex finally pushed by his brother and walked away.

Confused, Fitz was now determined he must speak with Mary tonight.

Mary made it through the introductions line and was trying to find a place to sit out of the crush of people when she saw out of the corner of her eye someone come up beside her. She turned. "Colonel; it is good to see you."

He bowed, "Miss Bennet, it is, of course, a pleasure to see you this evening." Just when she thought he would walk away, he continued, "I have heard you *do not* have a partner for the first set and I have made it my mission to insist upon your hand."

The look in his eyes was intense and she knew *he* would not take *no* for an answer, so she quietly replied, "Yes, of course."

With another short bow, he said, "Until then," and she was left alone again as he walked away.

Shaken by his harsh demeanor, she soon found the quiet corner she was looking for and sat until the dancing was to begin.

When the time came, he escorted her to the line, taking his place right beside his brother. Mary soon realized the placement would have her dancing just as much with her partner as it would with the viscount, and she had to give him credit for his efforts. What she did not realize was their cousin Anne was in on the scheme as well and chose this specific country dance to start them off at the request of Fitz. The third pair of dancers in their group was Charlotte and her husband. The two were not easily distracted from each other, as one would expect from a couple just married, and Mary soon found herself in a very uncomfortable situation with a gentleman to whom she could not allow herself to be drawn. It seemed as if his eyes continued to find hers, even when he was dancing with his cousin.

Mary was so discomposed by the second dance of the set that she asked Fitz to sit this one out. He escorted her out of the crowd and into the garden, and found a bench for her to rest upon among the primroses along the back wall.

Sarah Johnson

Stepping into the ballroom, Susannah saw Elizabeth and Jane standing up with their husbands for the second dance of the first set. Tears formed in her eyes at the love that shone from their husbands' faces.

Henry came up beside her and took her arm, "It is quite surreal to see three of our daughters dancing at such a place as this, is it not?"

"I never imagined it," she replied. They stood watching the dancers, swaying inadvertently with the music as they quietly observed all around them. Susannah sighed and hugged her husband's arm a little tighter, quietly saying, "We are soon to be grandparents."

"Yes, and it seems, once again, I was right," he replied. "And I dare say it will not be long before our eldest daughter is to bless us even more abundantly."

The music ended and Bingley led his wife over to the two, greeting them warmly. "Are you enjoying the evening?"

"Yes, it is quite the crush," Mrs Bennet said, then began to look around the room with a worried look on her face. "Have you seen Mary? I thought she was dancing the first with the colonel, but I do not see her now."

Knowing her sister's aversion to crowds, Jane replied, "She *was* dancing with him, but perhaps she was in need of some air?"

"It is entirely possible," Henry said.

Jane, seeing the pained look on her father's face, reached for his hand, "Charles and I are not engaged for this next dance, so we will go and find her while you rest."

He squeezed her fingers, "Thank you, my dear."

The Bingleys watched as Susannah helped a struggling Henry to a seat, both smiling at the care with which she gave him.

38

"It is wonderful to see such a loving marriage after so many years. One day, my love, we too will be their age, and I dare say we will be just as in love as we are today."

Jane looked at her husband, "Or more."

"Or more," he said, barely above a whisper. "Come, we will search for your sister."

Sitting down beside her, Fitz asked, "Why did you lie to me, Miss Bennet?"

"I did not lie, Colonel. You asked if I talked with your brother, and I assured you I had," Mary replied.

"I will accept that, but you *did* deceive me."

She looked down at her hands, folded in her lap. "I did, and I do apologize, Colonel."

He tapped her chin, causing her to look up at him, "I only care for your well being. You are practically my cousin now, after all. Family means a great deal to me."

She nodded, "Thank you."

"I truly wish I could call you my sister. Are you certain you cannot give my brother the chance he needs to earn your respect?"

"I do not see myself in the position you seem to see me in, sir. Your brother did not have any problem filling his dance card adequately," Mary explained.

Fitz was just about to advise her of how it came about when he heard someone walking along the path. He looked up to see the Bingleys standing there. He stood and bowed to them, "I see the set has finished."

"Yes, and we were sent to find my sister," Bingley said, his chest puffing out just a little, though it did nothing for his lean figure compared to the colonel.

Mary tried not to laugh at the spectacle the two men posed. She stood, "I was in need of some air, and the colonel escorted me out here."

Jane walked over to Mary, removing her glove and pressing her hand against Mary's forehead. "You do look pale. Are you feeling well? Do you need to lie down?"

Immediately the two silently dueling for the position of brother turned, concern filling both of their features as the two nearly tripped over each other to get to her side, each grabbing an elbow.

"Yes, yes, you must rest…"

"My mother keeps her private sitting room available…"

She interrupted them both, "I am well. Thank you though." she smiled a little, "We cannot miss the entertainments inside. Come, it is time we return."

Jane, seeing the small smile, pulled her glove back on, "If you are certain you feel well enough?"

"Yes, Jane, and Charles," she said, looking at each as she said their name, "and Colonel," she chuckled, "I am perfectly well and wish to rejoin the festivities now."

The colonel stepped back and gave an exaggerated bow, just like the ones he would often give to Georgiana, making Mary smile even more broadly than before. His hand extended out and he said gallantly, "May I have the honour of escorting you back to the Ball, Miss Bennet?"

Now in a much better mood, she gave a deep curtsy, then took his hand, "Why certainly, Colonel."

The two walked off, leaving the newlyweds alone, Jane chuckling at the display both had made. She was about to follow when her husband's hands wound around her waist and he leaned down to her ear, whispering, "Since we are alone, and amongst such beautiful flowers…" His words faded as they both leaned closer, their lips meeting in a sensual exchange.

It was another ten minutes before the Bingleys appeared back inside.

"Lord Primrose, what a pleasure it is to see you here tonight."

Bowing to the three ladies as they came up to him, he replied, "Miss Bingley, Miss Morley, good evening. Miss Bennet, always a pleasure."

"It is a pity I was unable to join my brother last week for Lord Ashbourne's wedding," Caroline said, letting go of Mary's arm and trying to attach herself to him.

"I believe it was my own fault," Bingley said as he joined the group, "as I forgot to extend the invitation early enough to account for travel time." He eyed Caroline, warning her to watch her tongue. They had already exchanged heated words earlier today about her behavior at the ball tonight. Bingley informed her of this being her one and only chance to prove she could be civil, and if she stepped out of line in any way he would have her on the road back to Scarborough tomorrow morning.

Caroline opened her fan and fluttered it in front of her face, sure of its covering her sneer. "My, it is warm in here," she looked at the viscount. "Perhaps someone would not mind getting some air?"

"That is a lovely idea, is it not Mary?" Jane ran her arm through Caroline's. "I have yet to see the tea room. Will you not join us Miss Morley?" she asked sweetly.

Alex let out an obvious sigh of relief when Mrs Bingley led the other ladies away. "Thank you Bingley." Looking at their retreating backs, Alex wished Mary had stayed with him, but he would not force his presence on her.

"I saw my sister coming your way, but could not stop her in time," he said. "I have only seen you dance the first tonight; are you not feeling up to it this evening?"

Alex ran his hand through his hair, "I was obliged to start the first dance, and my aunt insisted I partner my cousin."

"I have never seen you so distracted at a ball before; you are starting to remind me of your taciturn cousin over there," Bingley looked towards Darcy, "although it seems he is a different person now that he is married."

"Yes, isn't he lucky," Alex murmured under his breath.

"What was that," Bingley looked back to his friend.

"Nothing," Alex said, patting his shoulder. "I will see you later." He pulled out his pocket watch as he strode through the crowd, *why does time drag on tonight? Only an hour longer, and I am not obliged to dance with any other ladies as my mother has seen fit to have an abundance of gentlemen here tonight.* Seeing his Aunt Catherine up ahead, he stepped into the card room to avoid her. He recognized the man standing nearby. "Mr Bennet, I trust you are enjoying the entertainments this evening?"

"Of course, my lord, of course. Would you care for a game?" Henry asked.

Looking back out the door and seeing his aunt looking all around, he quickly turned and ushered Mr Bennet to a table, "I believe I would, sir." *If I cannot have the pleasure of a dance with Miss Mary, at least I can enjoy talking with her father for a time and avoid the clawing and insipid creatures on the prowl*, he thought.

CHAPTER V

Wednesday, April 8, 1812

Mary was sitting outside in the garden at Darcy House, her journal opened on her lap, when she felt a familiar presence engulf her in a hug from behind, kissing her forehead in his fatherly manner.

"I did not mean to disturb you, my dear," Henry Bennet interrupted his daughter, "I just wanted to visit my girls once more before we leave tomorrow morning."

"You are going home early?" she asked.

"Yes, it seems your mother is not as fond of Town as she thought she would be, and my leg is starting to bother me with this much activity. The Lucases left this morning and we have been invited to join them tomorrow evening to celebrate Mr Lucas's twenty-fourth birthday." Raising his eyebrow, he said, "It seems he *specifically* asked if your sister *Katherine* would be there."

"Do you think he is interested in her?" Mary asked.

"Perhaps when she is out he will approach me. We will just have to wait and see," Henry replied. "Your mother sends her love and promises she will be over later to say goodbye. She seems to think the maids are not folding the clothing properly in the trunks, so she is personally seeing to the packing this morning."

Mary chuckled, "She has to have something to fuss over, does she not?"

"Just be glad it is not you," he kissed her cheek and stood. "I expect to have at least two letters about the many beaus you turn away during your time in Town."

Mary chuckled again as her father left. Looking back down to the words on the page to which her journal was opened, she read through them again, trying to decide what she should allow her heart to believe about the viscount.

***

Friday, April 10, 1812

G.W. was hiding in the park across from Darcy House when he saw the couple exit the house and cross the road. He was well hidden in a grouping of bushes, but he was a bit worried when they seemed to be walking directly towards them. His heart nearly beat out of his chest until he realized their destination was the bench located right next to the bushes he was hidden within.

"Your aunt has stolen my sister away for another day at Rosebery House," Elizabeth said as she sat.

Darcy smiled, "Aunt Helen takes great joy in having a young lady around. If she could get away with it, I think she would find a way to keep your sister there for the whole Season instead of just a few days here or there."

"I am sure she would, if she did not think Georgiana would miss Mary's presence," Elizabeth smiled. "Your aunt can be quite persuasive when

44

she wants to be. She maintains we need to visit my uncle's warehouse again next Tuesday morning, and I could not talk her out of it," Elizabeth said, winding her arm through her husband's and resting her head on his shoulder. "I have purchased enough for five girls' Seasons in Meryton, but your aunt insists my wardrobe is still not enough to get me through the next two months here in Town, nor our time at Pemberley."

"I did warn you, my love," Darcy said.

"Well, as it turns out, my dresses *are* becoming a bit snug," Elizabeth replied.

Smirking, Darcy replied, "Yes, I have noticed."

Shocked, Elizabeth lifted her head and looked into his bright green eyes, "Why did you not tell me?"

"Because I saw no good reason in telling you," he said. "I quite like the changes your wardrobe has taken with the addition of our child growing within you. If you feel uncomfortable in your current gowns, by all means, purchase more. What good is having money if I cannot allow you to spend to your heart's desire?"

"It is a good thing you did not marry a spendthrift, otherwise that attitude would run you into the ground in no time," Elizabeth joked.

"Are you ready for Monday?"

She giggled, "Yes, William, I am ready."

"Are you certain you wish to take your curtsy this year? You do not have to, you know. Everyone will understand, especially with your condition." He looked worriedly at his wife, drawing his arm a little tighter around her shoulders.

"I am not worried about falling, and honestly, I would rather get this done and over with as soon as may be. It would drive me to certain distraction if

I had to look forward to such an event for twelve months complete." She shook her head, "No, Monday is perfectly well with me."

"Come," he said, gently kissing the back of her hand and helping her up from the bench, "we have just enough time for a leisurely stroll around the pond before we are needed back at home."

G.W. watched as they made their way to the other side of the park. *Tuesday morning at her uncle's warehouse is it? We will be ready.* He snuck out of the park and made his way across Town, his mind already forming a plan. His first stop was a specialty shop he had used several times in the last few months.

"Mr Wilkerson, it is always good to see a returning customer, sir," the owner said when he entered. "I see your newest piece is working out quite nicely."

"Yes, the fit is amazing. No one can tell it is not my real hair, and it has saved my having to admit I am going bald too early" he replied, pasting a fake smile on his face.

"Well what can I do for you today, sir?"

"We have been invited to a masked event, and my wife insists on my dressing as the partner of her chosen character. She says this color will not do and I must obtain a blonde wig," G.W. told the man.

Rubbing his hands together eagerly, the man turned towards the array of wigs displayed on the shelves, "I think we have two in your size already made. When is this event?"

"It is next week," he answered, "so whatever you have ready-made will have to do."

Looking at his customer, the man tapped his chin as he thought aloud, "Hmmmm, I think the lighter of the two would work with your features. Right this way."

"My wife will be happy I have purchased such a fine work of art, my good man," he complimented the proprietor.

"Anytime, anytime," the eager salesman replied.

G.W. started to pay and then stopped, "You would not happen to have something in red to fit my wife, would you?"

"Let me check my records for your wife's size, and I will see. We may have just what she needs as well."

The man checked his records and was soon leading him to the back of the store, "Do you know which length she would prefer?"

Fingering the long tresses of the darker of the two wigs, G.W. replied, "This one will do nicely I think."

"Capital! I will have that wrapped up for you as well. Will that be all, sir?"

"Yes, I believe that is all for now." G.W. smiled at the jovial man.

"If your wife finds this does not fit well, she can come back any time to have it adjusted."

"I am sure it will work perfectly for its intended use," he said as he handed the man a coin for the two packages and left the store.

When he arrived at Mrs Younge's boarding house he was led into the drawing room where she sat. When tea was called for and the butler was dismissed, he held up the two packages, tossing one onto her lap, "I have some information, and a plan." He pulled off his dark wig and placed the blonde one on his head, looking in the mirror on the wall to adjust it then turned to his accomplice. "How does this look?"

She stood, circling around his figure to examine him from all sides, "It is amazing how well you look in that color. You almost look like that image you have of... well, never mind."

With a cold stare, he pulled off the wig. "Do not bring up *that man* to me."

Wanting to change his darkened mood, she smiled, "So what did you bring for me?"

"You and I have some warehouse browsing to do. It seems a *certain person* will be at *Gardiner's Goods* next Tuesday, and we may be able to separate her from her party fairly easily. First we need to know what we are dealing with in the layout of the store."

Mrs. Younge unwrapped the red wig and turned to the mirror on the wall, fitting it onto her head and tucking her own brown hair beneath the soft curls. Turning back to him, she asked, "Does it become me?"

"It will do," he smirked. "Sit, and I will explain my plan."

***

Mary was enjoying her visit to Rosebery House. The Countess was such a genuine person and Mary truly took delight in being around her. The ladies were drinking tea in the garden when a visitor was announced.

"Miss Anne de Bourgh to see you, madam," Simms said as he led the petite lady through the door.

Standing, Helen greeted her niece with a hug, "I have missed having you here with us. Please tell me your mother is treating you well and you are not too weak from your travels?"

A small smile crept to the corners of her mouth as Anne replied, "I am well, Aunt."

"Please sit and take tea with us," Helen said.

Looking at Mary, she replied, "I do not wish to intrude."

Squeezing her niece's hand, she replied, "I have a feeling you and Miss Bennet will get along famously and before long you will have a great deal to talk about." Helen suspected the feelings of her eldest and would be glad to one day welcome Mary into the intimate family circle.

Sitting back down to their tea, Helen said, "I am surprised your mother did not accompany you today."

"She has a headache." With a somber look, she quietly continued, "She has them more frequently now, and sometimes cannot even get out of bed."

"Oh my!" Helen's shock was evident. "I did not know they were so bad. If only your mother would allow Doctor Eaves to see to her care while she is in Town."

"She will not hear of it." Anne turned to Mary, "My mother is not very trusting of the new medical techniques used by the younger doctors."

"I understand," Mary quietly replied. "My sister has seen Doctor Eaves since coming to Town, and he is quite the personality."

Anne smiled, "Yes, it is hard not to like the man, but somehow my mother chooses not to."

"Would you like me to request he see you here at Rosebery House," Helen asked her niece.

"Maybe that would be best. I know my cousin has said he would like me to be checked over, and you know he will not give up on such a suggestion until it is completed," Anne said.

"It is settled then," Helen replied. "Maybe my husband can help me distract his sister sometime next week, allowing you to visit me alone again."

"I look forward to days I can visit here," Anne said.

"I know dear, I know," Helen lovingly took her hand again. "Now, we must not discuss this any longer. I have some fabric sets I need some opinions on, and you two would be just perfect for that purpose." Pulling out a stack of several pieces, Helen turned to include Mary, "What do you think of these colors?"

"What are they for?" Mary asked.

"Oh, I am sorry; I just assumed you already knew. My eldest son is to take over Dalmeny, so my husband and I are moving to the Dower House. It has not been redecorated in many years and will require many changes. I intend to start with the drawing room, and I thought these would bring out the bright morning sun well as it shines through the east facing windows."

Mary and Anne each gave their opinions on the fabric choices, and Helen pulled out another set of fabrics. "I absolutely love this," Anne said of one piece, running the soft velvet over her cheek. "This would be perfect for the small sitting room off the mistress' chambers."

"You think so?" Helen asked. "Yes, I can see how it would frame those windows nicely, though my husband would not have preferred this color in there. Maybe once my son marries, the *new mistress* will redo that room." Helen quirked her eyebrow and Anne understood immediately that she hoped *Mary* would one day fill that role. Mary, on the other hand, was convinced it was yet another small sign that *Anne* was meant by the family to marry the viscount.

The two were becoming fast friends by the time Mary returned to Darcy House, and she was looking forward to their scheduled shopping trip next week as Anne would be joining them. Mary wrote in her journal,

I feel such happiness for Miss de Bourgh and the changes to soon come to her life. If only I could reconcile within myself *who* she is to marry. Perhaps this is a blessing in that I will better be able to put my feelings aside. Feelings… do I have feelings for him? I shan't think about that. He is to marry his cousin, and that is how it should be.

She quickly closed her journal, trying to forget the person who had taken over her every thought once again.

CHAPTER VI

Tuesday, April 14, 1812

Elizabeth woke to her husband lovingly caressing her stomach. As she laced her fingers through his, he kissed the back of her hand and placed their conjoined hands back on the bulge and kissed her cheek. "I was just having a little talk with our child, thanking her for not causing you to fall yesterday when you took your curtsy," he said.

"And does *he* need to have his father talk to him of such important details already?" she asked.

"Absolutely; *she* will never tire of hearing her father's words of wisdom," he smiled.

"I see you are *still* determined we will have a girl," Elizabeth said.

"And *you* are still determined we will have a boy," he answered.

"Well, at least one of us will be right." Hearing the clock chime, Elizabeth groaned, "As much as I would love to stay here in your arms, your aunt insists on shopping today." Pulling away from his embrace, she stood, stretching her aching back. "If this is what I have to look forward to every morning, I am not certain I am meant to have a baby."

Running his hands over her form, he said, "If *this* is what *I* have to look forward to, I am certain to never let you leave our chambers, Mrs Darcy."

Swatting his hands away, she gave him a serious look and went into her dressing room.

Darcy lay back in the bed and was nearly back asleep when he heard an exasperated grumble come from the other room. Going to the doorway, he asked, "What is wrong, my dear?"

"What is *wrong*? What is *WRONG*? *THIS* is wrong! I cannot even clasp this dress that fit just fine a few days ago!" Elizabeth huffed as she removed the offending item and threw it on the dressing table.

"You will be going shopping today and will have some more clothes to choose from soon," he said as he tried to comfort her.

"But what am I to wear in the meantime? I cannot go around Town in my chemise and stockings," she sat on the chair as tears started to form in her eyes.

"Where is Annette?" he inquired.

"I did not call her yet," Elizabeth wiped her cheeks with the back of her hand.

Pulling the cord to call her maid, he handed her a handkerchief and lovingly kissed his wife's hair, "I will be right back."

A few minutes later he reentered, followed by Annette who had four gowns draped over her arm, "These are Georgiana's. I know she is not out so they are a bit more conservative, but she is a little larger than you and Annette assures me they should fit nicely until the gowns you purchase can be completed."

Elizabeth looked up at his face, the love he had for her evident in his eyes, and tears again threatened to spill from her eyes. Wiping furiously, she said, "Thank you. You will never know how much this means to me."

With Annette's help, she was soon dressed in a green dress that brought some color to her cheeks. Stretching her arms, she made sure there was room enough to not burst a seam on the shoulders, and she smiled at William as he looked on from the doorway. "What has caught your attention, *my husband?*"

Why, you, of course, *my wife,*" he said teasingly.

Dismissing the maid and stepping behind her, he wrapped his arms around her waist, resting his large hands on her protruding abdomen. "Please purchase what you need, and, more than that, purchase whatever my aunt suggests. I plan to take you out a few times while we are here in Town and I would not have my wife appear lacking in the eyes of the Ton.

"I promise to do just as you say," she turned and kissed him.

<hr />

Maddie Gardiner smiled as she saw the group of five browsing her husband's warehouse. She joined them, "What a lovely color on you, Mrs Darcy."

Elizabeth recognized her aunt's voice and spun around, "Aunt Maddie! We did not expect to see you today."

"I was feeling better than I have been, so I decided to see what I could find in the newest shipment." Turning to greet the others, she hugged Mary, then Jane, in turn, "It is good to see you too, Mary and Jane." Nodding to the other two ladies, she said, "Lady Rosebery, Miss de Bourgh, it is always a pleasure to see you as well." Turning back to Elizabeth and Jane, she grasped their hands, "Oh you simply must tell me how your curtsies went yesterday?"

Elizabeth giggled and Jane's face shown a simple smile, Jane saying, "It was all I dreamed it would be."

"Yes, well, seeing as I have never dreamed of taking my curtsy before, I cannot say the same, but it was not a cruel experience," Elizabeth said.

"I am so proud of you both," Maddie said, trying not to cry, "so very proud." Again speaking to the whole group, she asked, "Now, is there something particular you require, or is this just a fun excursion?"

Helen wound her arm through Maddie's and turned to face Elizabeth, her chin stuck out as she said boldly, "It seems our niece has grown too large for her clothes, so we have been sent with specific instructions from her husband to not return until she has purchased enough gowns, and other accoutrements, to see her through this Season and the summer at Pemberley." She turned back to look at Mrs Gardiner, "I was told you have fabric that would fit every need?"

With a gleam in her eye, Maddie smiled, "We may just be able to help you. My husband has several crates of fabrics yet to be put out. If you will come with me to the back, I think I can talk them into letting us peruse them to see if there is something serviceable for such gowns."

The two people who stood with their backs to the group listened intently to what was being said. G.W. leaned over and whispered into his companion's ear, "You try to distract her from the rest of the group, and I will see where I can hide up ahead of them to steal her away. Keep her alone!"

He quickly made his way through the aisles, hiding from view of the others in the warehouse. Looking back, he noticed the women slowly coming his way, stopping to look at a few items along the way.

"Oh, pardon me," Elizabeth felt someone bump into her. Turning, she saw a woman with red hair and dark, almost black eyes, addressing her. "Are you all right Miss?"

"Mrs—if you please," she answered, "and yes, I am well."

54

"Mrs? Oh yes, of course," she said, her eyes being drawn down to the obvious bulge under her dress. "Perhaps you can help me for just a minute. You see, I have never been to this particular warehouse before and I am looking for a specific item."

Looking towards the others of her group as they continued to walk away, Elizabeth had an uneasy feeling about this woman. "Just a minute," she said. "My aunt and uncle own this warehouse and I am certain they can find someone to help you."

As she started to walk away, the lady grabbed her arm, squeezing it hard enough to leave a bruise. "No, no, that is quite all right, there is no need to get someone else."

All of a sudden Elizabeth heard a blood curdling scream. The stranger was shaken enough for Elizabeth to pull her arm away, and she turned to see Anne de Bourgh lying on the floor. Quickly making her way to the group, she heard the others as they called for smelling salts and Mrs Gardiner sent someone to fetch her husband.

"Sir, your wife needs you downstairs," the employee said, slightly out of breath.

"What has happened? Is she ill?" Gardiner replied as he quickly followed the young boy.

"A young lady shopping with her has fainted, sir," the boy answered.

Making haste, he had to push his way through the crowd that had gathered. "What has happened?" he questioned his wife.

"Please, we must get Miss de Bourgh to a quieter place," Maddie replied.

Easily picking up the small, frail lady, Gardiner followed Lady Rosebery as she made a way through the crowd, then he led them to his office and laid Anne down on the sofa, calling for some fresh water and towels.

Helen pulled a vinaigrette from her reticule, then leaned over her niece and opened it. Anne was soon revived and sitting up, taking deep breaths to calm her racing heart as her aunt rubbed her back and encouraged her to take her time.

When she was recovered well enough to speak, Helen asked her niece, "Please tell us what happened?"

"I… I was walking along, speaking with Miss Bennet about a fan I liked, when I looked up and saw… *his* face!" Helen noticed Anne's cheeks go pale with just the mention of it.

"*Who* did you see?" Elizabeth asked.

"*My… my… father!*" Anne said, grasping her chest as she felt it tighten.

"Now, take a deep breath, my dear," Helen said, calmly wiping her brow with the cool, wet cloth. "Your father has been gone for many years, so we know it was not him. Did you sleep well last night?"

"No…no, I am *certain* it was him! It is the same face I have seen so many times in the portrait that hangs in the library at Rosings Park. It was him… it had to be him…," she replied, her voice becoming more frightened as the words came out. "Un… unless it was… *could it have been a specter?*"

"Now, now, my dear, we do not live in a gothic novel." Helen turned to Elizabeth, "Please have one of the footman sent from the carriage and we will take Anne back to my house to rest."

"Yes, of course, my lady," Elizabeth said as she turned.

"I will take care of that," Gardiner replied, leaving and soon returning with the footman.

Shortly the women were back at Rosebery House and Anne was settled into a guest room with Mary sitting by her bedside. Lady Rosebery went to speak with her eldest son and husband, who were in conference with the steward from Dalmeny. Elizabeth and Jane stood in the doorway looking on as Anne finally began to calm.

Elizabeth was not sure what happened, but she remembered distinctly the feeling that something was very wrong when that woman grabbed her arm. *Could the two events be related? Is it possible someone was trying to restrain me for nefarious reasons? Could it be that Anne's screams saved me from such an event taking place?*

Jane wrapped her arm around her sister's shoulders, "I think it is time I return home. Please let me know what has taken place when it is finally determined."

Elizabeth hugged her, "Oh, I will. Expect to hear from me this evening and I will let you know how Anne is recovering."

With a smile of affection, Jane turned and left, passing Darcy in the hall and taking her leave of him as well.

Elizabeth turned back to look into the room, and when her husband's arms wrapped around her she could hold her emotions in no longer. A flood of tears began to pour from her eyes and her husband turned her around and embraced her tightly. "What is wrong, Elizabeth?"

The tears kept her from speaking, so she just held him as close as she could and cried. Seeing she would need some privacy to compose herself, he ushered her into a nearby empty bed chamber and over to the sofa. He urged her to sit, then he went to the windows and opened the curtains, allowing light to fill the room. He then returned to close the door then went to sit beside his wife, who by now was well on her way to ruining her sodden handkerchief. Pulling his own from his pocket, he replaced the cloth in her hand, and wrapped his arms around her, pulling her closer and soothing her until she was calmed enough to speak.

When she had finally calmed, she explained all that happened with the lady with the dark eyes, telling him of the dread she felt wash over her when the lady looked at her. She even removed her pelisse to reveal a bruise on her arm where the lady gripped her so tightly.

"You think Anne's fainting saved you from whatever this woman had in mind to do to you?" he asked.

"Yes, I do; oh William, she had such a look in her eye. I am certain I will never forget it as long as I live. I just knew she wanted to harm me in some way," Elizabeth began to cry again.

"Shhhh, it is all well now. You are here in my Uncle's home, and safe in my arms. No one will do you harm here."

Darcy stepped over to the desk and pulled a piece of paper out.

"What are you doing?" she asked.

"I am writing to Fitz. I think we may need his help today."

When the note was completed, he pulled the rope for a servant, giving the note to be dispatched to Colonel Fitzwilliam immediately when the footman arrived.

Fitz arrived just as the footman was leaving to dispatch the note to him. He opened it, and upon reading that something had happened to Anne and Elizabeth, he rushed inside, taking the stairs two at a time and meeting Darcy in the hall. The details were explained to him quickly.

"I need to speak with Anne," Fitz said nervously.

"Mary is sitting with her still," he nodded towards the chamber where Anne had been taken.

When the knock came at the door, Mary answered it, "Darcy, Colonel, come in."

Darcy and Mary stood back as Fitz went to Anne's bedside and picked up her hand and sat on the edge of the bed. "Are you well?"

Darcy gently pulled Mary out into the hall and asked how Anne fared.

"She is complaining of a headache, but otherwise she seems to be just shaken."

"Come," He said, "I need you to help me get Elizabeth back home and sit with her. I have some business to discuss with my cousin when he is finished with Anne."

Confused by his statement, Mary asked, "What has happened to Elizabeth?"

Alex walked decidedly down the hall, having just heard from his mother what happened to Anne, and was close enough to hear Mary's question, so he stepped up to the two and asked, "Am I needed?"

Darcy turned to include him in the discussion, explaining to them both what Elizabeth revealed about the woman and how Anne's scream may have stopped a much larger nefarious plan from taking place.

"Oh, no! Who would want to cause harm to my sister?" Mary was shocked.

"I do not know, but I am determined to find out. I need you to help me return Elizabeth to Darcy House and sit with her until I come home."

"What are you going to do?" Alex asked.

"I do not know yet, but Fitz is already here discussing what took place with Anne. If it becomes necessary, we may have to leave Town early and go to Pemberley where I can be assured of Elizabeth's safety," Darcy mused.

"Yes, of course," Mary replied. "Whatever is necessary is what must be done."

"Please mention this to no one," Darcy urged the two.

"Yes… of course." Alex patted his cousin's shoulder, "I will sit with Anne."

Mary's heart tightened just a little more as she thought of the two sitting together alone in Anne's chambers—it was quite clear the two would be married. Darcy retrieved his wife from the chamber across the hall and he and Mary returned Elizabeth to Darcy House to rest.

Alex stood at the door to Anne's chamber, his mother joining him while Fitz finished speaking with Anne, explaining that Darcy was taking Elizabeth home to rest. As promised, he did not mention the version of events passed on to him by his cousin.

Lady Rosebery replied, "Yes, I passed them in the hall downstairs. Elizabeth was quite pale—I do hope this outing was not too much for her at this time."

"Miss Mary will see to her care," he said in assurance.

Fitz joined them in the hall. "She says she has seen her father. Did anyone else see this man?"

Lady Rosebery shook her head, "No… we were all too focused on Anne to notice anything else." Her hands began to shake, and the composure she had held so far began to drain from her body as tears filled her eyes.

Alex reached around her shoulders, taking her arm as he urged her to her chambers, assuring her he would remain by Anne's side.

When he returned, Fitz was still waiting in the hall, standing in the doorway and just staring in on their frail cousin. He stepped beside him, "There is more, but I will let Darcy tell you himself."

It was only a few minutes more before Darcy joined them and told Fitz what Elizabeth revealed and the fear she had over the encounter.

"So do you think Anne was simply a diversion? Could someone have been dressed like her father just to frighten her?"

"It is a possibility," Darcy replied. "I think we need to look further into this incident."

"Yes, I agree. Can you join me?" he asked Darcy.

"Yes; Mary is sitting with Elizabeth."

Fitz turned to Alex, the words not even past his lips when Alex replied, "I will not leave her side until you return." He then went into the room, pulled a chair over to the bedside, and settled in for a long wait as Darcy and Fitz left to see what else they could find out about the incident.

Sarah Johnson

CHAPTER VII

Darcy and Fitz made their way through the crowded streets of the commerce center of London looking for Fitz's contact. The two had already returned to the warehouse, but learned nothing new, and, having no time at present to look into the matter further, Fitz had suggested they hire this person to do the investigating for them.

"Are you certain you know what he looks like?"

Stopping his horse and looking around, Fitz rubbed his chin, "Well, maybe not." Seeing a familiar shop, he pointed, "There, I am almost certain he will be inside the tea shop."

Clicking his tongue, Darcy urged his horse forward as they slowly made their way through the crowds.

"It would have been better to leave our rides and just walk through this section," Fitz replied.

"Yes, now I see why you suggested just that earlier," Darcy looked around. "I have never been here before."

"Oh if you think this is bad, you should see the crowds in the early morning." Fitz jumped off his horse and tied him to a post. He found a boy standing nearby and gave him a coin to watch the two horses, then said to his cousin, "Come, we will wait in here." They found a table and sat, ordering something to drink, while they waited.

Half an hour later a thin man of average height knocked into Darcy's elbow, "Oh, I am sorry, sir. Please accept my apologies for nearly ruining your coat."

Putting down his tea, Darcy brushed at his coat with his fingers, "That is all right; nothing spilled."

As soon as the man walked away Fitz stood, "Come on."

Nearly tripping over the chair, Darcy tried to catch up to his cousin. "Why the rush? Where are we going?"

Fitz weaved through the crowds outside the shop, "That was him; now keep up."

If it were not for his unusual height, Darcy would have lost Fitz within minutes. *For a man of such large size, he has amazing agility and can blend into a crowd remarkably well,* Darcy thought of his cousin. The thin man ducked between two buildings and disappeared. The two followed, and when Darcy's eyes adjusted to the dim light of the alley, he pointed to a door at the end, "There."

"Yes, come," Fitz said. When they came to the door he knocked twice.

When there was no answer, Darcy said, "Should we not just follow? Why must we stop to knock?"

"I can guarantee there are at least three pistols aimed at the other side of this door right now, and unless you want to lose your life tonight, I say we wait for it to be opened." Fitz watched as the color drained from Darcy's face. "Breathe, Darcy; the last thing I need is to have to haul you back home over my shoulder. You insisted on coming with me to meet him even when I told you it might be dangerous."

"Is this the kind of work you do often?" Darcy asked.

"You know I cannot talk of what I do." Hearing a noise inside, he shoved his cousin behind him, "Duck down if you hear shots."

The door creaked open just a tiny bit and a small child asked, "What ya want, mister?"

From behind the child he heard a gruff voice say, "Let the men in, son. I know 'em."

Darcy found he could not stand up straight in the small room and was glad when they were led to a back room where a large round table dominated the space. Fitz pulled his cousin around to the other side, "Sit here; do not ever sit with your back to the door unless someone you fully trust is watching it for you."

The thin man from the tea shop came in the door a minute later, sitting across from them. "What do you need?"

"My family seems to be the target of someone; we do not know who or why," Fitz said.

"Tell me all you know," the thin man said as he pulled out a notebook and pencil.

"My mother, our cousin Anne, and my cousin Darcy's wife and her sisters," he said nodding to Darcy, "were shopping in *Gardiner's Goods* when his wife was approached by a lady. It was obvious to her the lady wanted to separate her from the group, and the only thing to save her was my cousin Anne's screams. She fainted after seeing what she swears was her father. My uncle has been dead twenty years at least."

"What was his name?"

"Sir Lewis de Bourgh," Fitz replied.

The man cocked his eyebrow to the two men as he wrote something down. "And then what happened?"

"Darcy's wife is related to the owners of the warehouse, so they took Anne to Mr Gardiner's office until she was composed enough to take her to my parent's house," Fitz explained.

"And were any of these ladies harmed?" the thin man asked.

"My wife has bruises on her arm from the woman's grip," Darcy said. "Our cousin is recovering. She was not physically harmed, but is quite shaken."

"What of this woman? Can you describe her?"

Pulling out a piece of paper, Darcy handed it to the man. "This is what my wife told me of her. It is not much."

Reading the description, the thin man nodded and added it to the notebook.

"And what of the man?"

"What man?" Darcy asked.

"The man your cousin saw," he replied.

"We are not certain she actually saw someone," Darcy said.

Putting the pencil down, the thin man shifted in the chair and looked at Darcy intently. "Has your cousin ever seen an image of her father appear before her prior to this?"

"No."

"And is she given to flights of fancy and storytelling?"

"No."

"And does she often faint in the middle of a shopping excursion?"

"No."

"Then what makes you think she did not see exactly what she thinks she saw?" he asked. He put his hands up to stop the words he saw forming on Darcy's lips, "Now I am not saying she saw her father, but it could very well be someone dressed to *look* like her father."

"For what purpose?" Darcy asked.

"That is not known yet, but I can assure you, I *will* find out. I take my job very seriously, and I get results. I am sure this is why the colonel has come to *me* with this task."

"I could not have my men compromise *our own* investigation without knowing if this was connected," Fitz replied.

"Wait," Darcy turned to Fitz, "you think this is connected to the case you are working on for the Army?"

"No, not at this time, but the possibility is always there," Fitz said.

The thin man made another note, "Is there anything else you wish to add?"

"Two months ago I was in Brighton," Fitz explained, "at the same time as Mrs Darcy's youngest sister, and I noticed someone following her and her friend. The same man was then seen in the wood that runs along the back of their father's home just a few weeks later."

"WHAT? Why did I not know about this?" Darcy nearly exploded.

"Calm down!" Fitz's commanding tone made Darcy flinch. "Mr Bennet was aware of these events and has been keeping an eye on his daughters. Until today, there was no indication your wife might have been a target also. The man did nothing more than watch Longbourn, and I have had my own men watching him since we learned of his presence."

"And where is he now?" the thin man asked.

"I can say he is in London, but I am not at liberty to divulge anything more than that," Fitz said. "If we find a connection between this case and my own, I will gladly cooperate, but I cannot let two and a half years of work be destroyed because of a lack of security of such vital information."

The thin man nodded in understanding and wrote some more in his notebook. He stood, putting his notebook back in his pocket, "I will find you; do not try to contact me. We will be in touch when I know something more."

When the two cousins were again alone in the room Darcy asked quietly, "Why would you keep such information from me?"

"It was not necessary to tell you until now." Fitz turned towards his cousin, "Darcy, please understand me—I do not want harm to come to any of our family, including your wife's family, but my first priority is to my own investigation. It is possible there is a connection, but until that link is found we must treat them as separate events." He put his hand on Darcy's shoulder, "My suggestion to you is to hire some extra *footmen* to accompany your wife and her sister wherever they go. I can give you some names of a few former soldiers that do this kind of work."

Darcy nodded, "Yes, thank you; I will do just that." He ran his hand over his face, "Do not tell Elizabeth; with her condition I do not want to add any stress to her already fragile emotions."

"I understand and will abide by that for now, but if something more happens she will need to be told."

"For now, I will protect her," Darcy stood from the table feeling years older than when he had come in the door.

"You cannot be around her all the time, Darcy; keep that in mind," Fitz stood also.

"We will be leaving for Pemberley early; I can keep her safe there," he said firmly.

"See if you can take Anne with you," Fitz's emotions were evident in the intensity of his eyes.

"I will see what I can do," Darcy assured him. "Aunt Catherine and I have . had little contact over this last year and she may not allow me to host her daughter, but I am certain your father can talk her into letting Anne go to Dalmeny."

"Thank you."

The two made their way back through the diminishing crowds to their horses and silently rode back to a more familiar side of London. Darcy went home and Fitz went back to his office to go over all his notes and see if he could find a possible connection between these two cases.

✦

Thursday, April 16, 1812

G.W. received a note telling him to be at this posting stop, dressed exactly as he was now, at this specific time. He knew the posting schedule and the next carriage would not be by here for another hour, so why must he be here now?

Pulling out the watch he won in a card game last night, he opened it–*right on time*. Snapping it shut, he saw a carriage coming towards the deserted station. The shades were drawn, and there were no specific indicators on the outside to tell him to whom it belonged. He did not even recognize the livery. He was nervous as the door opened and a gruff voice said, "Get in!"

He stepped into the dark carriage and the door was barely closed when the team of horses set off again. Falling into the seat, he realized there were three others with him. Once his eyes adjusted to the dim surroundings, he asked, "Where are we going?"

The gruff voice answered again, "NO talking! My orders are to shoot any of you that say a word. You will get no other warning."

G.W. sat back and tried to calm his racing heart. He had been in much graver circumstances before and made it out alive; he would just have to keep his wits about him. He could talk himself out of just about any situation, and this would be no different.

They rode in silence for over an hour before he felt something touch his foot. He assumed it was one of the other passengers trying to stretch their own legs, so he slid closer to the middle of his own seat giving them more foot room. He felt the person next to him slip a piece of paper into his hand. Feeling some raised bumps, he silently ran his rough fingers across the scrolling hand etched into it. It was the size of a calling card, and after a few minutes, he recognized the name his fingers traced—*Lady Catherine de Bourgh*.

His heart nearly stopped with the realization they were being taken to see her, probably at Rosings Park. It would explain why he must be dressed as he now was—she did not want him to be recognized. He now also knew two of the other occupants of the carriage were his comrades. Evidently, the great lady heard of their misdeeds from two days ago, and she had something to say about it.

Knowing it would be a few more hours until they were anywhere near Rosings Park, he decided to sit back and rest in the dark carriage. He leaned back into the corner and was soon asleep.

"Wake up," someone kicked his foot, jarring him awake. They were now on a rut-filled road, and soon they stopped. The door was flung open and light filled the inside, blinding the four occupants, three of which were pulled out of the carriage and pushed into a building, where they were left alone for a few more hours. G.W. recognized the place as the hunting lodge he had hid out in a few years ago.

When the door opened again, Lady Catherine waltzed in and sat on the edge of the best seat in the room, leaving the bed for the three conspirators. "Sit," she ordered. When they did so, she looked them all over, sneering at something "Are you three quite proud of yourselves?" In a false sense of joviality, she drew her hand to her chest, "I have heard some fabulously entertaining tales of what you are all about these days."

She turned her steely eyes to the first on the bed, "George *Wilson*, is it?" She waited for him to nod. "Well, *George Wilson*, I believe you have been wasting your time gallivanting about the countryside following a young lady who would not give you the time of day when you were in Brighton. So, how is it going?" Her voice was so steady it sent chills down their backs. "Well? Are you to answer me?"

"I have been... unable to... to form any kind of..."

"Stop stuttering, boy! From now on I will be very clear as to what your job will entail, and if I hear of your deviation from what I say *this* time, I cannot guarantee your safety from my men," she looked over to the large frame of the man who took up the entire doorway.

She turned to the second person, "Now, *G.W.* is it?" At his nod, she continued, "I do not see why you two boys must change your given names in such a manner—what *would* your father say?" She tapped her fan in the palm of her hand, "Well, no matter; it does not change who you are. I believe we have *you* to thank for my daughter now believing her *dead father* is alive and haunting her. While I am sure it made for a good show, *that* was not the purpose." She looked intently at him, "I will be sure to make it very clear to you as well what your role is to be from now."

She turned to the last person seated on the bed, "Now, Mrs Younge—the only one of you who seems to know her own name." She glanced at the other two then back to the woman, "I have given you many months now to carry out an act which should not take this long. My nephew's wife is now with child, and if that child is born, he or she will be the next heir to Pemberley. I think I was very clear when I said, *the heir must come from my daughter*, not from *her*."

Lady Catherine then turned to address all three of them, "It seems you need my guidance, just as you always did." Lifting her chin, she continued, "My daughter has been invited to stay with my brother for a few more weeks in Town, and then they are to go to Derbyshire to his estate. The Darcys will also be leaving in a few weeks to return early to Pemberley. Obviously this incident has frightened them enough to wish to remove from Town early. You will never find a way to overtake Mrs Darcy while they are in Derbyshire as my nephew is now suspicious of someone trying to do harm to his wife, so I suggest we wait until they return to Town. They are expecting their child to be born in the autumn, and will return to Town for its birth to be near the best medical care possible. That gives us several months to come up with a fool proof plan. I expect my *parson* to show back up for a visit with his *cousins* around the first of August. That will give us much needed information into their particular travel plans, and then, if they will be visiting her family, we can plan something in Hertfordshire instead of in Town, where obviously you lack the skills necessary to pull this off."

She stood, her steely eyes making all three shiver. "I will have my revenge," she replied, then left them alone in the cabin, with instructions given to the footman that they were not to leave until she returned to Rosings in a few more weeks. "See to it they are cared for, but not overly so," she said as she left the three alone.

"Something is wrong with her," George lay down on the floor of the hunting lodge they would be staying in for a few more days, it seemed.

"Yes, I cannot determined what it is, but there is something very odd about her behavior today," G.W. turned over and stared at the ceiling. "*It was something about her eyes.*"

"You two are ridiculous—there is nothing awry with that woman, other than her thirst for revenge," Mrs Younge replied, the springs of the bed on which she lay squeaking when she turned to face the wall. "Now go to sleep."

"No, it is something," G.W. said. "She has never had that look about her in all the years I have been acquainted with her."

CHAPTER

VIII

Thursday, April 30, 1812

Over the next two weeks tensions were high for Darcy, but he refused to reveal to his wife that anything was amiss. He took Fitz's advice and hired two new *footmen* to accompany them whenever Elizabeth or Mary left the house, but so far, their presence was not needed.

Darcy hired Madam LeFevre to come to their home and Elizabeth was able to purchase enough clothing to see her through to the end of her confinement.

Tonight they were to go to the theater, and Darcy was on edge knowing the attention they would receive at such a place. He tried to cancel, but Fitz cautioned him that changing their normal routine could prove even more dangerous than going, and these plans had been made weeks in advance. This would be their only trip to the theater before they left for Pemberley, and he was determined his wife would enjoy these last few days in Town.

Mary was nervously fidgeting while Claire fixed her hair. Tonight would be the first time she saw the viscount in over two weeks. Every time she visited with his mother he was away on business, and Elizabeth's condition, and the ill health that came with it, meant they did not leave the house often. Mary did not mind, as she was able to spend much more time with her dear friend Georgiana.

Her musings were interrupted by the maid's question, "Do you not like this look, Miss?"

"Oh, I am sorry—yes, it is lovely," Mary answered.

"You are nervous?"

Mary blushed, "Yes, just a little."

"Over this evening's trip to the theater?" Claire fussed with one curl that would not stay in place.

"No, not exactly," Mary answered.

"Ahhh, I see; then it must be nerves over a beau?" Claire asked.

"*Yes*... I mean... *no*... I do not know," she stammered.

Claire squeezed her shoulder, "It will work out, Miss."

"Thank you, Claire." Mary stood and dismissed the maid, gathered her things, and went downstairs to meet her sister. She found her sitting in the library reading. "I did not mean to disturb you," she said as she entered, "I just needed to return this book."

Elizabeth patted the sofa beside her, "Please sit with me, Mary. William will be a few more minutes yet, and we have not had the opportunity to talk today."

Sitting down, she noticed what Elizabeth read, "Ahhh, I see you are expanding into love poems now. It must be your husband's influence."

74

Elizabeth laughed and hugged her sister. "Oh Mary, I cannot tell you how much my perception of love has changed since I met William. I always said I would not marry for anything but the greatest of affection, but I never knew I would feel as loved as I do when he looks at me. No words are necessary; it is all spoken in his eyes. Just one look and I know what his heart is saying, even if his lips are silent."

Mary thought of what she said for a minute. "Do you really think the old saying is true about the eyes being the window to the soul?"

"I know it is for my William," Elizabeth closed her eyes, imagining her husband in her mind. "One day, when you meet someone who catches your attention, look into his eyes and see for yourself if it is true."

Mary's heart beat rapidly. She often saw a certain look in the viscount's eyes, but he could not truly feel for her. *He is engaged to his cousin, and even if he was not, his family must expect him to marry much higher than a simple country gentleman's daughter with little dowry. Wait a minute—what am I thinking? Marriage! The man is infuriating at times, and I have numerous reasons to not be attracted to him. No, it is best we meet only as common and indifferent acquaintances.*

"Mary? Are you well?" Elizabeth was patting her arm.

"Oh, yes, I am sorry Elizabeth."

"I was just saying you look lovely this evening, but you seemed preoccupied. Is there something you wish to talk about?"

Mary shook her head, "No, it is nothing." With a small smile, she asked, "Have you been to this theater before?"

Darcy found the two a few minutes later. Kissing his wife's cheek, he complimented both on their appearance. Mary was soon sitting in the carriage, once again thinking of all Elizabeth said about love being seen in the eyes.

⁂

"P*ssst... Claire... come here,*" she heard Miss Darcy whispering.

Looking around, she saw her husband Joseph at the end of the hall with his charge in his arms. She went up to the younger girl. "Can I help you, Miss Darcy?"

Georgiana looked around and whispered, "I must speak with you… *privately.* Follow me to my room."

When Georgiana was comfortably seated and Joseph left the room, Claire was bid sit in the nearby chair. "Now, you must tell me what you know."

"What I know, Miss? I do not understand," Claire responded.

"Yes, what you know about Mary… Miss Bennet. She has been *despondent* lately. Not very much so, just enough to catch my attention, and I cannot determine why. Do you think she misses her family?" Georgiana queried.

With a small smile, Claire said, "Ahhh, I see. Well, I cannot say for certain what is bothering Miss Bennet."

"But you have your suspicions," Georgiana goaded, carefully watching the maid's eyes. "Does she have a suitor?"

"I have not been told of one," Claire answered.

"Oh but you must know! No one has come to visit her here, but I do not accompany them when they leave Darcy House." With an exasperated sigh, she continued, "Oh you simply *must* tell me what is wrong."

Claire patted her hand, "I do not know if it is a matter of the heart."

Excitedly bouncing, Georgiana said, "Oh, it must be! How happy I will be when she marries! I wonder if I know him?"

Claire stood, "Do you need anything else, Miss Darcy?"

Georgiana smiled, "No, thank you Claire. I am certain you have some things to do in Miss Bennet's room."

"Yes, Miss." She left to complete her work and wait for Miss Bennet to return from the theater, smiling as thought of the loving family she now worked for. *It is rare to find a place like this*, she mused.

Fitz knocked on his brother's door, opening it and sticking his head in when no one answered. Alex was standing in front of the mirror.

"I think you fidget more with your cravat than any other gentleman I know," he teased.

He pulled the knot out to retie it again, "Yes, well, it is better than *some* who let their appearance go when not in uniform."

Standing tall, Fitz pulled down on the front of his jacket, "I happen to like these clothes; Mother picked them out."

"So you are telling me *your mother* still chooses your clothing? How old are you again? Are you out of leading strings yet?" Alex smiled.

"It is good to see you joking again, even if it is at my expense. I have come to deliver some good news; it seems since Aunt Catherine has decided, rather unexpectedly I might add, to return to Rosings Park on the morrow and will not be joining us at the theater this evening. Our parents have decided to stay home as well."

"Truly?" Alex finished the knot and stepped back from the mirror.

"Yes, and even more, if you promise not to tell anyone your plan, I can promise to keep Anne by my side so you are available to sit next to Miss Bennet," Fitz countered.

A small smile alit on his face, "I believe we may be able to come to an agreement for once." Alex turned towards the door, "Come on, we are wasting time up here."

Hmmmm, all he needed was a small boost, Fitz thought, *and if that boost also allows me to sit beside my Anne, I cannot complain.*

"What has urged so many changes in Aunt Catherine? First to allow Anne to stay here, even allowing her to return to Derbyshire with them, and now she is leaving us alone without her constant overseeing? It is quite odd, do you not think?"

"Odd… Hmmmm… yes," he murmured.

"Ready?"

"Oh, yes… of course."

<hr/>

Mary was trying to read the playbill in her hand, but the carriage proved to be too dark even beside the window. She looked up when she heard Elizabeth say, "Oh, that dress is divine."

"Which dress?" Mary asked as they waited in the line of carriages in front of the theater.

Elizabeth leaned over and pointed to a statuesque figure by the doors. Her light blue gown shimmered in the light of the lamps, set off by the soft white cape she wore around her shoulders. *"Oh my,* she is *lovely,"* Mary replied.

Darcy looked out the window, "That is the Lady Elaine Stalwood, daughter of the Duke of Norfolk."

"She has Jane's coloring," Mary replied.

"Yes; she is simply *breathtaking*." Elizabeth turned to her husband, "Do you know her William?"

He sat back away from the window, "We were acquainted, but I have not seen her in a couple of years." Under his breath he continued, "*I hope Alex does not notice her presence here tonight.*"

"What was that?" Elizabeth asked.

"Oh, nothing; she is not someone you would want to meet," he explained.

"Well, she *is* lovely."

"Looks can be deceiving, especially among the Ton," Darcy said quietly.

The carriage continued to inch its way forward and soon they were ready to disembark. Darcy helped Elizabeth down then stepped away from the door. Mary did not expect to see the hand that reached out for hers, but she recognized it immediately. She would know those fingers anywhere— *Viscount Primrose.*

When she was safely on the ground, he bowed and greeted her.

With a curtsy, she replied, "My lord."

Alex wound her arm through his as he followed his cousin through the crowd and into the theater. Mary felt her heart start to race as more people pushed into the foyer. Her breath caught in her chest, and Alex noticed her distress immediately. Quickly making his way to a door, he led her into a smaller room.

"Are you well, Miss Bennet?" Alex held the hand that rested on his arm.

"Thank you," she closed her eyes and started to fan herself. When she was sufficiently calmed, she opened her eyes only to find the viscount staring at her. *Just one look and I know what his heart is saying, even if his lips are silent.* Elizabeth's words ran through her mind and she could not turn away. It *was* as if his eyes were saying words his lips could not form, and Mary's heart understood those unspoken words all too well. Her heart began to beat even more rapidly with this knowledge, tears starting to form in her eyes.

All of a sudden the door flew open and someone nearly stumbled into the room, "Oh, pardon me." Lady Elaine Stalwood raised her eyebrows to Alex, "I see your proclivity to be found in places such as this, alone with a *lady*, has not changed since I last saw you, Lord Primrose."

His grip on Mary's arm tightened, fury evident in his eyes. Mary felt herself being pulled back into the foyer as he harshly replied to the woman, "You will excuse us, *my lady*."

Looking over her shoulder at the statuesque creature who stared after them with a gleam in her eye, Mary did not know what to think. *What did she mean about his proclivity to be found in such places alone with a lady?* Mary was so preoccupied with what was running through her mind she did not even notice the crowd as they pushed their way through and climbed the stairs. When they entered the box, Fitz, Anne, Darcy, Elizabeth, Bingley, and Jane were already seated, and Alex led Mary to the last bench, where he quickly sat beside her.

Fitz was sitting in front of him and stiffened when he felt his brother lean in and whisper, "Lady Elaine Stalwood is here."

He turned and quietly asked, *"Did she see you?"* At his nod, Fitz asked, "Did she *approach* you?" At his nod again, his face turned red. Turning to Anne, he said, "I will be right back." He grabbed his brother's arm and dragged him through the curtains. "Now tell me what has happened."

Alex explained what took place downstairs, and Fitz cursed under his breath. "Wait right here." Fitz soon returned with Darcy, and Alex explained again what had occurred.

Darcy's jaw tightened and he patted his cousin's shoulder, "It will work out. We will be leaving for Pemberley right after Georgiana's birthday. What rumors could she possibly start in a week?"

"She has made my life a nightmare before," Alex explained, "and it will not take much to embroil me in more with only a few words spoken to certain people."

"Yes, I agree," Fitz stated. "The Ton feeds off the gossip she seems to love to spread."

Darcy rubbed his hands together, "If we leave right now it will make whatever rumor she starts seem possible. We will wait until intermission and all go back to my house as if that was the plan all along."

The three gentlemen joined the rest of their party in the box, and Darcy explained to Elizabeth their need to leave at intermission.

His eyes pleaded for her to understand without explanation, and she quietly acquiesced, "When we return home I expect to be told what is going on."

"Of course; please tell your sister of our changed plans."

Elizabeth leaned over and explained all she knew to Jane, who nodded her assent and relayed everything to her husband.

Anne leaned over, quietly asking Fitz, "What is going on?"

His simple reply, "*Lady Elaine Stalwood is here,*" made her pale.

Only Mary was left in the dark as to what had occurred. She was so distracted with this being her first trip to the theater, she did not notice the somber moods of all the others in their box.

Alex leaned closer to her and held out his hand, "My mother insisted I bring these for you to use."

She smiled and took the offered opera glasses, thanking him, then continued to read the playbill until the actors took to the stage.

All throughout the first few acts of *Macbeth* Alex tried to pay attention, but the situation made him very nervous. Noticing Mary's enthusiasm starting to diminish, he leaned near her and asked, "*Macbeth* is not your particular favorite of the Bard's plays, is it?"

"No, not really," she answered.

"Which do you prefer?" he asked.

"I actually like the comedies more than the tragedies," Mary lowered the glasses to her lap.

"Somehow I thought that about you."

The act ended, signaling it was time for intermission. The four ladies were soon being led through the crowd and back out to their carriages. Darcy and Elizabeth rode alone, allowing them the opportunity to speak of what took place in the theater, and Mary found herself sitting next to Anne and across from the Fitzwilliam brothers in the viscount's carriage, though she was still confused as to why it was necessary, though she did not question anyone.

Arriving at Darcy House, the gentlemen once again helped the ladies down from the carriages, and Mary *once again* tried to calm her racing heart when the viscount escorted her inside and into the drawing room. No matter how often he performed this task, it always had the same affect on her.

Anne sat next to Mary on the sofa. The men were talking on the other side of the room, and Anne turned towards Mary, "I have enjoyed being in Town these last few weeks and will miss it next week."

"Do you prefer Town to the country?" Mary asked.

"My mother has rarely allowed me the opportunity to come, but if I were to choose, I like the diversions Town has to offer. It is also easier on my health than the country as the best doctors in all of England are here," Anne replied.

"Yes, that is why Elizabeth's plan is to return when it is closer to time for her to have their baby," Mary explained.

Anne looked at Darcy, "I am not surprised; my cousin will do anything to see a safe delivery, especially after all his own mother went through to have Georgiana."

Having heard the tragic tale of Mrs Darcy's difficult pregnancy, as well as the delivery that led to her death, Mary did not need any further explanation. "Are you returning home next week?" Mary asked.

Smiling and looking down at her hands, Anne said, "No, I am to go to Dalmeny with my aunt and uncle. My aunt insists on showing me the results of our redecorating excursions."

"Oh," Mary said, "I did not realize you were traveling with them."

"It is a recent development," she replied, not wanting to recount the tale of the rather loud conversation this morning in which her uncle insisted to her mother that she accompany them instead of returning to Rosings Park.

Elizabeth joined them and sat down beside Mary, reaching for her hand, "I am sorry we were unable to stay for the whole play, but I am sure you understand why we had to leave, right?"

Mary was saved from answering when Anne said, "I cannot believe *she* is back in Town."

"Yes, well, we will all be leaving within the next week, so she will not have time to cause any more trouble," Elizabeth assured her.

Quietly, Anne said, "You do not know how fast the rumor mills can start."

"I am certain it is no faster than in Meryton," Elizabeth said. "I will be right back," she said as she went to her husband's side. By the time she returned, Mrs Benson was ready with a small repast, so they all removed to the dining room where no more was said of the trip to the theater.

Mary retired that evening unsure of what to think. She knew what she saw in his eyes, and yet he barely spoke with her all these weeks in Town. She was also extremely confused at the *situation* everyone kept speaking of, but not explaining. She got the impression something was going on with the viscount.

CHAPTER

IX

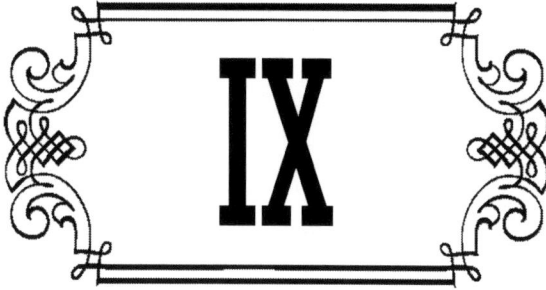

Friday, May 1, 1812

Darcy was sitting in the dining room when Alex came in, a box in his hands. Darcy's eyes got big, "Please tell me I am not seeing things."

Alex smiled, "No, you are not seeing things. I thought Miss Bennet might enjoy one of the rare treats of Town since she has never been here for a Season before, so I brought enough for even your appetite to be appeased."

Darcy ate his treat in silence, his face showing the delight it brought, and Alex had to laugh. "You know, Chelsea is not that far from here. You could go purchase these treats yourself instead of waiting until I bring them to you."

"If I started doing that I would want to go every morning," he said. "No, I do much better in leaving them as a treat for only when you take the time to go." He finished his last bite, "Georgiana and Miss Bennet have already broken their fast; they are now out in the garden."

"Then to the garden I will go," Alex said. "Here," he gave Darcy one more before he closed the box, "that is for your wife, so do not eat it yourself."

Looking at his cousin's face, he opened the box once more, "No, your poor wife will never know what she has missed. There, now you can enjoy one more, and leave your wife's treat alone."

Darcy laughed at Alex as he left through the doors that led outside to the garden. He could hear Georgiana's squeals of glee when she recognized what was in his hands.

Alex bowed to the two, "Miss Bennet, I must offer my apologies for your ears being deafened by my young cousins' exuberant cries, but as you see, she knows what I have with me."

"*Hot Cross Buns!*" Georgiana said excitedly as she bounced on the bench in anticipation.

"Yes indeed," he answered with a smile.

"Have you ever had *Hot Cross Buns* when you were in Town before, Miss Bennet?" Georgiana asked.

"Not that I remember," she answered.

"Well then, be prepared for a treat the likes of which you will compare all others to from now on," Alex said gleefully.

"You think very highly of these buns, my lord," Mary said with a small lift of her eyebrow.

"When you have tasted them yourself, I am certain you will agree," he nodded to the footman his thanks for the dishes being placed on the table, then helped Georgiana and Mary to their chairs, sitting on the other side of Mary as the footman served the two ladies their buns. Georgiana took a deep breath of the confection and cut into it with all care, savoring the flavor of each bite.

"I could not imagine you being here for your first Season in Town without trying one of the most delicious treats London has to offer. Chelsea Bun

House serves these buttery buns with raisins and currants rolled on the inside and covered in a sweet glaze," he explained as she took her first bite. Mary's face showed her delight in the treat, and Alex smiled. "Now you see I have not lied to you, Miss Bennet."

"Oh, these *are* delightful," she said between bites.

Georgiana quickly finished her own bun and sat back into her chair, "If I had known you were to bring these I would not have broken my fast already. I do not think I can eat another bite now," she joked.

Alex smiled at his young cousin. "I may just have to bring you some more on Tuesday for your birthday."

Smiling, Georgiana asked, "Are you not going to enjoy one?"

"I have already partaken of one myself—my mother insisted on me eating with her, my brother, and Anne this morning," he explained.

"The colonel was here a few minutes ago taking his leave of us," Mary said, then took another bite.

"Yes, his work is taking him to Brighton for a few weeks," Alex said.

"Does he travel often?" Mary asked.

"Sometimes, though his usual assignment is here in London. He has been known to be gone sometimes for weeks at a time," Alex answered.

Darcy came out to the table, "I hate to be the bearer of bad news, but Georgiana, Mrs Annesley is waiting for you in the music room with your tutor."

"It seems I must leave you to my cousin's hands now," she said to her friend as Darcy came over and picked her up.

Mary took another bite of her bun before pushing the plate away, "As much as I adore these, I doubt I can finish the whole thing."

"Well then, would you care to take a stroll in the park across the way?" he asked.

"Yes, that does sound nice," Mary replied. "I have some scraps I have been saving to feed to the ducks."

"Do you go over there often?" he asked as he pulled out her chair for her.

"Georgiana and I try to go a couple times a week. We planned on going this morning, but did not make it there yet," Mary said, indicating the bundle of scraps on the bench. She gathered her things and they went back inside.

"I will return in just a minute," Alex went to find Darcy and let him know where they would be. When he returned, Mary had her spencer on and was tying her bonnet. He put his arm out to her when she was finished, "Are you ready?"

"Yes, thank you," she answered. Noticing Claire following them, she smiled at his solicitous gesture; *that is why he left for a minute—to have someone walk with us.* Mary felt her heart start to beat wildly as it always did in his presence and she could not help the blush that overtook her cheeks when she almost stumbled and his arm tightened to keep her from falling.

"Are you uninjured, Miss Bennet?"

Finding her footing again easily, she answered, "Yes, thanks to your arm, my lord."

Alex smiled as they quietly walked across the park to the bench beside the pond. When they were seated he asked, "Did you enjoy the performance last night?"

"I have never been to the theater before, so it was quite an experience," she replied.

"But it was not your particular choice of plays," he took the offered bread and broke it up, throwing the pieces to the ducks.

"No, I have never really enjoyed Macbeth," Mary threw her pieces one by one out into the pond.

"Which would you have preferred to see?"

"My favorite of the Bard's works is *Much Ado About Nothing*," she answered. "What about you?"

"*As You Like It*, though your favorite and *The Taming of the Shrew* come in close behind for me," Alex answered.

"Ahhh, now any of those would have been delightful to see," Mary chuckled.

The two sat talking in companionable conversation for a few more minutes before they decided to take a stroll around the pond then return to Darcy House. Mary later reflected on their walk and was confused. He gave particular attention to her last night and today, even though he was seemingly engaged to his cousin. In her heart she almost wished he were not engaged, but she could not allow herself to become attached to such a man. *He is only being amiable*, she tried to tell herself. He was, truly, an amiable gentleman. If only she could reconcile all these different qualities others told her about with what she saw herself. The situation truly baffled her.

***

Monday, May 4, 1812

Mary was quietly reading in the library when she heard a disturbance in the front hall. She poked her head out the door to see Lord Primrose asking anxiously, "Where is my cousin? I must speak with him immediately!"

"Right this way, my lord," the butler said as they turned her direction. Not wanting him to see her, she stepped back into the library as they passed. The butler passed again not even a minute later and returned to his post by the door. Raised voices in the study left her intrigued, and she sneaked down the hall to Darcy's study, putting her ear close to the door and trying to determine what could be so upsetting. What she heard sent cold chills down her back. Lord Primrose was speaking, the words cutting into her heart.

> ". . . and she is now with child. Her husband refuses to stand Moses for the child, and the possible results could tear our family apart. What are we to do? We must hide this information from the Ton. I have convinced her husband to allow his last name to be used for the child, but he refuses to do anything more than that. His wife has now been sent away to live with her uncle. He will not divorce her, but he also will never allow her back into his house again. She is practically destitute."

Mary retreated back to the library, shocked at what she overheard the viscount professing loudly through the study door. She was unable to hear *all* of what was said, but what she *did* hear left her heart reeling. All of a sudden, she heard the two come out of the study in a fury, the viscount quickly leaving and Darcy marching heavily up the stairs. Mary retired to her room, and all of Lady Catherine's and Caroline Bingley's previous warnings and pronouncements about the viscount came rushing back into her mind.

She sat down on her bed, not understanding what was going on around her, and began to cry. Reaching into her drawer, she pulled out a handkerchief. As she wiped her eyes with the cloth, she realized it was the one *he* had given her when he returned her glasses.

After all the warnings, after all the stories I have been told, even after knowing of his family's expectation of his marriage to his cousin and Miss de Bourgh's own confirmation of their attachment, I still allowed a small part of my heart to dream the impossible. Now those dreams are crashing down as he is to be a father and will more than likely be marrying his cousin soon in order to avert any sandal that is sure to come to the family because of his actions.

Mary curled up in her bed and cried so much she made herself sick. Over the next few days she only left her room when it was necessary, counting down to Thursday morning when they were to leave for Pemberley and she would not have to see the viscount again for a long time.

***

Thursday, May 7, 1812

Alex was dressed early, and ready to accompany his cousins to Pemberley. As he descended the stairs, he saw his parents in the breakfast room, and entered to bid them farewell.

"Oh, there you are," Helen said to her eldest son. "Have a seat, and eat something before you go."

"No thank you, I haven't much time—you know Darcy and his punctuality with all things, especially when leaving on a journey. I just came to wish you farewell. Do you know yet when you will be returning to Dalmeny?"

"Our travel plans are not yet fixed, as we are hoping to have the doctor look at Anne once more before we leave," Hugh replied.

Alex nodded, "I will be at Pemberley for a few weeks, then will be going to Dalmeny so I shall see you when I arrive. Goodbye Father," he reached over to firmly shake his father's hand. "Goodbye Mother," he was quickly embraced in a tight hug from his mother.

"Alex," Helen said when she pulled back, "promise me you will win her heart."

He started to say, "I do not know who . . ."

"Yes you do, son," Hugh interrupted. "You know exactly who we are talking about, and we want you to know you have our full support. She is just who you need, and just who Dalmeny needs."

"I know she is intimidated by the prospect of marrying someone of your rank in society, but I am certain she will come around," Helen assured her son. "Love will triumph, after all."

Alex looked down at his hands and took a deep breath, "I hope so."

Helen rose and took his hand in hers, drawing his eyes up to her face, "Have patience with her, and she will see what you have to give to her. You have to understand how she grew up. She has always known she was without many prospects. She is the middle of five girls, without much of a dowry and given a minimal education at best. As a naturally quiet person, she is often overlooked and not used to receiving specific attention. I can imagine she is probably scared of what life would be like if she accepts your attentions."

"Yes, we once talked of her life and how she was reared is a vastly different story than my own."

Hugh firmly grasped his son's shoulder, "She needs to understand her own heart before she can accept yours, son. Give her time and she will see what you are about."

The few minutes he had while waiting for the occupants of Darcy House were just long enough for him to think of all his parents said to him. *I think I am starting to finally understand why it is so hard for you to accept me Mary Bennet,* he thought, *and I will not let you go this time. I will fight for us no matter what walls you put up because of your own fear..*

Mary was taken aback when she realized the viscount would be accompanying Darcy on horseback as the ladies rode inside Georgiana's carriage. They were also to stop in Meryton for a few days before leaving Monday morning for Pemberley. Mary was looking forward to seeing her family and watched out the window as the buildings of Town slowly disappeared and the roads became windier. Before tea time they were pulling through the town of Meryton on their way to Longbourn, and Mary could not help but smile as her home came into view.

When they dismounted, Darcy saw the distressed look on his cousin's face as he patted his horse's neck and spoke to the stable hand. When the boy walked away with both their mounts, Darcy came up beside Alex, "He will understand."

"I hope so," Alex said somberly, "I truly hope so."

"Mr Bennet is a fair and perceptive gentleman; this is not like before," Darcy tried to assure him.

"No, it is nothing like before," Alex followed the others into Longbourn.

When the pleasantries were exchanged and tea was served, Henry asked the two gentlemen if they would care to join him in his study.

"Actually, I had something I wished to discuss privately with you, if you do not mind, sir," Alex said.

"Yes, of course, my lord," Henry answered, leading the viscount to his office, curious as to what it could be. If the look on his face told anything, it could be nothing good.

The two were ensconced in the study alone for over an hour, and when they came out at last, Bennet asked to speak with Darcy for a minute. Alex excused himself to go for a walk and was not seen again until it was well past dark outside.

Darcy met him at the door when he returned, "How did it go?"

"He was understandably upset by the situation, but was glad nothing has come of it so far. I explained why I was worried something would, but he does not think any further action is needed," Alex explained. "He and Mr Gardiner will keep their eyes open for anything appearing in the papers."

"If nothing has been posted yet, I doubt it will be," Darcy said.

"I can only hope you are right," Alex said as he slowly went upstairs and retired for the night.

CHAPTER

X

Sunday, May 10, 1812

Georgiana was sitting outside in the garden when the others returned from services. Kitty and Lydia eagerly went to sit next to their friend, greeting her with a hug.

"You promised me details of your birthday, and I am prepared to be amazed," Kitty said excitedly.

"Well, my day started with my cousin personally delivering Hot Cross Buns for me. *Oh they are so good!* I could eat them every day if it were not for my figure." She turned to her friend, "When you are next in Town you must go to Chelsea and purchase some."

Georgiana then went on to describe what she did all day, giving particular attention to the foods served that evening for a small family supper and the gifts her family lavished upon her. Kitty was awed by Georgiana's new locket, and both giggled and talked for another hour, before they were interrupted by Mr Bennet.

"Kitty, your mother wishes to speak with you," he said to his daughter.

She turned to her friend, "I will be back in a few minutes."

Henry sat, "I will gladly keep you company while you wait, Miss Darcy."

"Thank you, sir," Georgiana smiled. The two formed a close relationship when she stayed here a few months before.

Henry looked in Joseph's direction, "I see you still have your carrying service with you."

Putting her nose in the air as her Aunt Catherine would do, she joked, "Yes, well, you know us of the *Haute Ton*—so spoiled we dare not soil our shoes with walking!"

Henry laughed heartily, "I see you have not lost your sense of humor." He looked at the young girl beside him, "In all seriousness, how is your recovery going?"

"You know how it is—some days are good and others are not so good."

"Yes, I know that all too well," Henry rubbed his own aching leg. "Are your doctors hopeful you will gain more strength over time?"

Georgiana looked out over the flowers, "No, they are almost certain I will never walk again."

"How are you handling that knowledge?"

"I know I must make some decisions that have been put off for far too long, but I just do not know if I am ready yet," Georgiana said.

Henry leaned over to look into the young girl's face, "Promise me you will at least try to accept the changes before you return in the autumn." At her nod of acceptance, he continued, "And, promise me you will not forever rule out using your bath chair to get around."

"I do not know that I am ready for that," she replied.

"Just promise to try," he tapped under the chin as he did with one of his girls when they were down. "Life will be much easier if you are able to get around—think of all the shops you could once again visit, or church services every week instead of just when you are strong enough."

Georgiana smiled sweetly, "I promise to *try*."

"Good then," Bennet sat back. "Now, tell me which flowers you have talked my wife into giving you cuttings of from our garden? I hear you have your own retreat at Pemberley that you have created over the years?"

Kitty returned a few minutes later, and they talked for only half an hour more before they returned inside for tea. Georgiana knew the next few days would be hard on her, so she retired early that evening to rest for their trip back to Pemberley starting tomorrow.

Wednesday, May 20, 1812

Jane and Bingley were seated together in the study when the mail was delivered. Bingley went through the stack, amazed at the invitations they were still receiving for events in London. "What do you want me to do with all these, Jane?" he asked.

"I will respond to them tomorrow. I do not have much time today; Mama and I need to work in the stillroom on a few medicines for the tenants."

"Do you enjoy doing that?"

She smiled sweetly, "Lizzy is much better at that particular job, but I do enjoy being in the stillroom. It always reminds me of my Granny Bennet."

Setting the invitations aside, he continued through the slowly dwindling stack. The last one was for Jane from Elizabeth, and Bingley smiled and handed it to his wife.

"OH! Elizabeth has written!" Jane tore into it nearly ripping the paper in her excitement.

Bingley watched as her mouth moved when she silently read, smiling when the letter revealed something funny.

Jane looked up and saw him watching her, "What is wrong?"

"Oh, nothing," he said, "I just like watching you when you read. Your lips move as you read along, and you smile, especially when the letter is from your sister."

Jane blushed, "Lizzy is so descriptive of the details. It is as if I can see Pemberley unfolding before my very eyes."

"One day we will have to go up there," Bingley said. "It is the most beautiful estate. Darcy's mother and grandmother were both accomplished at planning the most fantastic gardens throughout the park."

"Lizzy says maybe the family can make plans to go there for the Christmas season," Jane said.

Bingley smiled, "Darcy is brave wanting to invite the family at such a time as to ensure they will be snowed in for a few months."

"Does it snow so very much in Derbyshire?"

"Yes, absolutely; one year we were so snowed in when visiting for Christmas that we could not return to school until two weeks late," Bingley replied. "We had the most wonderful ice fort and snowball fights you could ever imagine while we waited for the roads to be passable." Chuckling, he said, "My good aim came in handy and the viscount and I won against Darcy and the colonel at the last minute. Of course, it helped that their fort collapsed, taking half their prepared snowballs with it."

Jane squeezed his hand and smiled, "I love hearing stories of when you were younger. A house full of girls is very different then a bunch of boys."

"We will just have to make sure we have a house full of boys then so you will forever be smiling and laughing at their antics," Bingley kissed her cheek. "Come, I want to show you a book I found at the circulating library yesterday. I am certain you will know which flower this one particular picture is of and I want to see if we can plant some in the garden."

Wednesday, June 3, 1812

The days seemed to be passing quickly for some, but life was not as favorable to Caroline Bingley. First the Darcys, along with the viscount, left Town earlier than expected, then when Charles and Jane left Town as well, Aunt Hamilton saw no point in continuing on there, especially because no one would extend invitations to Caroline on her own. So, against the advice and cajoling of her niece, she insisted upon returning to Scarborough.

Caroline was once again thrown into the company of the neighbors, including one particular gentleman—Mr Curtis Wildsmith. He had a small estate on the outskirts of town, and though not exactly the highest of rank in the area, he did hold enough land to be worthy of attention from all the local young ladies. Those he grew up with did not turn the gentleman's head though, and when Caroline Bingley, with her light blonde hair and tall, lean features, came into town, he was taken with her beauty. He did not know anything about her personality, but she would do nicely on his arm, and her dowry of £20,000 was enough incentive for him to put his suit forward to her.

Caroline was not impressed with the gentleman. He wore glasses, had bright red hair and freckles, and was constantly rubbing his hands on his pants and twitching his fingers, and the one time he touched her hand ungloved she was repulsed by his excessively sweaty palms. No, Mr Curtis Wildsmith would get no attention from her. She often turned around and walked away when she saw him coming her way. She could not, however, avoid the teas he was invited to by her Aunt Hamilton, or the card parties her aunt seemed to favor. Often the two were partnered for cards, and twice he asked to stand up with her for a set at a local dance. Caroline endured his attentions without giving him any reason to hope she would accept anything more.

He did not take a hint very well though. Today she found herself sitting in the garden next to the man she spent too much time trying to avoid. His demeanor and anxious stuttering worried her. *Oh, if only something would interrupt this interview and I could get away from this man,* she thought. Just then a servant walked up to her and delivered a letter, offering her the opportunity to walk away without having to hear his ideas on marriage partners.

She excused herself and returned inside to find the missive was from her brother. Eager to see if he was to extend an invitation to her again, she quickly went upstairs to her room and closed the door, tearing into the letter. *No, of course he could not host her again—it would be too much strain on his wife at this time.* She balled the letter up and threw it into the fire, watching the flames engulf the pages, turning them to ash.

Caroline stared off into the fireplace until late into the night, trying to work out just how she could get away from here. *There must be a way back into my brother's good graces,* she thought. As time passed, she became incensed at the new family to which he attached himself, and as morning's rays began to peek through the curtains, she vowed reprisal on the lot of them for ruining her life and causing such distance from her brother. She would find a way to talk Charles into an invitation to Netherfield Park, and then her revenge would be great. *Hmmmm,* she thought, *maybe I should take the time to return my recent correspondence from Mrs Miranda Philips.*

Thursday, June 4, 1812

Bennet received a letter from his brother and sat down to think of all he suggested once again. They had yet to hear from Mr Collins with an answer to the papers the solicitors drew up. Gardiner suggested from the beginning that a date be put in them stating how long the offer would be open for consideration, but Bennet did not think it would be necessary. Who would possibly be so daft as to let such an offer go unattended for such a length of time? Now he realized he should have listened to his brother-in-law all those months ago. It was five months later, and his cousin had still not sent his answer. Now it seemed the man was away on a particular mission for his patroness, and any correspondence would take weeks to reach him and be returned with an answer.

Well, there was no way around it. Bennet sat down at his desk and took out the necessary accoutrements, trimming his quills and laying them out on the desk next to his ink well, then pulled a blank piece of paper out and began to put all his thoughts into the missive, scratching this part out, or underlining that part. After over an hour he felt comfortable with the words he penned, and he made two exact copies—one to be sent to Mr Collins from his attorney and one to keep in his records, giving his cousin three months—until autumn—to make a decision and either accept the terms or reject them. If he did not answer, it would be assumed he was rejecting the terms and no future contact would be made about this matter.

After writing a letter of explanation to his attorney and another to his brother, he set them aside to be sent out tomorrow, and wearily climbed the stairs to join his wife in their chambers, hoping he would have this whole mess behind him soon. If Mr Collins was not going to sign the papers, then he would need to make other arrangements for his family, and Darcy already said he had a few ideas to discuss with him when they returned to Town for Elizabeth's confinement, if this did not become a reality as he hoped it would.

His mind was a whirl of activity still when he lay down next to his sleeping wife. As she turned to cuddle into his arms he kissed her cheek, "*I will do my best to provide for you, my dear,*" he whispered. "*I promise.*"

Sarah Johnson

Tuesday, June 9, 1812

Alex walked to the library door knowing Mary was in there reading, as she was nearly every night at this time. She had avoided him for weeks now, since before they arrived at Pemberley, and he could not determine why. The last civil conversation they had was when he walked with her around the pond more than a month ago in London, but since then she was back to ignoring him, and being barely civil when she did deign to speak to him. Business kept him and Darcy busy during the month of May, not allowing him very many opportunities to even see her. He knew it was time to put this behind them, and he hoped she would not do as she did in the past and just ignore his plea that they talk. With a deep breath, he turned the handle on the door and entered the library. She was sitting on the sofa on the other side of the room and looked up coldly from her book. *Is that hurt I see in her eyes,* he wondered to himself. *When have I hurt her?*

Alex closed his eyes and swallowed the lump forming in his throat as he walked over to where she sat. "Do you mind if I sit?"

"Actually, I was just about to retire," she said shortly.

"I will not take up much of your time, but there is something I wish to discuss with you, and I have brought Claire along so we are not alone," he said, trying to ease her mind.

Claire stood by the door giving them privacy, and Mary decided, seemingly against her own will, to listen to him. "As you wish," she said, though her actions did not show her being very open to hearing what he had to say.

He sat next to her on the sofa, "What have I done to offend you?"

Mary looked down at the book in her hands, "What makes you think I am offended?"

"Miss Bennet, may I speak plainly with you?" he asked. At her nod, he continued, "I do not understand you. One day we are discussing Shakespeare while amiably strolling through the park, and the next thing

I know you are avoiding me for weeks on end. It was the same last year when I stayed at Netherfield Park, and I simply cannot fathom what I could have done to deserve such censure from you."

Mary did not move.

"I only want to understand, Miss Bennet. *Please?*" he pleaded. When she still would not say anything to him, or even look at him, he stood and bowed, "I do not wish to distress you and will leave you now. I truly am sorry if I have done something to offend you, but as I said last year when you also refused to speak with me, until you tell me what is bothering you, I will never know."

He left the room dejected.

Mary was not aware of the tears streaming down her cheeks until Claire pressed a handkerchief into her hands. Putting the book aside, she thanked the maid and dabbed her eyes.

When Mary calmed a little, Claire asked, "Would you like me to help you upstairs, Miss?"

"No, not just yet; I will be up shortly" Mary said, dismissing the maid. She sat looking down at her hands as her mind tried to find a solution to the problems that plagued her about the viscount.

Mary sat thinking of all her interactions with him over the last seven months. *Why am I offended? From the very beginning of our acquaintance he has been solicitous of my needs. Oh, I know the stories I have heard, and they frighten me, but after what Elizabeth said about the eyes—I just cannot put aside what I see in his. While he said I looked almost wild to his cousin, his eyes told something different when he returned my spectacles. While I have struggled with Miss Bingley's assertions of his being a rake; that is not what I see of him. I question even my own ears and what I heard through the door about his fathering a child and causing a scandal. He has never looked at another as he looks at me. Even with his cousin it is simply a familial look of mutual camaraderie, not what I see in either of my sister's or their husband's eyes when they look upon their spouse. But when he looks at me, it is as if the world stands still.*

Sarah Johnson

When he reaches for my hand or places my own on his arm, it is as if my heart will beat through my chest. I cannot refrain from thinking about him, even though I do not understand what he is about. What are his intentions? His family's expectations must be fulfilled in his choice of a wife, and I know I do not fit what is necessary for such a person of distinction.

Even so, he does not deserve my wrath. If his life's choices lead to his marriage to Miss de Bourgh, or to someone else entirely, I cannot let it affect me as it does. I must put this behind me and allow my own heart to heal from this pain. My own feelings for the gentleman have taken so dramatic a turn that it frightens me. If only I knew what his intentions were, I could better manage this anguish. If only I could be so brave as to ask—oh, but I dare not be so brazen. No, I must just put this behind me and go on with my life, letting him go on with his as well. He at least deserves my civility when we are forced together, and I will have to purpose in my heart to give him that, she decided, tears once again overtaking her eyes at the finality of her decision. Before Mary knew it, she fell asleep in the library.

CHAPTER

XI

Fitz arrived at Pemberley late after riding hard all day. He was just about to retire to a nice hot bath and soft bed when he saw his brother come stomping out of the library. "Is something wrong?"

"Not now, Fitz," Alex said gloomily, pushing past and going to the music room.

He could barely discern Mary crying in the library and Fitz ran his hands through his hair and groaned under his breath, "Why must I be the one to remedy everything?"

Sighing at what he knew he must do, he went to his room to refresh himself, quickly washing up and brushing the dust from his clothes as best he could. Then upon returning to the library, he found Mary asleep on the couch.

Fitz could hear the far off notes his brother banged out on the pianoforte, the tension in the air making him realize just how desperately he was needed. Fitz pulled up a chair from near the fireplace and sat across from Mary, then he gently reached out his hand and woke her.

She opened her eyes, groggily wiping at them, though it only made them sting even more. Then she began to realize who was seated directly in front of her. "Colonel, I did not expect to see you," Mary's greeting was solemn.

"Are you feeling well, Miss Bennet?"

"Yes, thank you," she answered.

"Your face is flushed, though I have a feeling it is not from exertion, but instead from crying," he stated.

Sitting up, she asked, "How did you know?"

He folded his arms across his wide chest, "Darcy and I have had charge of Georgiana since my Uncle George passed away, and if there is anything I have learned to discern over the years, it is tears." Pointing to her face, he explained, "Your eyes are red rimmed and swollen, and a handkerchief is clutched tightly in your hand."

Mary looked at her hands and began to fold the handkerchief, smoothing out the wrinkles left from her tight grip. "You are very perceptive, sir."

Taking on a naturally authoritative stance, he said, "Now, let us get down to business. What has my brother done to cause you to cry?"

"What makes you think your brother had anything to do with it?"

"Listen," he said, indicating the music that played in the distance. "He only plays like that when he is upset, and I saw him exit this room earlier in quite the temper." Looking at her, he said, "Do you want to talk? It will make things easier on me if you do."

Wringing the handkerchief in her hand again, Mary timidly said, "I do not understand..." she stopped, not knowing what else to add.

"You have not had the privilege of being raised with a brother," he stated.

"Yes, as we have discussed before. I find myself very confused," she replied, quietly adding, "around men in general, but especially your brother."

"Well, as the person who knows him better than any other, let me assure you, his intentions are not to confuse you," Fitz said.

"But what *are* his intentions, Colonel?" she asked.

"Only he can tell you, when he is ready," Fitz stated. "My brother has, unfortunately, been through some very trying situations over the years which have wounded him deeply. He may put on a nice smile, but inside he is as unsure of himself as you are."

Caroline Bingley's words of warning came back to her. "*What* has he been through?"

"That is not a story for me to tell," Fitz replied, "but believe me when I say he truly is a good man, despite what has happened in the past."

"I do not know if I can trust him," Mary quietly said, "not with what I have heard of his past."

Fitz sat forward, leaning his forearms on his knees so he could look directly into her eyes, "Miss Bennet, if we truly were siblings, we would have a rapport which I know we do not yet possess, but please trust what I say to you. When my brother is ready to speak of all he has been through, he will. No one can force him, and what has happened needs to come from him, not me. What *you* have heard, unless it came from someone in our family, is probably nothing more than a rumor started by a spiteful person."

"You speak as someone who has his own story to tell, Colonel," Mary stated.

He nodded, "I have had to learn to talk to someone also, about things I did not even know were holding me back. My own story is very different from my brother's, but we all carry the scars of the past. I am certain you have your own to tell, and one day, when you find the right person and the right time, you will learn to move on from your past also. Talking to my Anne has truly taught me a lot about myself."

"Anne? De Bourgh?" she questioned quickly, clearly taken aback.

"Yes," he was confused at her question. "She told me you knew of us?"

Realization dawning, Mary quickly went over all Anne had said to her. *She was not staring at the viscount that evening when he came in the drawing room door, she was staring at the colonel who stood beside him,* Mary thought. "But her mother said…"

"My Aunt Catherine is not well. As I am sure you have heard Anne say, she often has headaches. She speaks of things as if they were the truth when they are nothing more than her own fantasies." Looking down, he continued, "I do not wish to draw you into a family dispute, but you cannot believe what she says. One minute she will claim Darcy was intended for her daughter, still insisting he marry her even though he is happily married to your sister now. Then the next minute she insists it was my brother for whom her sister and she always spoke of being united. This is all her own fantasies though and the family has never had an expectation of such a union for any of us. They want us to marry for more heartfelt reasons than simply obligation."

"So your brother is not engaged?" Mary asked.

"Miss Bennet, let me assure you, my brother is quite unencumbered and free to make his own choice," Fitz said.

Mary sat stunned as she thought back to how she treated him over the last month—really over practically their entire acquaintance. "But what about the scandal that caused him to leave London?"

"I know of no scandal that came from his Season in Town," Fitz said, continuing under his breath with, "*though we did expect something to come from that wretched woman again. Thank God it did not.*"

"What wretched woman?" Mary asked.

Looking at her quizzically, he finally said, "I will leave that for my brother to tell you when he is ready."

"But I know what I heard him say, Colonel. I heard him speaking to William of... *of a woman*... who was *with child* and sent away to live with her uncle," she said quietly.

Realization dawned and Fitz immediately knew to what she was referring. Pulling a letter from his pocket, he asked, "May I read you something we recently found among my father's things? It is a letter from Darcy's father to mine written when my brother was just a babe himself. It is dated December 29, 1782."

At her nod, he asked for her silence to all others of what he was to tell her, then quietly read.

> "You cannot imagine the week I have had, brother. Lewis and Catherine have finally left, and my dear Anne is resting after so emotional an upheaval as was thrown upon us this last week.
>
> It seems Lewis' visit to Pemberley just a few months ago for my wedding produced a situation we are now left to handle. Our brother seduced the wife of my steward, and she is now with child. Her husband refuses to stand Moses for the child, and the possible results could tear our family apart. What are we to do? We must hide this information from the Ton."

Mary's heart beat wildly as the words she heard the viscount say that day through the door were now read aloud from the paper in the colonel's hand. Mary's hand went to her mouth as a look of shock overtook her face.

Fitz stopped reading, "Are these the words you heard him speak, Miss Bennet?

"Yes," she managed to whisper.

"May I continue now?" he asked.

Mary took another deep breath, calming her racing heart, and replied, "Yes, please continue."

> "I have convinced her husband to allow his last name to be used for the child, but he refuses to do anything more than that. His wife has now been sent away to live with her uncle. He will not divorce her, but he also will never allow her back into his house again. She is practically destitute. I have convinced Lewis of his duty to provide for the child, and he has finally agreed to my plan.
>
> Attached are the documents I had him sign. I am sending a copy to you to keep, and I have the other copy here at Pemberley, as he does not want Catherine to learn of the particulars. Lewis has agreed to make some amendments to his will to provide for his child, and those changes have been sent to his solicitor in Town."

Fitz looked up to Mary, "My brother found this letter and told Darcy about it right before they left London. He changed his own plans of returning to Dalmeny and has been here this last month going through all my Uncle George's old letters and business papers with Darcy, trying to see what else they can learn of this situation." Fitz waited for her eyes to meet his before he continued. "I would not wish to burden you further, but I think you need to know something else I immediately thought of when this letter was finally sent to me last week, and thus why I have come to inform my brother and cousin of my suspicion and help with the search. I have reason to believe the child that resulted from this situation may be the same man who caused Georgiana's accident."

Mary drew in her breath and put her hand to her mouth, "Are you certain?"

"Not yet; we never thought before of a possible connection to Pemberley's steward as we knew he did not have any children, but *Wickham* is not that common of a name and the baby mentioned in this letter, if it lived, would now be the right age as the man Georgiana described to us after her accident. We need to find something with the child's name, or at least its gender, but so far nothing else has been found."

Fitz sat back and watched as Mary absorbed the shocking information he presented to her. When color started to return to her cheeks, he said, "My brother truly is a good man—*please give him a chance to prove it to you.*"

Mary looked down at the handkerchief still tightly clutched in her hand and quietly said, "That sounds like advice Elizabeth would give to me."

"Well then, I am in good company," a small smile formed on his lips. "I truly do care for your well-being," he added seriously, "as I would if you *were truly* my sister."

Mary looked up into his warm blue eyes, "Thank you—for everything."

Fitz stood, "I have done my duty and will leave you now to retire along with the rest of my family; well, all except *Mr Brooding*, that is," he said, again indicating the music still ringing through the halls.

"Do you truly think he is brooding?" Mary asked.

"Just as you did not grow up with brothers, we did not grow up with sisters. He is just as fearful and confused as you in some ways," Fitz explained. "I will see you tomorrow," he placed the chair back against the wall, bowed, and left the room.

Mary knew he was right, and she also knew she would not be able to sleep until she set things to right with the viscount. She stood and walked from the library down to the music room, listening to the melodious sounds of his playing ringing throughout the lower level of Pemberley.

Sarah Johnson

Alex sat with his back to the door, so engrossed in the notes he played that he did not hear the creaking of the floor when she walked in.

"Sir?" she said quietly when he did not look up. "My lord?" She walked over to the pianoforte and lightly touched his arm.

Alex recognized the hand that stilled his arm and he closed his eyes, swallowing hard the emotions rising in his chest. When he looked up, he saw compassion in her face.

"If you are not too busy, I wanted to speak with you now," she said.

"Oh, of course," he stood. Realizing he did not have his jacket on, he rolled his shirtsleeves down and pulled the jacket back over his arms, then indicated the sofa nearby.

When she sat, Mary spoke immediately, "I need to apologize for how I have acted towards you, my lord."

"That is not necessary," he said "It is I who need to apologize."

"No," she said firmly, "I must take the blame laid at my feet. I have treated you abominably and I am truly sorry for what I have put you through, my lord."

Alex sat as if in a daze, his hand resting on the sofa between them, and his head spinning with her complete change from just an hour before.

Mary lightly placed her own hand on top of his, and when he looked up at her she squeezed his fingers. "Please, accept my apology."

Feeling his heart start to race, Alex swallowed hard and managed to say, "I accept, Miss Bennet, but only if you accept my own apology also for whatever has caused your offense."

"I was wrong," she said. "Your brother has made me see that some things

I have let cloud my judgment were simply misunderstandings on my own part. It was nothing you did, my lord."

Alex turned his hand over and clasped her fingers, bowing slightly over it as he drew it to his lips, kissing the back ever so gently. "Thank you for giving me the opportunity of which I have dreamed for a long time."

Mary was confused by his profession, but did not have the chance to ask him about it before he stood, pulling her to her feet also. "May I walk with you tomorrow, Miss Bennet?"

"Yes, of course," she replied.

"I think there are some things I need to tell you," Alex said, "and an apology I owe to you, though if I do so now you will not understand why. It is late, and I think we both need a clear head to continue this discussion." He put out his arm to her, "May I escort you to your room?"

"Yes, thank you," she wrapped her arm around his and walked beside him quietly as they made their way upstairs. Alex noticed she did not stand as far away from him as she usually did, and he smiled at the small acknowledgment of acceptance he found in such a tiny act.

When they reached her door, he bowed over her hand, "I will see you when we break our fast tomorrow, then we can choose a path you have not yet had the opportunity to see, and we will explore the beautiful grounds here at Pemberley." At her nod of approval, he replied, "Until tomorrow," then he bowed over her hand once again before letting it go.

"Until tomorrow, my lord," she curtsied and disappeared into her room.

Alex retired to his own room, excited about the prospect set before him, and yet dreading what he must tell her tomorrow. All he could do is hope she would be as understanding when she found out what he purposely kept from her, even going so far as to insist upon silence from her father.

Sarah Johnson

CHAPTER

XII

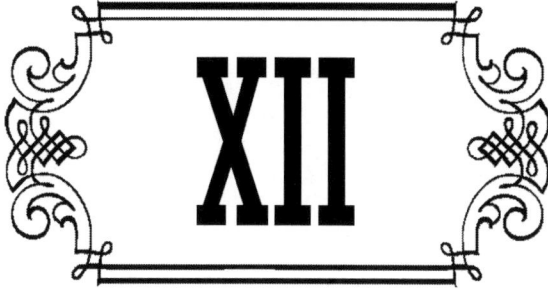

Wednesday, June 10, 1812

Alex took a deep breath as he stood in the hallway, his hand poised on the door handle to the breakfast room. *Please be kind to me today, Mary Bennet*, he thought. Turning the handle, he entered the already occupied room and sat down in his usual chair. Tea was drunk, toast was eaten, and conversation was entered into—and then the time came for their walk. Alex had already spoken with Darcy and Fitz early this morning telling them of his planned excursion with Mary, so he was not surprised when the two of them were left alone in the breakfast room when everyone was finished.

"Are you ready, Miss Bennet?" he asked.

Pushing away the plate she had hardly touched, she replied quietly, "Yes, just let me retrieve my spencer and bonnet."

"I will meet you at the door then," he bowed.

Alex was pacing in the front hall when Mary appeared on the stairs. He smiled and put out his arm, "May I escort you, Miss Bennet?"

She took it and he picked up the basket Mrs Reynolds packed for them, "I thought we might want a bite to eat or a drink while we are gone."

"Just how far do you plan on us walking, my lord?"

"Actually, I thought we might take a ride first. I would like to show you a part of the park that is too far to walk to from here, but it is a most enjoyable area. Is that agreeable?" he asked.

"Yes," Mary answered with a small nod.

"Georgiana has even given me permission to use her phaeton and ponies for our excursion."

Mary soon found herself sitting beside him quietly as she watched the grounds of Pemberley slowly pass by. The addition of the basket made it a tight fit on the phaeton seat, and Mary blushed when her knee touched the side of Alex's leg. He immediately drew his leg away, placing his foot up on the dash rail to give her more room, and apologized profusely, to which she accepted and they again sat in silence.

Alex rounded a bend in the road and pulled on the reins, bringing the ponies to a stop, "We will have to walk from here." He offered his hand and helped her down.

Mary looked around at the beautiful rolling hills and trees while Alex unharnessed the ponies.

When he was finished, he turned to her and said, "I hope these ponies do not make you as uneasy as I have seen you with larger breeds."

She chuckled and looked down to the ground. "I cannot say I would wish to be standing next to you right now, but they do not cause as much distress as *your* horse did."

Alex smiled when she brought up their meeting—it was something he thought of often, but he was not certain what her feelings were about that day. That she was willing to jest about it was enough to appease his curiosity for now. "We will have to take them with us a little further, but I hope you trust that I will have them well in hand."

With a small nod, she quietly said, "I trust you, sir."

He retrieved the basket from the phaeton and put his arm out to offer his escort. They began walking slowly through a field, the ponies positioned on the viscount's other side away from Mary.

Sheep grazed off in the distance, and soon a river came into view. "Oh how lovely," Mary said.

"We will be following the river until it curves up ahead, then we will be at our destination," Alex explained.

"The hills here in Derbyshire are very different than the Hertfordshire landscape."

"Last autumn was the first time I have had the opportunity to spend any time in Hertfordshire, and it left a lasting impression on me," Alex unintentionally drew her a little closer when he spoke.

"I hope a good impression, my lord?"

With a small smile on his lips, Alex assured her, "Of course, Miss Bennet. I enjoyed the countryside and beautiful weather, though it was the neighborhood itself I shall not soon forget. I am not often able to just be myself, with preconceived notions of my rank and wealth the usual topic of discussion wherever I go. Meryton is different. There I am invited to shoot and fish with the local gentlemen because they enjoy my company. I am not hunted by the matrons, their single daughters presented before me at every opportunity. My time in your neighborhood was very relaxing."

I never thought of it that way before, she thought. "I would not like to be treated as you describe. It is a good thing I have nothing with which to induce so much attention."

"You have more than enough to induce the right person's attention, Miss Bennet."

Mary blushed at such a pronouncement.

They rounded the bend, giving them a wonderful view of an old mill that sat right by the water's edge. "My uncle used to bring Georgiana out here often for picnics."

Mary let go of his arm as he set the basket down, "It is quite lovely indeed! Is it no longer in use?"

"Oh, no, it has not been used since before I was even born," Alex explained. "There was an especially wet spring about forty or so years ago, and the flooding made the river change its course. This original part now cuts around and meets back up with where the river is much stronger a few miles north of here." Alex pointed in that direction. "Since the mill works off running water, a new one had to be built where the river could better accommodate its needs." Turning back to the large stone edifice, he continued, "Darcy was worried he would have to tear this down, but the man who surveyed it says it is strong enough to stay for now, it just needs some specific repairs made to ensure it will last. So, he had a new roof put on last month, and plans are being made to redo the inside and possibly make it a small, cottage style retreat."

"Can we go inside?" Mary asked.

"Darcy would prefer that we not, as the inside part is in need of the most repairs," Alex explained.

Alex set the basket down next to the tree and tied the ponies to a low tree branch allowing them room to graze, then he turned to his companion, "Come Miss Bennet, I wish to show you my cousin's garden." He pointed to a small garden at the end of a path. Mary once again took his arm as he led them around the large building to a picturesque glen with a stone half-wall surrounding a garden. "Georgiana has been planting this since she was very little, adding to it every year."

"Oh, is this the place she speaks of so often? She talked my mother into giving her some flower clippings, insisting they would be perfect for her garden. She planted them in some boxes for now and said when she is better able to reach her garden she will plant them in the ground. Now that I see it, I can understand why she says it is too hard for her to come here at this time."

"Darcy is working to have a road cleared all the way to the mill so she can come any time," Alex said.

"She will love that," she said looking around. "It is not as grand as the gardens surrounding the house, but this is quite lovely," Mary leaned down to smell some flowers.

"Yes, my cousin has my aunt's touch. My Aunt Anne could make anything grow. I once saw her take a single small twig from a particularly lovely bush, and when it was large enough she planted it in the ground. It still grows in her rose garden today."

"I do not have such luck with plants," Mary replied.

"The gardens at Longbourn are charming," Alex indicated the path to the right when they came to a split.

Following his lead down the path, Mary answered, "My Granny Bennet put her mark on Longbourn's gardens throughout her long lifetime there, and she taught all she knew to my two eldest sisters. Elizabeth especially enjoys making mixtures of plants into usable cures for all manner of ailments, and Jane is known far and wide for her scented waters and oils."

"And what are you known for?" Alex asked.

"In the garden? Killing things," she smirked.

Alex laughed, "I doubt you are that bad."

"Oh, you have no idea. My Granny Bennet finally gave up on my ever growing even a simple bush or wild flower bed. No, my talents are better displayed at the pianoforte."

"Yes, you play beautifully. I remember hearing you when we first met," Alex looked off in the distance as he remembered that day vividly.

"I did not know until last night that you play as well," Mary said.

He blushed slightly, "I do not tell many people. My Aunt Anne taught me when I was young. I have never had formal lessons, but she always said I had natural talent."

Mary knew she could put off her apology no longer. "I... I have to say that... I am *truly sorry* for how I have treated you, my lord. When your brother informed me last night of all have I misunderstood, I felt horrible. I cannot imagine you being so civil with me when I have treated you so abominably." She grew somber as the path once again joined together, leading back to the front of the garden.

"May we sit," Alex indicated a large tree near the entrance. "Wait, I will be right back," he said as she started to sit on the ground. Mary watched him walk over to check on the horses. Then he picked up the basket and walked back. "I am certain Mrs Reynolds will have a blanket in here." He opened it, "Ahhh, see, she has never let me down yet." He pulled it from the basket and Mary helped him spread it out on the ground and they sat, she with her back against the tree and he facing her.

"Miss Bennet..."

"Please, my lord, I believe we already agreed months ago that you would call me by my name. I am still not used to being referred to as *Miss Bennet.*"

Alex smiled, "I will agree only if you refrain from saying *my lord* to me. Is it a deal?"

"Yes, of course."

"Now, where was I. Oh yes—*Miss Mary*," he lifted his eyebrow when he said her name, "I am not certain what *exactly* my brother has enlightened you about."

Mary looked down at her hands, a blush taking over her cheeks. "I have treated you horribly for many months now, and I am ashamed to say, it was because of lies."

"What lies were those?" he asked.

"I cannot say exactly, as your brother would not tell me all. I only know the little bit he did tell me of that disabused me of a most recent development in my dislike of you."

"I think it might be best if we start from the beginning," Alex suggested. At her acceptance, he started, "When we first met you were open with me and it drew my attention, but then that evening, upon us being together in company, you seemed to be a different person. What did I do to set you against me almost from the beginning of our acquaintance?"

"I was first taken aback at your not telling me you were titled," Mary replied honestly. "Then when I overheard you telling your cousin about how you found me that day, it just... it felt like a betrayal and my feelings were hurt."

"Telling my cousin about how I found you? I do not remember saying anything to him about how we met that afternoon."

"Yes, I remember your words exactly," Mary said. Sitting up, she closed her eyes and repeated the words that cut her to the core that night so many months ago, *"She had no bonnet, and her dress was at least six inches deep in mud. How she could have thought to be out like that is beyond me. She looked almost wild."*

"You heard me?" he replied quietly, confusion evident on his face. *"And you thought I was speaking of you?"* Scooting closer to her, he touched the back of her hand drawing her gaze to his, *"Miss Mary, I was not speaking of you. Those were not even my own words."*

"But... I heard you say it," she said barely above a whisper.

"Yes, I did say that, but not about you. My cousin and I were speaking of a letter I received from my Aunt Catherine in which she told of a young girl whom she chastised in the middle of the streets with those very words. I would never tell anyone, *not even my cousin,* such a thing about you," he said.

"You have never told anyone of how we met?" Mary felt tears welling up in her eyes.

"Only Fitz knows some of it, and he will keep silent. I did joke with some people of all the misadventures I had that day before arriving in Meryton, but meeting you was the highlight of my trip. No one else knows we met on the road that day, or what condition your dress was in when I came upon you."

"You are certain?" Mary asked.

"Yes; I have spoken to no one else. Only what you have said to others is what is known," he assured her. "I know what it is like to have vicious rumors spread about you, and I would not wish that on anyone. No rumors came of our meeting, but if anything had, I would have made it right." With a small chuckle, he said, "To own the truth, I was a bit anxious when your father asked to speak privately with me that evening when I arrived."

Mary looked up into his eyes, "I am sorry for how I treated you because of my own misconception."

Alex squeezed her fingers lightly, "Let us not think on it any longer. We both have things for which to be sorry, and I am sure this conversation will be just as enlightening for me as it has been so far for you." He sat back again, "Now, was there something else which led to your dislike of me?"

Mary again looked down at her hands and blushed, "Yes, though this is harder for me to say."

"Would you feel better if I guessed?" Alex asked.

"I am not certain you could," Mary replied.

"Maybe not, but it would make for a very diverting conversation, wouldn't you say?" he smiled.

Mary giggled, "I thank you for the offer, but I believe I owe you the truth from my own lips." Taking a deep breath, she continued, "Miss Bingley told me you had a reputation around Town and were a *known... flirt... and... and more.*"

"A known flirt? Really? A flirt? *And more?* What is that supposed to..." realization dawning, his mouth opened in astonishment, "*She said I was a RAKE?*"

"Yes," Mary replied. "I took what she said as being the truth, and a comment Georgiana put in her letter seemed to only confirm Miss Bingley's words."

"What would Georgiana say of me that would point to my being a rake?" Alex asked in exasperation.

"She wrote of your distraction when you were back in Town, and said your own mother assured her it was nothing more than your looming birthday that would put an end to your *wild ways.*"

Throwing his head back, he let out a loud exasperation. "Did *everyone* put such notions in your head? No wonder you wanted nothing to do with me." Alex closed his eyes and pinched the bridge of his nose tightly.

"Are you well, sir?" Mary's concerned voice cut through his thoughts.

"What? Oh, yes, sorry. I have an odd habit of doing that when I am overwhelmed."

"Well, we both know I hide my eyes when overwhelmed," Mary joked.

Alex smiled at the memory of her burying her face into his chest when the horse they rode together scared her the day they met. "Yes, I remember well."

Mary blushed deeply and Alex knew she was embarrassed, so he continued, "My mother's comment was in reference to something not many outside the family know yet. Because of a scare a few years ago with his health, my father and I agreed I would take over the running of Dalmeny when I married or upon my thirtieth birthday, whichever came first. My mother was only making a joke with my young cousin, who obviously did not have much understanding of it, about my taking over Dalmeny soon, not leaving me as much time for the social scene," Alex explained. "That is what I have been so busy with these last few months."

"Oh, well that *does* explain her comment," Mary replied. "That is not all I held against you though."

"I do not see how it can get any worse than this, so go ahead," Alex replied.

"Unfortunately, it does," she sighed. "When I arrived in Town, I had the privilege of sitting next to Lady Catherine de Bourgh during your birthday dinner."

"*Oh, no!*" Alex cried.

"*Oh, yes.*"

"I forgot about that."

"She certainly made quite the impression. She told me of the family's wish for many years of joining the two estates of Dalmeny and Rosings Park, and of her expectation of your proposal to her daughter any day." Mary shifted positions on the uncomfortably hard ground, drawing her legs up under her and leaning over onto her arm. She played with the wrinkles in the blanket as she continued, "Later that evening I asked your cousin Anne about it, and I mistook what she said to mean she was secretly attached to you."

"Me? What could she possibly say to make you think such a thing?" Alex asked.

Mary remembered her promise to tell no one of Anne and the colonel's secret engagement, so she shrugged her shoulders, "I cannot say. It is just what I thought after listening to your aunt expound upon the match for nearly two hours."

"I take it this is what my brother cleared up for you last night?"

"Yes, that was part of it."

"There is more?"

Taking a deep breath, Mary once again closed her eyes as she explained, "I was in the library when you visited William a few days before we left Town. I heard raised voices and went to see what was wrong, and I heard part of what you said through the door."

"Part of what I said? *What* did I say?" he asked.

"I now know it was part of a letter you were reading, but I thought... that is... what I heard was about a woman who was now..."

"Oh... *there is no need to go on, Miss Mary*," he said quietly, "I know what you heard."

"Yes, well, as you can imagine, after everything else, it just seemed to be one more mark against you," she said.

"While most of what you have said can be attributed to misunderstandings and other's lies, there is one thing I must confess to you. I know why Miss Bingley thinks me a rake." Alex looked down at his hands, trying to gather the courage to continue.

Mary understood and gave him time to collect his thoughts.

Taking a deep breath, he looked back up, meeting her eyes, "Two years ago there was a young lady determined to marry me at whatever cost to her own reputation. At the beginning of the Season we met at a ball and she insisted in front of a group of others that we were meant to dance the first together. I did not want to embarrass her by saying it was untrue, and it *was* only a dance, so I partnered her for the opening set. I usually do not dance that set at such events because of the perceived notion of it being a set for lovers."

Having never heard of this rule before, she drew her breath in, "If that is true, why would you ask me to dance the first with you—*three times?*"

"Oh no, I mean, Almack's Assembly Rooms is so very different than a private ball or a country dance. There are rules for so much more, and that is one of the unspoken ones—dancing the first set is seen as one gentleman telling all others this is your girl. While in the country you may be able to get away with a second dance without it being perceived as much more than a close friendship or amiability, while at Almack's it would indicate you were surely engaged."

"Oh, I understand," she quietly replied. "Please continue."

"We danced the first in the set, and during the second she became ill, so I escorted her out of the ballroom to catch her breath. She indicated a certain room, and I foolishly led her in without thinking of us being alone. She nearly fainted and her cousin then opened the door to find her in my arms. I now realized this was her ultimate goal all along, and I quickly left the ball."

"I do not see how this would make Miss Bingley believe you to be a rake, sir," Mary said.

"I am not finished with the tale yet, Miss Mary. You will see how this is connected to you momentarily." At her nod, he continued once again, "Word soon spread that the lady was with child, and she insisted it was mine. Her father came to me and demanded I marry his ruined daughter, but I refused. The lady was then sent away to stay with family in the north, and I later learned both she and the child did not make it." Alex looked anywhere he could but at Mary as he continued his story. "Her cousin vowed to ruin me no matter what the cost, but my family and friends stood by my decision. Before leaving Town she said she would have her revenge on me some day. I have not seen her again until the night we went to the theater." Looking into her face once again, Alex quietly said, "*The cousin of whom I speak is the Lady Elaine Stalwood.*"

"The lady who came upon us at the theater!" Mary's face went white and she closed her eyes, her head immediately starting to throb and tears welling up in her eyes.

"Yes," Alex was heartbroken at her reaction, "unfortunately, there is more." Mary would not look up at him, so he too looked away and continued, "We left the theater early and I was prepared to do what was needed if any rumors started, but we did not hear of any before we left Town. I insisted no one tell you of her connection to me and that we travel through Meryton on our way to Pemberley so I could speak with your father." Alex stood and began to pace under the tree while he finished telling her what he must. "He was, of course, extremely angry with the possible compromising situation in which I placed you. He wanted to tell you of it, but I insisted he also keep silent as I was hoping the rumors would not start. He finally agreed only after my insistence that if anything were to come of the incident I would make it right immediately."

Fuming, Mary stood and stepped in front of him, making him stop his pacing and look at her. Her eyes became dark and cold as she said, "How dare you! What right do *you* have to *insist* I not be told of the possibility of rumors about a compromising situation that could very well alter, so dramatically, the rest of *my* life?"

Alex did not know what to say. *She is correct; I had no right to insist no one tell her.* He watched her walk away, angry steps taking her quickly along the garden path they had traversed together slowly earlier. Knowing she needed to compose herself before he tried to apologize for his underhanded actions, he walked back to check on the ponies, finally settling on the river's edge alone.

Mary walked on in silence, circling the garden path four times before she finally began to calm down. She needed to speak with someone, but there was no one here... no one except... *him.* She looked back over towards the river's edge where the viscount sat. Shaking her head, she thought, *perhaps we should return to Pemberley and I can speak with Elizabeth? No, I fear she would not fully understand. If any of my sisters could help me right now it would be Jane, but a letter exchange of all I must say would take a week at least. No, it seems I must work this out for myself this time.* Mary walked back over to the tree and sat back down on the blanket, drawing her knees up and resting her chin on them as she tried to think clearly.

Why am I so upset? Naturally, anyone would be upset to learn of the highhanded nature with which I have been left out of my own possible future. It was not just one person though. Elizabeth did not speak with me, neither did William, and my own father agreed to keep silent also. Why? Why would they not include me? Why am I holding one person more accountable than all the others? There is nothing I can do, but accept what is laid before me now.

What of the situation itself? Who was truly at fault? The viscount was only trying to help me in the unexpected crush of the crowd. He saw my reaction and knew he must get me to a place where I could regain my composure. I fear if he had not done so I would have fainted. No, I cannot fault him for his solicitous nature. It has been clearly displayed from the very beginning of our acquaintance.

A sudden thought startled her, *He did not know my family, or me, the day he rescued me on the side of the road, and yet he said he would have made it right if any rumors came of it. Even after being nearly trapped by another a few years ago, he placed his entire future in my hands that day just to help me home. If anyone was at fault it would be me. I chose to ride with him, and if anyone happened by and saw me with my face buried in his chest, I surely would have been ruined. Yet he did not push me away. He allowed me to take the time needed to soothe my nerves, knowing full well what could come of such a situation. He then bravely faced my father that evening instead of leaving town and ignoring what consequences might be forced upon him.*

How could I have been so fooled into believing him to be a rake when he has displayed to me, from the moment of our first meeting, the complete opposite? He truly is a gentleman, and I owe it to him to not become angry over one situation when it was me who placed us in a much greater situation many months ago. It is entirely my fault—not his.

Tears streamed down Mary's cheeks as her heart broke for how she had treated this man all these many months.

Finally calming after several minutes, Mary turned to look at the viscount again, whispering aloud to herself, *"He truly is an honourable gentleman."*

Mary dried her swollen eyes, then sat in silence, not knowing what to say to mend this situation. Suddenly her stomach rumbled, breaking the tension and causing her to giggle. *I was so nervous I hardly ate*, she thought to herself.

Knowing the viscount deserved an apology from her, she took a deep breath and stood, straightened her dress, and slowly walked over to the gentleman who sat by the water skipping stones across its surface. He looked dejected, and Mary felt compassion rise in her chest for him. *I owe him another chance*, she thought to herself. Kneeling beside him, she touched his arm and shuddered when he turned towards her, his green eyes piercing into her own. "*I* am the one who placed us in a compromising situation at the beginning of our acquaintance, so I cannot be unduly angry with you for what has come from this most recent situation without also being angry with myself. As it will do no good for either of us, I have decided we must put this all behind us and start over again." Standing back up, she took a step back, put a small smile on her face, and curtsied, "Good day to you sir, I am Mary Bennet, and who might you be?"

Alex could not help the smile that overtook his own features. He scrambled to his feet and bowed, "It is a pleasure to meet you, Miss Mary Bennet; I am Alexander Fitzwilliam, *Viscount Primrose.*"

Mary raised her eyebrow, *ahhh, he was listening when I said before how off put I was at his not telling me from the start of his title.* "I was just about to sit down to a picnic, and I wondered if you would like to join me," Mary asked.

He had to laugh at her continuing as if they just met, "Why yes, Miss Bennet, I would be honoured. May I escort you?"

He put out his arm and she wrapped her own securely around it as she replied, "Yes, of course. Please call me, *Miss Mary*, sir."

With a wink, he said, "With pleasure, *Miss Mary*," and led her back to the blanket, where they both enjoyed the treats Mrs Reynolds had packed, along with some amiable discussion that signaled the beginning of their friendship.

Alex and Mary returned to the house by tea time, and Alex once again helped in the search for more documents. Late that night the three cousins met in Darcy's study to discuss what they would do now with the little information they possessed.

"A month of searching in vain," Darcy paced the floor, agitated at their lack of progress.

"I have a feeling we will find more in Father's things," Fitz stood by the fireplace.

"I do not understand where my father could have hidden his papers," Darcy replied. "His death was not expected, and yet it is as if just those months of letters from your father are missing from these trunks."

"Wasn't my father here when Uncle George died?" Alex asked quizzically.

A sudden realization came to Darcy, "Of course; I was not able to come home for several weeks, and your father stayed with Georgiana until I arrived. He must have gone through these papers himself and pulled out what he did not wish me to find."

Fitz returned to his chair, "Did you pack Uncle George's things up yourself, Darcy?"

"No, when I arrived they were already in these trunks." Darcy also returned to his seat, looking at his two cousins, "We will find nothing more here at Pemberley."

"I doubt we will find anything at Dalmeny either," Alex interjected. "My father has been packing his things there for nearly a year now, and except the estate records I would need, his drawers have been cleaned out."

"Yes, well, he may have missed something," Fitz explained

"True—I say you two go on to Dalmeny tomorrow," Darcy suggested, "and I will meet you there next week."

"You cannot join us now?" Fitz asked.

"No, Elizabeth's birthday is Saturday and we have some special plans." Darcy leaned back into the wings of the large, leather chair, sighing loudly. "No, next week will not work either," he rubbed his tired eyes. "My steward is to meet with me Thursday and Friday. I cannot put it off, as it is to get the plans for the road to Georgiana's garden underway. We will have to leave the following week."

"That will work," Fitz stood.

"Yes, it will give Mother time enough to prepare for visitors." Alex interjected. "She mentioned in her last letter her desire to show Elizabeth, Georgiana, and Miss Mary her newly decorated rooms at the dower house."

Darcy slowly stood, placing his drink on the table. "I will check with Elizabeth about when we are available to join you. Mary's birthday is that week, and I do not know what my wife has planned."

"Which day?" Alex asked. "I am certain Mother would like to help put together something special," he added.

"Yes, she seems to like having my sister around. It is the twenty-fifth," Darcy answered. "I will let you know tomorrow before you leave what our plans are. Good night," Darcy tiredly walked out the door leaving the two brothers alone.

"Well, it is about time we retire as well, is it not?" Alex started to leave the room also.

"Not so fast," Fitz stopped him. "I believe *you* owe me some answers."

"Answers? To what question?"

"What happened with Miss Bennet this morning?"

A small smile alit on his face, "We discussed all that has held her back from giving me a chance, and we have now began anew with our friendship."

"So are you going to ask to court her?"

"Not yet."

"Why? She *was* more amiable towards you at supper," Fitz stated.

"She needs time—*we* need time. Her misconceptions of my character were because she does not know me, and I fear if I ask her now she will be too frightened to give me a positive answer. I hope she is able to visit Dalmeny. It will give me time to build our friendship and show her more of who I truly am."

"Why not stay around here and travel with Darcy when they leave?" Fitz suggested.

Alex rubbed his tired eyes, "No, I have been here for a month complete now and I really must continue on to Dalmeny. I have too much work to be done there. Darcy wishes to return to Town for the end of Elizabeth's confinement, and Miss Mary will be returning home then. I am hoping to be finished with business enough to return to Meryton and visit Bingley again."

"And, of course, visit the other local neighbors often, I am sure," Fitz smirked.

Alex smiled, "Yes, of course." He stood again, "I really must go to bed before I am too tired to walk up the stairs on my own. It has been a long day for me, and I feel as if I could collapse right here."

Fitz walked to the door, "Sleep well. We do not need to leave too early tomorrow, so maybe you can get one more walk in with *your lady* after we break our fast."

"Yes, perhaps."

The brothers retired, Alex falling asleep immediately and waking the next morning with a renewed hope for his future.

Sarah Johnson

CHAPTER

XIII

Thursday, June 11, 1812

"Miss Mary," Alex caught her attention just as she was leaving the breakfast room to go to the library, "may I have a moment of your time?"

"Yes, of course, sir," she stopped and looked up into his vibrant green eyes, her breath catching in her chest. *Why must I react so to him?*

"I wondered if you were too busy to join me for a stroll around the garden?"

"I am free from any obligations until after Georgiana has completed her practice," Mary said. "Just let me return this book to the library and gather my bonnet and spencer, and I will meet you outside.

Alex smiled, "I will be waiting."

When she arrived, the two walked around the gardens for a few minutes before Alex asked if she wished to sit. Upon her agreement, they sat. "My brother and I will be leaving in a few hours."

"Oh? I did not know," she looked down at her hands.

"It was just decided late last night. We have had no luck in finding the documents for which we are searching, and it is time I return to Dalmeny to take care of business. I hope to be finished in time to travel back to Meryton with my cousin, if that plan meets with your approval?"

Mary looked back up questioningly, "If it meets with my approval?"

"Yes, I do not wish to add undue pressure on you. I would like to get to know you, and you to get to know me, but I will travel there only if you wish it of me."

Mary did not know what to say. His solicitous nature could be what was pushing him to say this, or it could be something more. She slumped back against the back of the bench.

Noticing her reaction, Alex assured her, "You do not have to answer me now. Darcy plans on you all visiting Dalmeny in a few weeks, and you can give me your answer at that time."

"Thank you," she answered shyly.

Standing, he held out his hand to her, "Now, let us continue our walk. Have you seen the maze yet?"

Mary placed her own hand in his and stood, "I tried to find my way once, but fear of getting lost made me turn back almost immediately."

Alex chuckled, "As someone who is constantly losing his way, I can appreciate your hesitancy. However, having grown up here, I happen to know the right combination of turns to reach the middle."

"Ahhh, but the better question would be can he find his way out again?" they both heard Georgiana and turned to see her behind them being held by Joseph.

"As a matter of fact," Alex replied, "I happen to know both routes for Pemberley's maze."

"Then my friend will be safe with you as her guide," she teased her older cousin.

"I thought you were practicing in the music room?" Alex asked.

"More like becoming unduly frustrated with a particular new exercise. Mrs Annesley suggested I get some fresh air."

Alex replied, "Well then, would you like to join us on our walk?"

"Yes, please do," Mary agreed.

"I do not wish to be a burden…" she started to say.

"Nonsense," Alex indicated the bench where Joseph could put her down. "I would love nothing more than to lead you and Miss Mary through the maze on this fine summer day." He picked her up, adjusting his hold so she was comfortable in his arms, "Now, if Miss Mary would take my elbow," he waited on her to do as he indicated, "… then we can leave on our adventure, and pray we find our way out again."

***

Saturday–Sunday, June 13 – 14, 1812

Elizabeth lay with her head in Darcy's lap reflecting on all the things her husband did for her today. She awoke to his insistence on her not removing from their bed until after they broke their fast, provided for them in their chambers and consisting of everything she loved to eat these days, including those thing which he personally found a repulsive combination. When they did finally arrive downstairs, he ushered her to the music room where he insisted she unwrap several pieces of music she was recently eyeing at the shops. He then enthusiastically led her outside where he surprised her with her very own phaeton, packed for the two to disappear somewhere around the grounds of Pemberley—where exactly, he would not divulge.

Darcy spent some time teaching Elizabeth how to hold the reins and what to do in guiding the horses, insisting she had more natural ability than she would admit to owning. When he finally took the reins from her again, he led them to a secluded glen right next to the river.

"We used to come here as young boys and swim," Darcy said when they had eaten their fill and were lounging beneath the tree.

"My sisters and I dearly loved to swim, though my mother considered it scandalous behavior and refused to hear of our adventures."

"So do you wish to go swimming today?" Darcy's eyebrow rose in challenge.

"Are you certain this is a secluded spot?" Elizabeth looked around.

"Yes, completely; I come here often and the grounds keeper is under strict orders to not send anyone here unless I request their attention to a particular need." He looked around, "As you can see, the foliage coverage is practically a wall around this area."

Elizabeth slid over to her husband's side and reached for the buttons on his waistcoat as she kissed him fully on the lips. Within minutes the two were undressed and splashing around in the sun warmed water, Darcy once again grateful for his wife's unconventional character traits that endeared her to him so well.

An hour later they returned to the shore and dressed, then lay down to relax under the shade of the trees once again as the smell of summer flowers wafted in the air.

Darcy was leaned back onto the trunk of the tree, playing with Elizabeth's curls as they lay drying on his lap. His other hand instinctively reached for her stomach and made gentle circles where their child lay inside, and before they knew it the two drifted off to sleep.

The clamorous sound of a thunder clash and the sudden sprinkling of rain woke them. Quickly gathering their things, they barely made it to the safety of a nearby covering before the downpour started.

"We will be safe in here for now," Darcy replied, not seeing the ashen look that overtook his wife's face until he turned around. He only had a moment to react, and barely caught her as she fainted.

Elizabeth could not see anything around her, but she could hear the sound of rushing water somewhere nearby. She tried opening her eyes but that did not help. Dizziness nearly overtook her, and she quickly closed her eyes again, trying to keep everything from spinning. She could feel the pelting of rain on her face and then it stopped. The sound of rushing water drowned out everything around her, and suddenly she felt something wrap around her. The safety of arms, but whose arms were they? *It must be William,* she thought. She felt the warmth and comfort take over her being, and she curled up into her husband's broad chest. Soon she could perceive a pillow under her head and a blanket being drawn up over her body as sleep claimed her at last.

A knock came and Darcy answered the door. "Finally—come in Doctor."

"I am sorry for my delay, Mr Darcy. I had to wait for the rain to subside a little or risk losing my own life in getting here."

"I understand." He walked over to his wife's bedside, "We were caught out in this storm when it started suddenly this afternoon. We found shelter quickly, and I was assuring Elizabeth of our safety when I turned around and barely caught her. I could not wake her, so when the rain seemed to stop for a small break, I quickly returned to the house. We tried to make her as comfortable as possible.

"You did well, son," the older man patted his shoulder. "Has she ever fainted before?"

His mind went back immediately to the day they married and the events revealed to each of them upon her fainting—that of his father losing his life in order to save hers when she was just a girl. His voice cracked as he answered the doctor, "I know of only one time when she fainted. Would you like me to ask her sister if it has happened more often than that?"

"Her sister is staying with you right now?"

"Yes."

"I would like to speak with her."

At Darcy's nod, Mrs Reynolds left to get Mary. When she returned, the doctor was just completing his examination of Elizabeth and replacing the blanket.

"This is Miss Mary Bennet," Darcy said in introduction before he turned to her. "Mary, this is Doctor Foxx, and he has a few questions for you about Elizabeth."

"Oh, yes, of course."

"Has your sister ever been known to faint for no reason?"

"I only remember once when Elizabeth became so frightened, and it was during an especially fearsome storm," she answered.

"Just like this afternoon?"

"No, much worse than today's storm. My aunt and uncle were kept from going back to Town because of the flooding that took place. Lizzy stayed in her room for several days, and my aunt stayed with her most of the time. That was several years ago though."

"*Just as on the day we were married*," Darcy barely said aloud.

The doctor turned to him, "Was there a storm such as today when she fainted before, sir?"

He nodded, his brow furrowing, "Yes—yes there was. It brought back old, long forgotten memories for her of a time when she was a child and was caught out in a storm."

Mary looked at the pale face of her sister, "She has never liked storms."

He noticed where her eyes went, "I am certain Mrs Darcy will be well, Miss Bennet."

"Truly?" tears welled up in Mary's eyes as she felt Darcy's arm wrap around her shoulder.

"Yes, truly."

"Let me take you back to your room," Darcy offered, then led her out. When he returned the doctor gave him orders to have Elizabeth rest a few days, and to get some fresh air when the weather permitted it. "If she is still having dizzy spells in three or four days, I will return and check on her."

"What do you think has caused this?"

"Well, it is difficult to say for certain, but I think you may have answered that question yourself when you said she has had a trauma associated with a storm. This may simply be her body's way of dealing with a frightening situation."

"What can we do? Will this continue to haunt her forever?"

He thought for a moment, then answered, "I am certainly no expert on things such as this, but I wonder... does she ever talk about her experience as a child?"

"No… never. It has only come up the day we married, when she remembered the events."

"Perhaps it would do her good to talk of it then. I know she has had a difficult time of things lately, with this pregnancy, so it could just be that she needs the rest."

Darcy thanked him, assuring him of his orders being followed, and Doctor Foxx left. Darcy dismissed the servants, dressed for bed, and curled up beside Elizabeth, placing his hand protectively on her stomach where their child rolled and kicked at the pressure. He soon found sleep just as his wife, and neither woke again until the next morning when the sun came shining through the curtains, rousing both from their slumber.

Darcy was insistent upon her remaining in bed, and Elizabeth resisted his appeal, but after hearing the harrowing spin her husband put on the tale, she agreed to rest for a few days, just as the doctor suggested.

Deciding it would be the perfect opportunity to spend some time with her sisters, she gave Mrs Reynolds a list of needed supplies, and, later that day, surprised Mary and Georgiana with the activity of fashioning some bonnets.

Mary held her creation up, looking at it from many angles, "I do not see how Lydia produces such quality in her bonnets. Mine looks as if a blind person put it together."

Georgiana giggled, "Mine is no better."

"At least the ribbons on yours match the fabric on the brim," Mary started pulling her stitches out. "I do not know what made me think I could put this combination together, but it simply will not do even for a walk in the garden."

"Here, try this fabric," Elizabeth handed Mary a piece that nicely complimented her ribbon choice.

"Where was this when I was trying to find something?"

"It was right under my stack," Georgiana smiled. "I was trying to be sly, but it seems it is not in my nature to be duplicitous."

Mary held the fabric out to her friend, "If you would prefer it, I can choose something else."

"Oh, no, you can use it. I was going to make a hat for you out of it, but now that I have spent so much time on this one, I am not certain I want to try another one. We simply must insist upon Kitty and Lydia teaching us their methods next time we are all together."

Darcy walked in, followed by Mrs Reynolds who delivered tea and cakes. "Ahhh, I see you three are ready for the finest millinery shop window."

All three broke out in gales of laughter, and put their bonnets aside to partake of some refreshments, after which Georgiana and Mary retired to their own rooms to allow Elizabeth to rest again.

Monday, June 15, 1812

Swearing loudly, G.W. threw the glass into the fireplace, his hand wrinkling the paper held tightly in its grip.

"What is wrong?" his female companion asked, trying to sooth his obviously disturbed temper.

"It is none of your concern," he said harshly. He stood to pour himself another drink, swallowed the liquor in one gulp and sat back down with another full glass.

When he did not say anything else, she quietly left the room, running into the third of their band of misfits in the hall. "I would not go in there if I were you," she warned.

"Oh? Is he out of sorts right now?"

"He has received a letter that set him off, though he refuses to tell me the particulars. I think it might be best if we wait until he has drunk himself into a stupor, then we can sneak in and read the contents without him knowing."

"Why do we not just leave him to his own devices?" George asked.

"Because, you would be a fool to think what he does will not reflect upon *your* plight with Lady Catherine. I, for one, will not let him bungle up our plans again. You know our orders. We are to remain here until August, at which time Collins is to go back to Longbourn and find out when the Darcys will be returning from the north. Then, when the time is right, we will carry out our plan with the mistress and heir of Pemberley—this time without any problems arising."

He looked to the closed door, then back to Mrs Younge, "Very well. When he is asleep we will read the letter."

It was not much longer before they heard a crash from inside the room, and they went in to find G.W. had passed out, knocking over a tray. George took over the task of getting their drunken companion to his room, while Mrs Younge searched for the letter. Unfortunately, in his anger, G.W. had tossed it towards the fire. Luckily enough though, he was too intoxicated to let it find its mark easily, so only parts of it were charred, and not too much to still be read.

The letter was addressed to Reverend William Collins, and in it Mr Henry Bennet laid out the particulars of a plan in which Mr Collins would consent to giving up the land he was heir presumptive to inherit for a large sum of money.

It was an intriguing prospect—and although he was not inclined to see the positive, she was, and felt this could be their ticket out of England if their plans with Lady Catherine de Bourgh became too overly taxing. Surely the lady's hand could not reach across the sea to another land, and this amount of money would set them all up nicely in America.

She would just have to convince him of the wonders of the prospect set before them.

Sarah Johnson

CHAPTER

XIV

Monday, June 22, 1812

"William, I insist we go. I have not felt faint in well over a week." Elizabeth stood with her hands on her hips and toe to toe with her much larger husband, her protruding belly keeping the two apart and making quite the comical sight for Georgiana and Mary. Both girls looked to the floor trying not to giggle or make a move, as they did not wish to draw attention to their presence.

Finally, Darcy's features softened and he leaned down to whisper something in Elizabeth's ear, to which she laughed and kissed his cheek before she turned him around and scooted him out the door.

When she turned back around the two could hold it in no longer and burst out laughing. "I see my brother has finally found his match in you, Elizabeth." Georgiana nearly fell off the sofa she was laughing so hard.

Elizabeth tried not to join in with their laughter, "Well, it worked, did it not?" She nodded to Joseph who stood outside her door, "Now, you two must be packed and ready to leave within the hour, or I cannot guarantee he will not find another reason to stay here instead."

"It is a good thing we both saw to it that our trunks were ready last night," Georgiana said as Joseph picked her up.

"Where to, Miss?" he asked as he carried her from the room, leaving the two sisters alone.

Elizabeth drew her arm around Mary's shoulders, "Are you certain you wish to spend your birthday at Dalmeny?"

Mary hugged her sister and closed her eyes, as just the name of the viscount's home made her heart start to beat rapidly. "Yes, I have missed visiting with Lady Rosebery."

When Elizabeth pulled back and saw the blush on Mary's cheeks, she smiled and lifted her eyebrow, "Is that the *only* person you have missed visiting with?"

Mary did not know what to say.

"Do not fret, dear sister, I shall not tease you. I think if you and he are drawn to each other, it would be a good match."

"I have spent so much time being upset with him over misconceptions; it is hard for me to say whether I even know him."

"Well, now is your time to put all that is in the past behind you and begin again. Truly, the viscount is a good gentleman, and anyone who is around him when you walk into a room can see the affection he holds for you— well, all but my husband, as his attention rarely strays from me long enough for him to notice much of anything with his cousin. I thought you might be warming to the viscount's attentions though."

Mary's hands began to shake with the realization that others noticed how he looked at her as well. "It is just too much for me right now."

Elizabeth reached for her sister's hand, "Give him a chance, Mary, and let your heart lead you. I know how anxious you become when a big decision must be made, and I also know how often you talk yourself out of what you truly want because of your fears. Do not let that happen this time. When it is the right person, your heart just knows." She put her finger under Mary's chin, drawing her eyes up to look into her own. "Promise me you will only think of your own happiness and not be frightened at the unknown."

She sighed deeply and then finally said, "I promise."

Mary sat quietly, examining the landscape as it passed and listening to Georgiana chatter on about some of the delights of which Dalmeny boasted that they would have the pleasure of partaking in during their week and a half stay. Mary was trying to pay attention to her friend, but her mind wandered too often to catch everything Georgiana said.

Pulling around a curve in the road, they entered through a large iron gate and slowly made their way through a canopy of trees covered with beautiful summer blooms. The movement of the carriage caused those blooms that had fallen to swirl around, leaving an almost magical feeling to the place they would soon see. Finally coming out of the trees, Mary looked ahead and was just able to make out the outline of a very large estate, its grandeur evident in the massive structure and the park which surrounded it. Pemberley's façade blended in to the landscape around it, almost seeming to have sprouted from nature itself. Dalmeny, on the other hand, was more Tudor in style. Chimneys rose high above, some billowing smoke. Mary was awed at its size and the number of windows just on the front. She knew her father paid a hefty price yearly for the number of windows at Longbourn, but he insisted it was worth the cost to let in so much light. She could not fathom the price the viscount's family had to pay for all the windows at Dalmeny.

When they came to a stop, Alex and Fitz were there to greet the visitors. Fitz took Georgiana, and Darcy took Elizabeth's hand, helping her from the carriage in the way only a husband could with his precious wife. This left Alex to act as Mary's escort.

He reached out his gloved hand. Her light grip with no hesitation on her part was the surest sign that all was truly forgiven. The joy he felt at this small sign was nearly enough to make his heart burst.

When her feet were securely on the ground, Mary looked up and smiled, "Thank you." She was taken aback at the lovely lines that formed around his green eyes when he smiled back at her.

Neither of them moved. Both were entranced just looking into each other's eyes. The large estate that worried her faded from Mary's mind like a fog rolling in from the sea, until all she could see was the man who stood before her now. The servants removing the trunks and directions given by both Darcy and Fitz as to what would go where could not intrude upon the moment of time that held the two captive. A peacefulness she could not explain surrounded her, and, in that moment, Mary knew more about her heart than she cared to admit, even to herself.

Suddenly the moment was shattered when a trunk nearly came down on top of Alex and Darcy stepped in quickly to right it, knocking into his cousin and sending Alex to within a breath's distance from Mary. Neither seemed to mind the scuffle that had caused such an intrusion upon their moment, especially with this conclusion.

In all the commotion, Elizabeth reached for her sister's elbow, exclaiming, "Mary! Were you hit?"

Her voice was quiet as she answered back, "No, I am well."

Alex's fingers gave a light squeeze to the hand still encased in his own. "Welcome to Dalmeny." He then stepped back, taking his place at her side and revealing the grand estate that stood behind him—his family heritage for many generations.

This is a part of who he is, Mary thought as the fog lifted and the grandeur around was revealed once again. But this time it was not in a way that overwhelmed her as before. No, this time it was different. This time it was a revealing of the heart of the man who still held her fingers lightly in his own. Every stone carried a memory, every bush held a secret, and she was more than willing to find out all she could from this place about its master.

Darcy insisted Elizabeth rest, and Georgiana also decided to retire for a little while, but Mary was too excited and wanted to explore. Alex offered to be her guide, and so the two were seen going from room to room as he gave the long history of the structure, which parts had been built when, how many fires it had withstood over the years, and how many of his ancestors were raised here.

"This is quite the collection," Mary said as they entered the library.

"Yes, my grandfather was a great reader and collected most of these during his long lifetime. Would you like to sit for a few minutes? I can call for some tea?"

"Yes, that sounds nice." Mary chose a window seat that looked out over the gardens, and when Alex returned from speaking with the housekeeper, Mrs Simpson, he sat beside her.

"Did you enjoy your tour of my home?" Alex tried not to stare at her, but was all anticipation of what she would say.

"Georgiana told me of how different from Pemberley it was, but I was not as prepared as I thought. It is a little more difficult to navigate through and I hope I do not get lost."

Alex chuckled. "When we were younger, on rainy days we could often be found hiding in the closets and unknown corners of Pemberley, but we would have the most fun at hiding when we were here at Dalmeny. There are so many more places no one thinks about here."

"Longbourn does not have many places to hide, especially with five sisters vying for every available space." Mary felt herself relaxing more in the viscount's presence.

151

"My brother and I were quite alone, and other than when Darcy or Bingley visited, we often found ourselves bored in this large place. How did your sisters survive in such a small home?"

"Elizabeth took to walking out daily, sometimes vexing Mama with being gone all day. Jane was often found in the garden or the stillroom. Her flower gardens are the most beautiful designs and she has even won prizes at the local fair for her creations in the stillroom. My two younger sisters could usually be found together, designing new dresses to wear or tearing apart and redecorating bonnets. They are both quite talented in that regard. Lydia plays the violin; you may have heard her the night you were introduced to my family."

"Yes, I remember being regaled that night with her on the violin, you on the pianoforte, and Elizabeth singing," Alex affirmed with a smile.

"Lydia is very musically inclined, but cannot sing as well as my sister Elizabeth. Katherine is a gifted artist and can often be found with a drawing pad in her hands these days."

"You, too, are very talented musically," Alex complimented.

She blushed slightly, "I thank you, sir."

"And what about you?" Alex asked. "What area of the estate always drew your attention, Miss Mary?"

"I was often found at the pianoforte, of course, or hiding in the barn," she chuckled.

"That is not the place I would picture you being, especially with your fear of horses," Alex teased.

"Oh no, I stayed far away from the horses. I had my own area in the loft. One of my earliest memories is of nearly being trampled by a horse, so I learned very early on to stay away from their stalls when they were stabled within," Mary explained.

"Is that when your fear of horses began?" Alex asked.

"It could be. As I said, it is one of my earliest memories, so it could have played a part in my fear," Mary said, "I really do not know though."

"If it was not the horses, what drew you to the barn so often?" Alex asked.

"Kittens usually," she smiled. "Our barn cat would have a litter of kittens several times a year, and I could usually be found playing with them. My mother would not let me bring them into the house, but a few times, I snuck one in. She would find them in my room and I would be punished from the barn for a few days, but it never deterred me," she chuckled. "My mother finally agreed to allow me to keep a cat inside, and when I turned fifteen, my father presented me with the most perfect gift imaginable—a kitten of my own. My mother soon found that having a cat inside was a blessing indeed, as it kept the small critters away. Longbourn now has three house cats, one of which is my Beatrice."

"Beatrice?" he smiled, "I once had two dogs named Hero and Don Pablo." The two laughed at their both choosing names from Shakespeare's *Much Ado About Nothing*, but he noticed a slight sadness to her eyes. "You must miss her."

"Yes; I wanted to bring her with me, but Elizabeth says William does not think very highly of cats."

"My cousin has always been more of a large animal lover. He puts up with the barn cats because they catch mice, but will not allow them inside Pemberley. His favorite animals are horses and dogs. My Uncle George loved to go hunting every chance he could, so he bred several different kinds of hounds that are still in the kennels at Pemberley. Darcy does not like the activity as much as his father did though, and prefers the larger dog breeds. He has several Dalmatians, and just two years ago he started breeding his Boar Hounds with much success. I think he has four of those at Pemberley right now."

"A Dalmatian… is that the spotted dog?" Mary asked.

"Yes; Bingley had one at Netherfield Park when I visited."

"Ahhh, yes, I remember seeing it once." Mrs Simpson entered with the tea tray laden with treats, and the two sat in silence as their cups and plates were prepared to their liking.

When the housekeeper was once again dismissed, Mary turned to Alex to continue their conversation, "I have yet to visit the kennels at Pemberley. I did not want to go alone and no one else has had the desire to go with me." Mary said.

"So you have not seen Darcy's Boar Hounds yet?"

"I have never heard of a Boar Hound before today, sir," she stated.

"It is a very large dog, standing about this high," Alex put his hand out, indicating their height.

Mary's eyes grew large, "That is nearly the size of a small horse!"

Alex chuckled, "I *have* seen a few that would rival a pony in size. You will have nothing to fear from them when you are visiting the kennel. They may be large, but they are the most gentle of creatures."

"My father has always prided himself on his hounds, but I have not been around many other breeds," Mary said.

"Oh, well you are in for quite a treat then. My mother has two little dogs running around the Dower House. If you are up for some exercise, we can go for a stroll through the gardens." He pointed out the window, "The Dower House connects to the back of the gardens, so I could easily introduce you to my mother's dogs while the others are resting?"

Smiling, Mary replied, "Yes, I would like that very much."

Alex stood and put his hand out to her, "Come, then."

When Mary returned to her chambers an hour later, her cheeks were flushed from the exercise of playing with the two small terriers. *If I ever do have the opportunity to own a dog, I think a West Highland Terrier is what I want,* she thought. For not being a dog lover, she was surprised at the connection she had with the two white dogs. No other animal would hold the same place in her heart as Beatrice, but it did feel quite nice to play with the two pups for a little while.

More than anything, she was happy to see how Alex interacted with the two—throwing a rope for them to bring back and rubbing their heads in reward. When the games were over he knelt down on the ground and rubbed the dogs' bellies. It was a sight Mary would always remember—especially the joy she saw in the simple pleasure he found in something that she was sure was a daily ritual between them. It was another glimpse into the character of the man she had completely misunderstood all this time.

Mary was interrupted by a knock, and she opened her door to find a young maid with a candle.

"Miss Darcy wishes to speak with you, Miss Bennet."

"Yes, of course." Mary blew out the candle on her desk and followed the girl as she led the way through the maze of hallways, eventually opening a door and indicating Mary should enter.

"Isn't it so fun here?" Georgiana patted the seat beside her and continued, "Pemberley is larger, but I have always loved Dalmeny for its winding passages."

Mary sat down, "Yes, but it is quite difficult to navigate, especially in the dark."

Georgiana grabbed her friend's hand, "Oh Mary, I am so sorry for making you come all this way in the dark.

Mary squeezed her fingers, "Do not trouble yourself on my account; the maid seemed sure of where she was going, so I just followed closely behind her the whole way. Now, getting back may be a bit of a problem if I am to go it alone."

"I wish we could be closer, but my aunt insisted on you being put in the green room, and this one is easiest with all my… necessities," she waved her hand around the room indicating everything she needed because of her injuries.

Mary smiled understandingly at her, "It is not a problem, Georgiana— truly."

They talked for a few minutes about their first day, and Georgiana finally yawned, indicating to Mary it was time to return to her own room. She wished her friend good night and the maid once again led her through the halls and back to her own room. Mary lit her candle, thanked the maid and dismissed her, then sat back down at the desk where her journal lay open.

The pen held once again between her stained fingers, she poured her heart out. All her hopes and dreams as well as her fears and insecurities flowed from the end of her quill onto the white pages. When she finally finished, she noted that she was finally on the last page. *It is time for a new start, in more ways than just one,* she thought to herself.

She quickly changed and climbed into the bed, her head lying on the soft pillow for only a few minutes before sleep overtook her tired body.

CHAPTER XV

Tuesday, June 23, 1812

Georgiana felt her cousin's arms tighten a bit around her as he made his way along the garden path. Darcy and Elizabeth were off in the distance, winding their way along the outside path. Ahead of them, on the path they followed, she watched carefully as Alex led Mary, the two discussing something quietly as they walked along. "Fitz, do you think Alex and Mary would make a nice match?"

"Why do you say that?"

"There is just something about them," she indicated with her head, "that seems very comfortable and familiar."

"Would you like there to be a match between the two?"

"Oh yes! Their personalities complement each other, and they do make a handsome couple."

Fitz smiled, "I happen to agree with you. Maybe they will one day realize the same and make you very happy."

Georgiana studied the pair and the small ways they interacted, "Maybe they already do realize it but are just not telling others yet."

"You think?" Fitz watched the small signals both were giving off. "I think it is far more likely that they do not quite realize yet what others can clearly see forming."

"I will have to ask Mary what she thinks of your brother."

"You will do nothing of the sort," Fitz admonished. "There have been enough misunderstandings between the two, and it would be best if everyone else just left them to find their own way."

Georgiana looked up to Fitz's face and raised her eyebrow, "So you know more than you are saying?"

"I will not honor that with an answer," Fitz tried to look away from her eyes.

"That's what I thought. I will find my answers somehow; I am determined."

"Yes, you did always have my mother's stubbornness," Fitz smiled. "As you are my charge though, I expect you to listen to my instructions and let them be. Miss Mary has already had too many things to overcome in her opinion of my brother, and I do not need more messes to clean up because of someone else."

"What do you mean? Did someone try to hurt my friend's chances with my cousin? Who would do such a thing?" Georgiana was shocked at his statement.

"Just believe me when I say they need to find out for themselves what their feelings are for each other," Fitz said.

"But anyone can see they are the perfect couple," she again turned to watch the pair.

"Georgiana, I will not have you defy what I say," Fitz's firm voice made Georgiana look back at his face. He set his charge down on a nearby bench and sat beside her. "Last year when Mr Wickham tried to woo you, what did he do?"

She looked down at her hands folded in her lap, "He told me how pretty I was, and that he could not live without my attention."

"But did he know you? Did he spend time with you? Did he know your favorite color, or which flowers you prefer in nosegays?"

"He knew nothing of me," she answered.

"He knew nothing of you because he did not take the time to get to know you. That is why we have courtships," Fitz explained. Taking her hand in his, he continued, "What made you hesitant Georgiana? Why did you not allow him to pursue you?"

"I have watched your parents all my life, and it is clear they have a regard for each other that is not evident in much of our society," she explained.

"Yes, they love each other; as your own parents did also."

"Mr Wickham did not try to get to know me. He just said I was beautiful and he could not live without me in his life." Georgiana's trembling hands were calmed when Fitz's much larger ones again squeezed her fingers. She took a deep breath and continued, "He had such handsome features, and it felt nice to attract the attentions of such a man, but what caused me to step back and question everything was that he did not know me."

"That is what courtship is for, and people like him are the reason chaperones are most important. However, the strictures by which society has relegated the courtship phase have made marriage into a marketplace where no one can truly know another. Rarely in our society are gentlemen and ladies allowed more than just a brief conversation while dancing at a ball or stilted words in the presence of others in a drawing room. How can feelings deeper than attraction form when society says you are not to talk with the person? Marriage is hard enough when you have a mutual affection towards each other, but without it there is nothing that will bind you when things get difficult."

"Like when Mr Bennet had his accident?" Georgiana asked.

"Yes, that is the perfect example. If the Bennets did not have something deeper than a surface affection for each other there is no telling what may have happened because of that accident. Their deeper love made them come together and form even more of a bond than they had before." Fitz let go of her hand and lifted her in his arms once again. "For now, my brother and Miss Mary need to figure out for themselves if they are each willing to form such a friendship that could grow into love."

"Do you think they will one day marry?" Georgiana looked back to the far off couple.

"It is a great possibility they will, but it is all in their hands, not ours. Our job is only to allow them time to get to know each other in a proper setting," Fitz smiled.

"I will have to see if I can leave them alone more often," Georgiana replied.

Fitz laughed, "The matchmaker at work."

"Now," she turned to him again, "What do *you* want in a wife?"

"Oh no, your services are not needed by me," Fitz admonished.

"So you are saying you already know who you will marry?" When Fitz refused to answer, she drew in her breath, "You do! I cannot believe it. Who could it be? Is it someone I know? When will you marry?"

"Georgiana, I said nothing of the sort, and your assuming will only bring you trouble," Fitz said firmly. "Now please let it go."

"Yes, sir," she replied, contrition evident on her face. "I will try to patiently wait for you to tell me all." She looked back up to his face, "You will tell me all someday, will you not?"

"Yes, Sweetling, someday I will tell you all."

The group arrived at the dower house and the ladies joined Lady Rosebery in her private sitting room while the gentlemen went to the library to talk.

"Georgie and I had a very interesting talk on the way over here," Fitz said to Darcy.

"Really? What about?" Darcy poured three cups of tea from the tray on the side table and followed his cousins to the chairs near the windows.

"Wickham."

Darcy sat down and took a slow drink of the hot liquid, "Did she bring him up, or did you?"

"I did." He put his own untouched cup on the table, "She did not hesitate or become overly emotional in answering me though."

Hugh entered and, seeing the young men, came over to join them. "I see you are all enjoying my wife's fine choice of tea and cakes."

"Just the tea, sir," Alex replied, "as it seems the cakes were reserved for the ladies."

Hugh pulled the rope to call the housekeeper, "Oh, no, I will not have my wife shooing me away from those treats all morning just to be refused some now." When the housekeeper entered, he spoke with her. When he turned back to the younger gentlemen, he replied "It is always important to remember your place as the *master* of the house, son," he said to Alex with a certain authority.

"Mother would have your neck if she heard you giving us such advice," Fitz chimed in.

Hugh sniggered, "Yes, that she would. Well, what she does not know will not hurt me." He poured his own cup of tea and sat down, "So, what were you discussing?"

"Georgiana's recovery," Fitz replied. "She seems to be slowly accepting what life has dealt her."

"Yes, I am so very proud of my sister," Darcy said. "Elizabeth's father said he made her promise to start trying to accept these changes. She was hesitant, but she did accept his challenge, and I am finally seeing the sister I always knew start to emerge again."

"How is Elizabeth?" Hugh asked. "I heard she had a small incident a few weeks ago and needed to rest for a few days?"

"Yes, it was rather odd. We were out on a picnic for her birthday and a storm came up quickly. She fainted dead away and could not be revived until a few hours later. The last time she fainted like that was when..." he looked to his uncle's furrowed brow and did not finish.

"...When she remembered your father."

Darcy nodded. It was no longer a family secret, but it was still not something he and his uncle discussed. Perhaps soon it would be time to do so.

"She seems to be back to her old self now," Alex replied.

Hugh uncomfortably shifted in his seat, "Was it the storm?"

"Yes," Darcy took a sip of his tea, "I have been around her for numerous rain showers, but it is only the thunder storms that seem to affect her."

Hugh was grateful for the arrival of the tray of cakes, and took this opportunity to try to change the subject of their discussion. "I hear you will be returning to Town for Elizabeth's confinement?"

"Yes, we would both prefer to have the best doctors around in case of complications." Darcy's eyes misted over, "especially with how delicate her constitution has become with her condition."

Hugh reached over and grabbed his nephew's shoulder, "Nothing will happen to her, Darcy."

"Yes, that is what I keep telling myself, but my own mother…"

"My sister was not a strong lady. She was often sick, even when young, and so many attempts to have a child were just too hard on her frail body."

Darcy looked into his uncle's eyes and inquisitively asked, "What do you mean *so many attempts to have a child*? How many times was she with child?"

"Three, besides you and your sister, that I know of, but it may have been more than that," Hugh replied.

Darcy looked down to his hands as he nervously twisted his ring, "I was not aware…"

"No, they wisely chose to not burden you with such information. Did you never question why you and Georgiana were born so far apart in age?"

"No, not really," Darcy said. "You and Aunt Helen only had two children also, so I guess it never occurred to me that it was abnormal."

Hugh looked out the window as his eyes misted with unshed tears, "We have had our own struggles with which to contend."

Alex broke the silence in the room with the question no one else was brave enough to ask, "How many?"

"Seven—if all had been born healthy we would have seven children." Hugh picked up his tea and took a long swallow, then pulled out his handkerchief and dried his eyes and looked back to his sons, "Fitz, however, will benefit greatly from our misfortune, and for that I am grateful." Hugh looked at his younger son, "Now if he would just sell his commission so his mother would stop becoming so anxious every time the post is delivered."

Fitz chuckled, "I take it she has put you up to questioning me once again about when that will take place?"

"Yes. Her brother wrote to her a few weeks ago and asked when you will take over the estate from the Alexander side of the family that he is holding for you."

"Hopefully soon, Father," Fitz sighed, "hopefully soon."

"Well, whenever you are ready, the estate papers are ready to be signed. The money we set aside for our daughter's dowries has been collecting interest all these years, and it is a nice bit of money you will be coming into when you do finally sell your commission."

Darcy heard the chime of the clock, "I hate to break up this loving group, but Aunt Helen said she planned on giving the ladies a tour about this time."

"And of course you would love the opportunity to escort your wife through the rooms," Hugh smirked.

"Yes, I too am interested in the changes you have made here," Darcy tried to interject.

"No, no, please spare me the sentiment," Hugh replied. "We all know you do not care about fabrics and furniture. Your protective nature is admirable, son." He stood, "Well, come on then and we will join the ladies."

The two brothers were seated in Alex's study, a drink in hand, when Darcy came in. "You needed me?"

"We did not have a chance earlier to discuss some business, and while I appreciate you not wanting to leave your beautiful wife's side, we must get on with things," Fitz replied with a smirk.

"Oh, stop badgering the man, Fitz. If you were married you too would not want to leave your wife's side, especially to meet with two as dull as us," Alex took up for his cousin.

"Well, since I must stay," Darcy sat down, "please tell me how your search has gone."

"We have found nothing so far. We cannot confirm that the baby even lived or what gender it was."

"So we are no further along than we were when we came to Derbyshire."

"I did receive a letter from my investigator," Fitz said, "and here is what he says:

> I was able to track down this uncle and find where he lived, but he has long been dead. There are three churches that were close enough to his residence. One has since closed its doors. The second I visited, and the vicar was agreeable, but their records were destroyed in a fire many years ago, so he could not help. The third, I was unable to get any information from the vicar. Maybe if a peer were to be asking he would feel the need to bow to their superior level of condescension, but the third son of a simple country gentleman was not enough to impress him into spending the time to look through his books. If I can find a suitable companion to distract the man, I will go back next week to see if I can sneak a peek at the books. I will continue to keep you informed if I find anything out here in Town."

Clearly frustrated, Fitz lowered the letter, "It was another unfruitful endeavor. We will have to investigate further."

"Well, we will just have to double our efforts," Alex replied as he stood.

Darcy stood as well, "Do you think we could find the letters at the dower house?"

"If my father were not there it is a good possibility, but the servants they took with them are very loyal. I do not even know where his trunks of old papers have been stored. I can say for certain they are not here at Dalmeny though." He sighed heavily, "Why must he keep quiet about this for so long? He refused to even discuss it when I asked about old records."

"I am sure he has his reasons. Maybe we will get a lucky break soon," Fitz said. "I am off to bed, so I bid you two good night."

They all three went upstairs, Darcy finding Elizabeth fast asleep when he entered their chambers. He dressed for bed and curled up behind her, laying his hand protectively over her as slumber found him as well.

CHAPTER

XVI

Wednesday, June 24, 1812

Elizabeth was reclining on the sofa when she heard a knock on the door. "Enter," she called out.

Anne opened the door and stepped in. Seeing Elizabeth with a cloth over her eyes, she brought her hand to her chest and rushed to her side, "Oh, Elizabeth, if I had but known you were feeling so ill, I would not have bothered you."

Elizabeth removed the cloth, "Nonsense, this is just a cloth soaked in lavender water that my maid thinks will *rejuvenate my wan features*," she said in a slightly mocking tone as she sat up and made room for Anne on the sofa. "Please do sit. I would enjoy a few minutes alone with you."

Anne smiled and took a seat next to Elizabeth. "My maid has a mind to often see that I bathe in a deep tub of salted water. She thinks it does something to my spirits. Sometimes it is just easier to do what they say rather than to question such authority as they possess."

"Oh, yes, I have found that to be true… of my maid and of our housekeepers!"

Anne smiled broadly, "Mrs Reynolds is always in quiet command of every situation. Her care for the family is evident."

"Yes, it is as you say, and since my family has joined with yours, she has taken me under her wing and taught me what is expected of the Mistress of such a grand estate."

Anne sighed, "My mother has never allowed me to learn the estate matters for Rosings."

Elizabeth tilted her head, "I have been curious for a while, and please do not feel you must tell me, but what exactly is the legal standing of Rosings? Was it not your father's land, to go to you upon his death?"

"I do not mind sharing what little I do understand with you. Perhaps, having been Mistress of Pemberley for all these months now, you can advise me in what I should do." She took a deep breath, and then began. "My father died when I was young—I hardly remember him. It is only the portrait in library that I most associate with him. Even when he was alive, he was not often in Kent, as he preferred the diversions of Town. Not being of age when he died though, naturally my uncle—my father's brother that is—was put over the estate. He is a naval man, however, and is rarely in England, especially with the war, so naturally my mother has been left to continue to run it as she sees fit."

"I understand now. Your mother is quite… overpowering…"

"Overwhelmingly so," Anne said with a small chuckle. "I do believe you are being generous with such a description."

Elizabeth looked up to see that no one was in the doorway, and then she looked back to Anne, "While we are alone, I must ask if you are well recovered from the… *incident?*"

Anne's hands began to tremble and she clutched them together in her lap. "I know people do not believe that I saw my father…"

"Nonsense! I believe you know exactly what you saw. Whether it was your father or not, it was something that caused you to faint, and if not for the distraction, I fear for what could have happened to me."

"Does Georgiana know?"

"No, William and I felt she should not be told. So we just used my health as a reason to leave Town early. Mary knows some of the details though. We begged her to keep silent, and she has not said a word even to me about it since."

Anne's trembling hands clutched the fabric of her dress. "Has William mentioned any reason for concern since returning to Derbyshire?"

Elizabeth reached her own hand out to squeeze Anne's, "He assures me that Pemberley, as well as Dalmeny, are both very secure, and we are safe."

Anne calmed tremendously. "Thank you, Elizabeth. Richard has told me the same, but hearing it from you, and knowing it comes also from William, has calmed my nerves." She turned to look more fully at Elizabeth, "Your condition is more evident now than it was in Town."

Elizabeth lovingly ran her hand across her expanding stomach. "If only this little one would give me some reprieve. I am nauseous nearly every minute of the day, and feel faint often. Why, it is as if my body is not my own any longer. It is wearisome just doing the simplest of tasks. Yet, the most difficult aspect is that I love to be outside, and cannot fathom doing nothing, and yet I am bound to rest so often."

"I know the feeling. Being of ill health most of my life, it is often that I have had to take to my chambers for sometimes months at a time. It becomes such a dull and dreary burden."

Elizabeth stretched her aching back, "What did you do to pass the time?"

She blushed a little, "Richard and I have passed many a letter over the years, and he would often engage me in frivolous games. I am not much for chess, though he did try to teach me once, but we would come up with word games, or send backgammon moves back and forth. He has truly been my savior many times over."

Elizabeth stood, "Well, I am glad you had someone. William has been my constant companion these last few difficult months, and we have grown quite close because of the situation." She placed the now cold cloth back in the bowl of lavender water, then replied, "I feel well enough now to go for a walk in the garden. Would you care to join me?"

"Yes, of course," Anne said, standing. "Elizabeth, I am very glad to have you in my family now."

<hr />

Thursday, June 25, 1812

"Georgiana, I do not know if this is a good idea."

"Oh please go with me Mary! My Aunt has already promised to let Anne go and to let us use her phaeton," Georgiana pleaded.

"Is her phaeton like yours?"

"Mine is much smaller than my aunt's. Hers has a seat for a driver, and two seats for passengers. *Please, please, please,* say you will go? My Aunt will not hear of it if you do not agree." Georgiana eagerly bounced on the window seat on which she sat as she begged Mary.

"I do not know…"

"Will you go if I invite my cousins to join us?"

Mary thought for a full minute before she finally answered, "If your cousins agree to accompany us, I would feel better about going."

Georgiana picked up her bell to signal Joseph, who stood right outside the door.

"Yes, Miss Darcy?"

"I need to speak with my cousins."

"Would you like me to take you, or have them attend you here?"

"Just have them come here to the library, Joseph."

When they both entered, Alex looked to Mary and gave her a small smile. She returned it then looked away as the two brothers addressed their young cousin.

Fitz's own smile mirrored his cousin's, "To what do we owe the pleasure of that beautiful smile, Sweetling?"

"Oh Fitz, I have the most amazing idea, and have already checked with Aunt Helen about using her phaeton, and Anne will accompany me, but Mary says she will only go if you two will also join us. So will you?"

"Wait, I do not understand," Fitz said, sitting beside his charge. "Slow down and start from the beginning."

"Aunt Helen said we could have use of her phaeton to drive around Dalmeny Park today, and Mary says she would feel more comfortable if the two of you were to accompany us."

Mary blushed when she saw Alex look at her.

"Oh, please say yes! I have not been able to go hardly anywhere since coming back to Derbyshire, and it would be such fun to have a picnic and see the land, especially with today being Mary's birthday."

"And what of your brother; have you asked his permission yet on this scheme of yours?"

"No, he did not come down this morning."

Mary spoke up, "My sister is not feeling well. I visited her earlier, and she apologized profusely, but says she will try to come down to supper this evening. William said he wishes to stay at her side, and hoped I could find something else to fill my day as they remained in their chambers."

Alex stepped forward, "I think it is an excellent plan, Georgiana. I cannot imagine you having decided to do this on your own, but Miss Mary," Alex looked at her and watched as the blush deepened, "was correct in saying we needed to join you. Neither you nor Anne need be away from the house for such a length of time without us." He looked sternly back to his cousin, "You *were* going to ask, were you not Georgiana?"

"Oh my, yes! My brother would have a fit of apoplexy if I left without a word of where we were to go."

He chuckled, "Yes, *that* is putting it mildly."

Alex addressed Mary, "Would you care to join me in speaking with Mrs Simpson about a basket?" At her nod of approval he extended his arm, happy to have her accept his escort without a second thought. His heart beat wildly at the thought that she was finally giving him the chance for which he had so long hoped.

They spoke to the housekeeper, and when Mary returned to the library, Georgiana was alone.

Georgiana smiled at her friend, "You seem very impressed with a *certain gentleman* lately."

Mary blushed, "He is *certainly* impressive."

Georgiana giggled, "I would have to agree with you there. Maybe you will marry him, then we could be cousins as well as sisters!"

Amazingly, Mary felt no trepidation at such a statement. "You would not mind the connection?"

"Oh, how could I? He needs someone like you in his life."

Mary smiled, "Perhaps one day... for now, let us return upstairs to dress for our outing. Alex has ordered a picnic prepared that is worthy of our awe, and the twinkle in the housekeeper's eye when she turned to walk away revealed she may have a few surprises in mind for our fare as well."

"Oh, so it is Alex now, is it?" Georgiana teased.

Mary blushed at the slip of her tongue. In truth she had thought of him as such for many weeks now, but had yet to verbalize it until now. Not knowing what to say to Georgiana though, she instead asked, "What will you wear?" Mary rang for Joseph to carry Georgiana upstairs.

The two were soon dressed and back downstairs to await the others in the library. Mary was looking through the books in the far corner when she spotted something... *what could that be... is that a piece of paper sticking up from between these two books?* She tried to pull the paper out, but it was stuck so she pulled the two books off the shelf and tried to separate them. It looked like the tiny scrap of paper was sticking out the top where the leather casings came together. Turning them over, she realized they were not books at all; it was a box made to look like books. She looked back to Georgiana ensuring she was not paying her any mind, and turned back to the box in her hands. Opening it, she found the piece of paper inside. There was nothing written on it, so she put it back and returned the box to the spot on the shelf. *How odd? I wonder why someone would want to make such a box?* She continued down the line of spines, reading the titles, until one caught her attention. She pulled it out to thumb through it, sitting beside her friend once again as they waited.

They were soon interrupted by the joyous raptures of Fitz as he strode into the room, picked Georgiana up in his arms, and swung her around, her laughter filling the air. Mary giggled at the display and did not even realize the viscount also entered the room until he spoke quietly to her.

"He knows just how to cheer my cousin up."

Mary looked to her companion, "Yes, he is rather good at that job, is he not?"

He watched as Fitz strode from the room with Georgiana in his arms, and with a slight bow, Alex put out his arm, "May I escort you to your ride, Miss Mary?"

Mary could not help the smile that came over her face as she took his arm and they made their way outside to the phaeton where Anne and Georgiana were already getting settled on the seat. Mary sat beside them and the two cousins climbed onto the opposite seat, the basket provided by Mrs Simpson having been placed by the driver's feet, and they were soon off on their adventure.

***

"Have you had the opportunity to see the castle yet," Georgiana pointed to the structure as they passed.

Mary looked across to the viscount, remembering their conversation before about his castle, "No, I have not."

"We must remedy that during your visit, Miss Mary," Alex said, "if not today, perhaps on another excursion?"

"Yes, I would like that, sir."

Georgiana smiled at the shy reaction Mary had to her cousin's offer and drew their attention to another part of the park they would soon pass.

The drive was picturesque with the sun peeking out from behind the clouds, their white, billowy forms allowing the occasional break from its warm rays. Darker clouds just starting to gather to the west caught Fitz's attention. Having grown up in this area, he knew how quickly a few clouds could turn into a downpour of rain. *I will need to keep an eye on those throughout the day*, he thought. His attention was drawn to the three seated across from him. Mary was looking around the landscape to all Georgiana and Alex pointed out, and Anne was quietly sitting, a worried look on her face. *What is wrong, my Anne? What has caused your beautiful smile to fade today?* He caught her eye to see if he could garner a smile from her.

She tried to forget what worried her, but, even with the beauty that surrounded them, Anne could not seem to push the ominous feeling aside completely. Fitz smiled at her, and she felt the corners of her mouth turn up in response.

The smile does not yet reach your eyes, my love. What is bothering you today? Fitz lifted his eyebrow in question.

Anne slowly closed her eyes, the smile on her lips growing just a bit with his attention. When she opened them again, Fitz was watching Mary's reaction to something his brother said. Anne turned to see Alex's face as he nearly beamed with pride over the land they traversed. Looking back to Fitz, she indicated the two with a nod of her head and a questioning look on her face.

Seeing where she glanced, a sneaky smile appeared on his lips. *Yes, it seems my brother is completely taken with her*, he said internally to Anne.

With a small nod of understanding the two once again focused on their own situation. The sun came out from behind a cloud, and she lifted her face as its warm beams shone down onto her naturally pale skin.

Fitz's heart began to race when Anne lifted her face to the sky, her blonde hair glowing in the sunlight, and the gentle breeze playing with the curls around her face. Fitz wanted desperately to remove her bonnet and run his fingers through her tresses.

Looking back to her betrothed, she found him intently looking into her eyes, the rising tension between the two completely overlooked by the others in the carriage. She felt her cheeks blush into a fiery pink the longer his gaze held hers.

Sarah Johnson

Oh, how much life seems to radiate from your features when a blush touches your pale cheeks, my love! The ribbons of her bonnet fluttered in a gust of wind breaking their intense stare and he could do nothing but smile in response.

Her breath caught in her chest at his grin. *He is a naturally jovial person, but this look he reserves only for me.* She felt protected even in just his glance. Adjusting the shawl around her shoulders, she imagined his arms in its stead.

Fitz saw her pull the wrap closer around her small shoulders and his hand twitched. *If only it was my arms that surrounded you instead, my love. I must have some time alone with you today. I must find out what is troubling you so.*

Anne saw the gleam in his eye and knew immediately what he wanted. *Your kisses are all that will calm this foreboding in my heart; I so desperately need your arms around me, my love.*

He could not look away from the intense pleading in her eyes. *She needs my comfort today.* With a small nod of acceptance, he assured her that he understood and they would find some time alone.

She did not realize how very transparent her thoughts were until his small nod indicated he understood completely. The blush deepened in her cheeks and her heart pounded so hard she thought it might be visible through her dress. She drew in a deep, calming breath, trying to focus again on their companion's conversation before she was completely undone.

The rise of her chest with the intake of breath caused his own heart to race, and he looked away before their private *tête-à-tête* was seen by the others, feeling bereft of their secret moment immediately.

Another warm wind whipped around them all, and Anne felt Fitz's foot come into contact with her own boot. She looked down to her hands and closed her eyes, relishing in the small touch no one else noticed. *He always finds a way to reassure me, even when we are in the company of others.*

CHAPTER XVII

Georgiana was seated against a tree, sleepily looking out over the field before her. "I could easily fall asleep after such a satisfying repast."

Alex agreed, "Yes, my new housekeeper is still trying to impress me. It was a lovely fare."

"I think I would rather take a short walk and pick some flowers," Mary said. "Miss de Bourgh, would you like to stretch your legs also?"

"Yes, that does sound nice," she stood.

"Do you want me to join you?" Alex offered.

"I think we will be well enough without your presence, my dear cousin."

Fitz looked at the sky above, "Do not be long."

"We will be safe. I know these grounds well, remember?" She threaded her arm through Mary's and the two walked off down the path.

When they were far enough away from the group, Mary looked at her companion, "You nearly gave your secret away today with that display in the carriage."

Anne blushed, "Did we? I thought we did well to keep others from noticing."

"I noticed, but maybe it is because I know already. I doubt your cousins noticed though—they were both too busy pointing out interesting sights. What drew my attention was when you two were staring at each other without a thought to those around you."

"We will have to keep that in mind in the future," Anne replied demurely. "I dearly wished to have some time with him today, but my young cousin seems to need his arms more than I do."

"When we return I will try to distract the others so you can have a few minutes alone if you wish, Miss de Bourgh" Mary offered.

Anne smiled, "Oh, please call me Anne, and I would like that. Thank you, Miss Bennet. There was something in my mother's letter that worries me, and I wish to ask Richard for his advice."

"Please call me Mary," she smiled as they continued down the path. "Is it something you can share with me?"

"No, I really do not know how to put into words what worries me. I was just going to have my cousin read the letter and see if he caught the same thing I did."

"Is your mother well?"

"As well as can be expected; she has suffered from severe headaches this last year and they are worsening these last few months." Anne stopped and bent down to pick some flowers. "I am glad my uncle and aunt invited me to come here with them. My mother does not like me to leave her side and it can become burdensome."

"She is quite overbearing," Mary interjected as she chose some flowers of her own before they began to walk again.

Anne smirked, "Oh you do not know the half of it. She has her own opinions and does not care what others think, she will have her way. I was quite shocked when William and Elizabeth were able to marry without her interfering." Anne looked up to Mary, "She proclaimed for years her wish that he marry me."

"Yes, I was told just that by the colonel and the viscount."

"I wonder... well, never mind."

"You wonder what?" Mary asked.

"It is quite rude of me to voice, but I was about to say, I wonder what conversation you would have with the two of them that would bring up such a subject?"

Mary blushed and looked down to the ground. "I did not look favorably upon the viscount for many months," she dearly wished to call him Alex again, but with such a slip earlier she did not want to have even more questions when she was still unsure of so much. "It was because of some, like your mother, who filled my head with nonsense and lies about him. We finally had a chance to speak last month, right before he left Pemberley, and your mother's desire to see you two marry was one of the things that came up in the conversation."

Anne saw a spark of interest and thought she might question her a little further. "And now that these lies have been exposed, what is your opinion of my cousin?"

Mary's blush deepened. It seemed her purposely not using his Christian name would not stop the questions today. She stopped to pick some more flowers, "I... he is... he is very solicitous."

"Yes, that he is," Anne chided. "Is there, perhaps, the possibility of *something more*?"

"I do not know," Mary said intently. "For now, we are just starting over and getting to know each other. I do not know if he has intentions beyond just that."

Hmmmm, I have a feeling there is much more between the two, especially on my cousin's side. I will have to see what I can do to further the match. "I have all the flowers I need, if you are ready to turn back?"

"I just need a few more," Mary answered. As the wind began to pick up, she saw some petunias off in the distance and thought of the day she met the viscount. "I see some over there I would like to gather."

The two continued to walk, needing to hold onto their bonnets more securely than before. "Do you think it is going to rain?" Anne looked up to the sky as it grew darker.

"Yes, it looks like it might," Mary said. "Maybe we should turn back now."

"No, I am certain we have enough time to gather the flowers before we return," Anne hastened her steps, pulling Mary along with her.

The two picked some of the petunias and were just about to turn back when the sky grew very dark and they could see the rain as it came towards them. "Oh, we must hurry, Anne," Mary urged her friend.

"The rain is coming from the direction we must walk," Anne noted as she looked around. "Maybe, if we go this way and into the woods to cut around, we will stave it off for a little bit longer."

The two found the wooded area to be less windy and were able to gain the distance from the rain that was needed, but the dark clouds began to make it difficult to see beneath the cover of the trees. A clap of thunder made both stop in their tracks as they felt the rumble beneath them and heard the crack of tree limbs ahead.

"Maybe it would be best to be back out in the field?" Mary suggested.

"No, we will just have to be very careful. I am certain we are almost there now," Anne urged.

The two continued on for several more minutes until another clap of thunder even closer made the two stop again, frozen in fear. Far-off they could hear their names being called.

Fitz looked up to the sky a few minutes after the two ladies left on their walk. "Alex, I do not like the look of that sky." His brother did not answer him. When he looked over, he noticed Alex, along with Georgiana leaning against his shoulder, was fast asleep. Fitz stood and lifted Georgiana in his arms. "Alex," he gently tried to nudge him with his foot. Kicking him a little harder, he was finally able to get his attention. "We must get everyone to the safety of the hunting lodge. The wind is starting to pick up and those dark clouds are getting close."

Alex rubbed his sleepy eyes and looked off in the distance, "Oh, yes, we must," he stood quickly.

"I will go there with Georgiana while you alert the driver where he can stable the horses. We do not need them becoming frightened," Fitz gave his orders and immediately started walking with his sleepy cousin in his arms, quietly reassuring her as she awoke that everything would be well.

When Georgiana was safely inside the lodge, Fitz returned outside and saw his brother coming hurriedly from the stable. "Did you see the others returning yet?"

"No, we must go and find them. I fear they may get lost in this rain."

The two brothers hurried away from the lodge and within minutes the sky was dark, the rain starting to pour from the ominous clouds overhead. A loud clap of thunder made them hasten their search. First they returned to where they had their picnic, but did not see Mary and Anne anywhere around.

"Do you know the woods well enough in this area?" Fitz asked.

"Yes, Father insisted I know every inch of this park if I was to manage it properly one day," Alex replied.

"Then you circle around and cut through the woods and I will follow the path they took. Hopefully we will find them before we meet again."

"Yes, sir," Alex gave a mock salute. "I would not mind taking orders from you in a battle, little brother."

Fitz smirked, "If only all my soldiers felt the same as you do."

The two separated, both calling out the names of the two ladies as they made their way through the rain. Another clap of thunder seemed to be right over Alex's head, and he heard a nearby tree limb crack. His steps were quickened and he eagerly shouted, "MARY? ANNE? WHERE ARE YOU? CAN YOU HEAR ME?"

Far off in the distance he could barely make out his brother calling the same thing from the other direction.

Fitz heard the snapping crack of the tree when the thunder clapped again, and for a minute he was worried for his brother's safety, until all of a sudden he could hear him clearly calling out for the two ladies. *He is well*, he told himself as he trudged further down the path, now nearly invisible in the heavy rain. "ANNE! MARY!" He pulled the collar up around his neck a little more and continued on, "ANNE! MARY! CAN YOU HEAR ME? ARE YOU HERE?"

Anne's hand grabbed Mary's arm causing her to stop, "Do you hear that?"

"I can hear nothing over this rain," Mary replied.

"Stop and listen." The two stood still for a minute and could hear the far-off sounds of the two brothers calling their names. "It sounds like Fitz is calling from this direction," Anne pointed back where they had just come, "but Alex sounds like he is coming from that way," she pointed off into the woods ahead of them.

The two immediately started calling out to their searchers, "WE ARE HERE! IN THE WOODS!"

The sound of shouting got louder along with the heavy footfalls as the rescuers made their way to the two ladies. Within minutes the brothers converged upon Mary and Anne from both directions and everyone exchanged excited greetings.

"Are you hurt?"

"No, we are both unscathed, but a little wet," Anne replied to Fitz, her heart beating faster when she saw the anguish in his eyes.

Alex and Fitz removed their coats and wrapped them around Mary and Anne, then the four set off for the lodge.

Both brothers were certain where they needed to go, but Fitz's steps were sure and steady in the rain and he and Anne were soon outpacing their companions.

As Alex trudged more slowly through the wood, Mary clinging to his arm, he could not help the rising feelings in his chest. The only thing that would make this moment even better was if she stood beside him not as just a friend, but as his intended. However, he could blame no one but himself for that. He hoped all the misunderstandings were put behind them though, and they would now be able to build a friendship that he hoped would lead to such a union in their future.

Mary could hardly see through the rain that covered her spectacles. She clung fervently to the strong arm of her rescuer, remembering intently the emotionally charged moments of when they first met. Mary's feet began to slide in the mud and she held even harder to her companion.

"Are you well? Do you need to rest for a minute?" Alex halted their walking and leaned close to her ear to ensure she heard him through the pouring rain.

The feeling of his hot breath on her ear sent shivers down her back, but she answered, "I nearly slipped, but I have found my footing again."

They were not five steps further when suddenly Alex slipped on the mud. Unfortunately Mary's strength could not keep him from falling, and he pulled her down right along with him. Alex landed on his back, with Mary on top of him, her spectacles now splattered with mud.

Slowly Alex reached up and took them from her face, revealing the brown eyes that stared intently into his own green eyes. What he dearly wished to do in that moment was kiss her, fervently and passionately, but the sharp pain in his back as a tree limb poked through the thin lawn of his shirt brought him back to the reality of the moment.

The two were soon on their feet again. Mary removed her muddy gloves and placed them in the pocket of the coat still draped around her.

Alex wiped what he could of the mud from her spectacles and handed them back to her, "I wish I could better clean these for you."

Mary reached for them, her hand stopping as it came into contact with his and started to tingle. She leaned a little closer, her desire to feel more was overpowering.

Alex saw the slight gesture and his heart beat wildly inside his chest, ready to explode with joy over her acceptance of him at last. If not for his brother's voice filtering through his mind, he would have pulled her into an embrace this instant. He smiled and released the spectacles, the moment ending when he stepped away just a little and turned to call through the wood, "WE ARE COMING!"

Alex once again put his arm out, Mary accepting it, and both knew it was an acceptance of more than just his assistance.

When they came to the edge of the wood, Fitz was there waiting on them. "Anne is with Georgiana, and I came back to find you." He chuckled and shook his head, "Do I even want to know how the two of you became so covered in mud?"

Alex looked at his own clothing, then over to Mary, a smear of mud on her cheek and nose. He tightened his grip and turned back to his brother, "We may need to clean up a bit when we get to the cabin."

"Well, we might be there a while—this rain is still coming down too hard for the horses."

The canopy of the trees had sheltered them from the intensity of the downpour, but now they would need to make a dash across the field to the cabin. Alex turned to Mary, wrapping his arm under the coat that draped over her shoulders, and asked, "Are you ready?"

Mary closed her eyes and took a deep breath. When she opened them again, she leaned a little closer, nodded her head, and replied, "Yes."

Fitz watched the two and knew there was something that had happened between them in the few minutes they were alone. He was glad to see the change, but was curious what could have spurred something so dramatic so quickly. He would have to ask his brother later.

The three darted through the pouring rain as hastily as was possible without slipping. When they were safely on the porch, Alex said to his brother, "Give us a minute; we will be right in."

When the door was closed and they were, once again, alone, Alex turned to Mary, "I must know what has happened."

She looked up into his eyes, questioning her own heart.

Alex stepped just a little closer, his hand drawing up to touch her cheek. When she leaned ever so gently into his touch, he said, "Miss Mary Bennet, I have been enchanted by your charms from the first moment of our acquaintance. I never expected to feel such a change, and so dramatically, from just a simple meeting on the side of the road, and yet it was exactly that. Even through all our misunderstandings, I felt drawn to you like I have never felt for anyone else, and my heart nearly leapt from my chest when you stood before me that day at the mill and introduced yourself again, giving me a chance to try again what I so blundered from the start. I would be remiss if I did not take this opportunity to ask of you—will you stand beside me all our days on this earth? Marry me?"

Mary's whole body ached from her desire to hear the words that finally escaped his lips. She leaned into his touch and drew her hand up to his chest. His words were hardly out before she uttered, "I never knew until this moment how much I have longed to hear those words from you."

"You have?" he whispered as he came closer to her.

"My sister has counseled me that when it is the right person you just know, and I now know that I have felt it from the first moment of our acquaintance, but have just refused to admit what I did not understand, and therefore feared."

Alex's hand trembled, his mouth going dry as he whispered, "What are you saying?"

"Yes, I will marry you."

Alex felt as if his chest would explode, and he closed his eyes and leaned down, his lips descending upon hers. All the previous touches between the two were nothing compared to the fire that rose in his chest when Mary accepted his kiss and returned it with just as much fervor. All time stood still as the two were locked in an embrace that built in intensity with every second that passed. The passionate exchange left the two gasping for breath, and when they separated, Alex beamed with pride at having finally convinced her of his true character.

Mary chuckled at him. "If I had but known how happy this would make you…"

"If you say you would have answered positively from the first day of our acquaintance, I shall have to take you to task madam. You and I both know you were terrified of me that day."

Mary removed her spectacles and reached into her pocket to see if her handkerchief could clear the spots of mud still remaining on them. "I was never terrified of you—on the contrary, it was my own feelings that caused such confusion in my heart."

One of his hands stilled hers as his other drew her chin up so she was looking at him again, "Truly? Even from the beginning you were drawn to me?"

"My desire has never wavered, only my own acceptance and understanding of that desire."

Alex wrapped his arms around her, his lips hovering over hers. "You know not what it does to me to hear of your own desire from the beginning of our acquaintance."

She whispered back, "You know not how I have longed to say that from the beginning of our acquaintance, but propriety has kept me from uttering the words so deeply founded in my heart until this moment. It terrified me to know how I felt about a gentleman such as yourself."

"But your courage always rises…"

She chuckled at his use of the line she had given to him months ago, the laughter caught in her chest as his lips closed the last few inches and once again the two were joined together.

Alex leaned his forehead against Mary's and with heavy breaths said, "If we do not marry *soon*, I shall not be responsible for what happens."

Mary chuckled, "Will you be speaking with my father *soon* then?"

Alex blushed and stepped back to allow her to finish cleaning her spectacles. "Actually, your father and I have already spoken. You need only send a letter with your own desires, and his permission will gladly be granted."

Remembering all that was revealed of their trip from London and the stop in Hertfordshire before they went to Pemberley, Mary felt a blush rise in her cheeks. Somehow even his mistake in speaking with her father instead of her would work to their advantage. "I hope to do that today," she said, replacing the spectacles onto her face.

Alex reached for the wet handkerchief from her hand and drew it up to wipe the mud streak from her nose and cheek. "I hope this is a birthday you shall always remember."

"I forgot it was my birthday, but now that you mention it, I never expected such a gift as you have given me this day."

"And what gift is that?"

"Why, your heart, of course."

"My heart you have had for many months. It is only today that you have accepted my pursuit of your hand."

The two were interrupted by the door opening and Anne stepping out onto the porch. "The rain is still coming down hard, I see."

Alex stepped back from Mary and handed her back the handkerchief. "Yes, it looks like we will be here for a while longer."

Anne stepped over to Mary's side, looking intently at her cousin.

"I will be just inside if you need me." Alex retreated inside.

CHAPTER XVIII

Upon the door closing, Anne turned to Mary, "So, are we to now plan your wedding?"

Mary's answer was given in the deep blush that overtook her cheeks.

Anne smiled, "I am truly happy for my cousin and for you. Welcome to the family."

She chuckled, "I am already part of the family, as my sister is married to your other cousin."

"True, but now you too will be married into the family as well, and one day I hope we can be sisters."

"I look forward to that day."

Anne drew her eyes down to take in Mary's appearance, "Now, we shall get you dried off and hope your maid is able to save your dress. I must say though, you fared better than my cousin did—he was positively covered in mud! What happened?"

Mary looked down at her own dress splattered with mud, then pulling the rain soaked coat around her shoulders even more, she replied, "We lost our footing and fell."

Anne chuckled at her friend's embarrassment and placed her arm around Mary's shoulders, "Come, we must dry you off before you catch a chill."

"I intended to give you time to talk with the colonel when we returned to the others, but now we are stranded here…"

"I am certain an opportunity will present itself soon enough."

They entered the cabin and both went to dry off beside the fire that roared in the fireplace. "Where is Alex?" Anne asked, taking the rain-soaked coat from her friend's shoulders and replacing it with a nicely-warmed quilt.

"He has some clothing upstairs, so he went to change."

Georgiana spoke up, "I have never seen him so covered in mud. I can imagine he is glad to have a change of clothing here at the lodge."

Alex entered the room just as Georgiana spoke, "Yes, I am, but I must apologize for my appearance," he said, indicating his stocking clad feet and lack of cravat. "My valet will need to attend to the clothing that is here at the hunting lodge, as I could not find everything I needed."

Mary's heart beat wildly at the unkempt way in which the viscount appeared in the doorway. She could feel his eyes looking at her, and her own cheeks began to burn from his scrutiny. To keep from having to say anything, she turned back to the fire.

Alex went to Mary's side and asked, "Are you warm enough? Do you need anything?"

"No, I am drying off nicely."

Seeing that the others were talking amongst themselves and not paying attention to them, he leaned a little closer and said, "Perhaps it would be prudent to have a change of clothing for you placed here as well, once we are married."

Mary smiled, but did not look away from the fire. "I shall keep your suggestion in mind, my lord."

"My lord? Are we still to be so formal?"

"What would you have me say?"

"I can think of a number of things I would wish to hear from your lips, but I fear now may not be the time to discuss those in detail."

Mary felt a chill run up her back at his whispered words. "I promise to think of a more appropriate response in the future."

Alex heard the scooting of furniture and turned to see his brother coming towards the fire with a chair in his arms.

"We thought it might be best if we rearranged the furnishings a little so no one gets cold," Fitz said, setting the chair down for Mary.

"Yes, that is a worthy plan. Can I help?" Alex asked.

"I will get Georgiana's seat if you can pick her up for a minute."

"Yes, of course," he said, going to his cousin and lifting her into his arms so his brother could move her chair.

Georgiana eyed him, "Something is different with you, Alex."

Alex looked over to Mary, "Yes… yes it is."

Trying not to squeal in glee, Georgiana replied, "Are we to wish you joy?"

"Yes, I do believe you are," he said quietly, "but let us not spread that around too quickly as Mary has yet to write to her father, nor talk with her sister about our plans." Georgiana's smile was enough to make Alex chuckle. He placed her back in her chair and tapped her nose, "Words are not needed, Sweetling. I feel just as you do at this time."

When the three ladies were seated in chairs, Alex and Fitz took their places on the floor, Alex positioning himself as near to Mary's chair as he could without being called out by the others. The five began to talk of all that happened that day, but all left the discussion of the personal lives of Alex and Mary for another day. Alex would forever hold one special moment in his heart for all his days—the look in Mary's eyes when he asked for her hand.

It was another hour before the rain began to slow, but not enough for it to be safe enough to use the carriage yet. So they were all shocked when Darcy arrived at the lodge, drenched.

"What has brought you out in such weather? Do not tell me there is a problem?" Alex asked.

"My wife was worried, and, I must say, Georgiana's health, as well as Anne's, was on my mind as well, so I thought it best to see if you were sheltered here before we began a search party of the wood."

When he was assured of their safety, and when the servant with him was sent to return the message that all were well, they returned to their places before the fire, this time telling Darcy of the events which led to their being in the hunting lodge.

The rain finally stopped and they were able to return to Dalmeny, so the footman hitched the horses back to the carriage and everyone climbed in.

"I fear my mother will not be pleased that we have made such a mess of her carriage," Alex replied.

Mary inspected the seat cushion, "I will tell her it is my fault."

"Oh, but it is not your fault at all," Anne said. "If anything, the fault is mine for insisting we take that particular route instead of going around. The rain came upon us rather more quickly than I anticipated."

Fitz chuckled. "Of course, no matter what we say, Mother will blame my brother."

"Yes," Georgiana laughed, "that is because he always seems to get himself into situations such as these."

Fitz laughed heartily now, "He is the only person I know who can find a way to soil his clothing with a simple outing."

Alex looked at Mary and smiled, "I seem to have a knack for getting myself into a bit of a mess now and then," he blushed.

"Oh the stories I could tell you of my brother and his escapades, Miss Bennet," Fitz replied loudly.

"There is no need, Colonel. I am well aware of your brother's penchant for getting muddy." Mary smiled at Alex.

"Oh really?" Fitz eyed the two.

"Yes," was all Mary would add.

"And which story is it you have already been told?"

Mary did not say anything, but the small smile as she looked at the viscount made him blush slightly. "I believe the lady wishes to keep her silence on this one, Fitz."

"Sometimes the best stories are those kept between those involved," she said simply.

"I completely agree, Miss Mary." The two shared a look that did not go unnoticed by at least three in the carriage, though none chose to say anything of the couple's private moment. Darcy, on the other hand, remained in his own thoughts with worry over Elizabeth since he had to leave her alone during the storm.

By the time they arrived back at the house it was time to dress for dinner. Anne was taken to the dower house, Fitz offering to help her to the door then walk back through the garden as the others continued on to the main house.

When the four came in the front door, the state of their clothing instantly sent the maids and footman into a flurry of activity. Mrs Simpson was there to oversee the staff, and Alex quickly helped Mary remove her muddy shoes and offered to take her to her room while Darcy saw to Georgiana's needs.

"Thank you, Mrs Simpson," Alex replied as they started up the stairs. "We all appreciate your thoughtfulness."

The simple smile on her lips hid her elation over the compliment as she followed Mr Darcy up the stairs to see that Miss Darcy was well settled, her final instructions given to the maids to attend to the floor quickly. Her quiet control of the situation put Alex at ease and he was once again grateful for having found such a woman for the position of housekeeper after the one he had grown up with moved to the dower house with his parents.

Alex put his arm out and escorted Mary to her chamber, then went to his own room and called for a bath. When he was finally able to slip beneath the warm water, he sighed with great relief as the memories of the day flashed in his mind.

Hearing the clock in his bedroom chime, he realized the water had become cold. He dressed and returned downstairs to check on the dinner preparations. Though he had little doubt Mrs Simpson could handle such an event, he was nervous that everything go perfectly this evening. He awaited his houseguests in the drawing room, and the sight of Mary on Elizabeth's arm as they entered made him smile.

Alex bowed deeply, "Miss Mary, may I offer my most sincere felicitations on your birthday. I hope the evening is to your liking."

"Thank you, sir. I am certain it will be the perfect end to a wonderful birthday," Mary followed her sister as they sat to await the others.

Elizabeth said to the viscount, "I hear we are to offer you both joy, my lord."

Alex smiled as he sat on the sofa next to Mary, taking her hand in his own, "Yes, your sister has made me the happiest of men in accepting my hand today."

Elizabeth saw the blissful looks the two exchanged and remembered well those feelings from early in her betrothal to her husband. "I am only sorry you were caught out in such weather." Elizabeth tried not to show her own anxiety, but her hands began to tremble.

Mary saw the slight movement and she reached over to take her sister's fingers in her own, squeezing them gently as she said, "No harm came to us."

"Yes, for that I am grateful." She tried to calm her heart, "You know how I am with such weather as we are having today."

"Yes, I understand completely. Perhaps this evening's entertainments will help distract you."

The distant clap of thunder outside made her jump just a little and she felt Darcy's arm wrap around her shoulders. "Are you well, my dear?"

Elizabeth took a deep breath, "Yes, thank you."

"Lord and Lady Rosebery and Miss de Bourgh," the butler announced as the visitors from the dower house arrived.

Lord Rosebery put on a smile as he offered his felicitations to Mary and took a seat by his wife's side.

Dalmeny's cook did not disappoint, and Mary could not decide which dish was her favorite, though she was greatly leaning towards the puddings. When everyone's appetite was satisfied, they all removed to the music room where Georgiana and Elizabeth performed a song together. Fitz retold the story of their outing, with his own comical spin on the events of course, and Alex even joined the entertainments with a rare turn at the pianoforte to play a song he wrote when he was younger. When it came time for Mary to open her gifts, Alex led them back to the drawing room where a stack of beautifully wrapped presents sat on a crate by the sofa.

Georgiana sat beside her friend and eagerly chose which gift Mary was to open. When Mary came to the viscount's gift, she was not surprised to find it was a handkerchief, and the two shared a small smile about their private joke—memories of the handkerchief he returned her spectacles in, as well as the one she had given him for his birthday just a few months before, played out in both of their minds.

Elizabeth was excited to have Mary open the last gift from her and her husband. Darcy placed the crate in front of Mary, and everyone waited eagerly as Mary unlatched the lid, lifted it, and peered inside. Curled up in the corner was a small, white puppy.

"A puppy! Oh, Elizabeth, William, thank you!" Mary jumped up to give her sister a hug.

"I know you have missed your cat," Elizabeth said, "and when I saw your enthusiasm the other day when you were playing with Aunt Helen's dogs I thought you might enjoy having one of your own. It turns out a friend of hers had some puppies ready to be weaned just this week, so we had the pick of the litter. Do you really like him?"

Mary tried to stop the flow of tears that welled in her eyes. "Oh, yes, I love him. Thank you so much!" She turned to the others, "Thank you all. You have made my birthday so special, and for that I am most grateful. Thank you for the book," she looked at Georgiana, "and this beautiful journal," she ran her hand over the leather bound book Anne gave her. "I was in need of a new one as I just filled the last page the other day."

Anne stood and hugged her friend, "Now you have some very interesting stories to fill the pages, especially if you write of our day the way Fitz describes the events."

Fitz winked at the two, and Mary sat back down, her hand running over the fine handkerchief now laid out on her palm, "The stitching on this is very fine indeed." She looked at Alex, "thank you." Then she turned and smiled at Fitz, "and I do not know what I would do without a locket with your picture in it."

"Feel free to replace that with another anytime you feel the need—I will understand," he pretended to be upset and wipe a tear from his eye making everyone laugh.

Mary turned to the earl and countess, "Thank you both for the ribbons and the bonnet."

"I had nothing to do with the choices," Hugh joked, "If I had, you would have ended up with some dull colors indeed."

Mary could see where Fitz got his sense of humor. Once again she turned to her sister, "Thank you. I have had a wonderful day."

She picked up the sleeping puppy and watched as he yawned and stretched, curling up in her arms immediately.

It was not much longer before Elizabeth also showed signs of the fatigue she could no longer fight, "Oh my, I must be more tired than I thought," she exclaimed. "Just how my condition lends to so much more sleep I shall never understand."

The countess reached over and patted her hand in a motherly fashion, "Just think of all the growing your child is doing, my dear."

Darcy delicately rested his hand on his wife's expanding midsection just long enough to get a little kick from the babe within, then he took Elizabeth's hand in his and helped her to stand, calling for Joseph to take Georgiana to her room.

Helen stood, "We must be off too. It has been a long day for Anne and I am certain she is ready to rest as well," she looked to her niece who nodded her head.

"The rain has stopped for a few minutes, so if you do not mind, I will escort you back through the garden?" Fitz said to Anne.

"Yes, I would like that," Anne stood to take his arm.

"I think we will join you, Son," Hugh replied. "The fresh air and exercise will do us some good this evening." He put out his arm to escort his wife, then turned and bowed to Mary, once more wishing her continued good health.

When the others were gone from the room, Darcy turned to Alex, "Perhaps you could see that Mary does not become lost through this maze of hallways?"

Alex met his cousin's eye and knew this was a rare opportunity they would be given to be alone—he also knew not to waste it. "Yes, of course. You can trust that I will see her safely to her room."

Darcy gave a small nod and turned to lead his wife to their chambers.

Alex turned to Mary, "I hope you do not mind the gift."

"Oh no, it is perfect," she pulled the handkerchief off the top of the stack and fingered the embroidered 'M' in the corner. "Thank you."

Alex did not know what to say, so he just watched her in happy enjoyment of knowing she had said yes—they would soon be married.

Mary was feeling odd under his watching gaze, so she finally spoke up, "I wished to speak with you about something if you have a moment."

"Yes, of course. What is it you need?"

"I found something odd in the library this morning." She stood and placed the sleeping puppy back down in the crate before walking beside the viscount to the library. "When I saw this I thought this might be the solution to the problem you all have had in not locating the missing letters. I did not find a letter, but if there is one, there is likely to be others hidden right on the shelves as well."

"Other *what*, exactly? I am sorry, but I have obviously missed something," Alex replied.

Mary walked over to the far corner and pulled the two books off the shelf. "This morning I found this," she handed them to him as he inspected them. "They appear to be books, but if you turn them just so, they open into a box."

"The letters could be hidden right here in plain sight," he looked excitedly around the room at the numerous tomes on the shelves. "Did you find a letter in here?"

"No, just this scrap of paper that I left in the box," Mary indicated the small piece that originally drew her attention to the books. "I hope this helps you find what you need in your search."

"Yes, thank you! You might have just solved this puzzle for us." Alex placed the box on the shelf once more and turned to follow her from the room. "It looks like we will be very busy tomorrow searching these shelves."

"I thought you would say that," she smiled as they returned to the drawing room and Mary picked up her puppy once again.

"Here, let me help you with your other gifts," Alex picked up the stack of items and walked beside her as they wound their way through the halls to her chambers. When the door was opened, he handed the packages to Claire and turned back to Mary, "I hope your birthday was all you wished it to be."

"It was just perfect—more than I could have imagined," Mary answered, her cheeks blushing. "Thank you."

Alex reached out for her hand and bowed over it, his lips descending to place a small kiss on the back. They lingered just a few seconds before he rose again, "Good night, Mary."

———————————◈———————————

Fitz walked beside Anne as they slowly followed his parents through the garden. "What has been on your mind today?"

"You can read my thoughts so very well." She looked to the ground as she became more pensive, "I received a letter from my mother, and there is something about it that worries me, though I cannot say exactly what it is. I thought you could read it and see what you think?"

"Of course, I will gladly do that for you. Do you have it with you?"

"Yes," Anne pulled it from her reticule and handed it to him just as they were reaching the steps that led into the dower house.

Fitz bowed over her hand, "I will see you again sometime tomorrow."

"Thank you," she barely whispered out before she turned and quickly went to her room, watching from her window as he slowly made his way back through the garden. *How much longer must we endure this separation, my love? How much longer?*

———————————◈———————————

CHAPTER

XIX

Friday, June 26, 1812

Alex eagerly urged his brother and cousin to quickly break their fast, so it was not too much longer before all three were ensconced in the library and Alex was explaining what Mary had shown him the night before.

"Could it really be so easy?" Darcy asked.

Fitz looked around, "Well, considering how many books are in this room alone, it might be more tedious than you think, Cuz."

"No time like the present to get started," Alex rubbed his hands together in anticipation. "I will take this section, and you two take those over there," he pointed to the far wall. "We can work our way down and meet in the middle.

Four hours later they had found only one more box, and it contained nothing. Their spirits were starting to wane when Mary entered the library, "I do not mean to disturb you, but as I knew you would be in here this morning I decided to check out the books in the other parts of the house." She held up another box, "I found this, and there are a few missives inside."

Fitz took the box from her and opened the lid to see the writing on the envelopes, "Darcy, does that look familiar to you?"

"Yes, it is my father's hand," he took the letters from the box, three in all, and lovingly ran his finger over the ink.

"Come," Alex replied, "We will go to my study and see what these contain." As he passed her, he bowed, "Thank you, Miss Mary."

"I just hope they contain useful information, sir."

"As do I," he replied and followed the others to his study.

They settled into chairs, Fitz handing out the drinks he poured, and Darcy opened the first letter, looking at the date. "This one is not from the same time, but I would be interested in reading it later." He carefully opened the second letter and read through a few paragraphs before he set it aside as well with no comment. Picking up the third, they all held their breath as he again opened the missive and looked at the date. "I think this might be it," his eyes began to fill with tears at reading his father's words once again, and he handed it to Fitz to read aloud.

He scanned through the long letter and stopped when he came to the part they had been hoping to find for months now. "I think this may be more unsettling than not knowing, but here is what it says,

I have heard from Mrs Wickham and she has finished her confinement. She has delivered *two sons…* "

"Two? Are you certain?" Alex asked.

"Yes, that is what it says," Fitz replied. "Do you wish me to continue?"

"Yes, I am sorry, please go on."

"She has delivered *two sons* and, as her husband agreed, they have carried his last name instead of that of de Bourgh. During the ceremony last week, they were christened *Geoffrey and George Wickham*."

Darcy's face went white, "George Wickham! That *blackguard*!" In his fury, he rose from the chair, ready to find the man who had so altered his sister's life.

Alex tried to calm him, "I know how you feel Darcy. I too wanted to call the man out for his treatment of Georgiana, but now that we know of the definite connection, it is even more chilling than before."

Sitting back down in shock, Darcy ran his hands through his hair. "It was bad enough when he was just some random miscreant wanting to con my sister out of her dowry of £30,000, but to now know he truly is our uncle's son as well..."

"Yes," Fitz folded the letter and handed it back to his cousin. "I have some other things to take care of before I leave, otherwise I would set off right now. I can leave at first light and be back in Town by next week. I will find all I can of these two." He squeezed his cousin's shoulder, "Darcy we will find this man and I promise he will pay for what he has done to Georgiana."

Darcy quickly drank the brown liquid in his glass, proclaimed, "I must go find my wife," and left the library in a hurry.

"Do you think he will be well?" Alex looked worriedly at the door as it slammed shut behind his cousin.

"Yes, Elizabeth knows how best to soothe him."

"Should we confront our father with this information?"

"No, not just yet; let me see what else I can find out from my investigators first." Fitz stood, "Would it be too much trouble to borrow your carriage for my travel? This rain looks like it will not let up for several more days, and it would not do to worry our mother with my riding all the way back to Town on my own."

"Yes, of course; just leave it at Rosebery House when you arrive in Town. I will be going back with Darcy and Elizabeth anyway, so I doubt I will need it here."

Fitz thanked his brother then left him in the study in solitude.

Alex filed the newest letter away with the other letter they had found a few months ago, then rose to look outside as the rain came down, drenching the land he could see from his window and beyond. *It seems an ominous sign for us to find this missive on such a day as this,* he thought.

After making sure his desk drawer was locked, he left his study, determined to find something to make this day a bit brighter. As he walked down the hall he heard pianoforte music filtering out the music room door. He looked in to see Mary sitting at the instrument, her new puppy perched on the bench beside her. Sneaking in, he sat down in the chair by the door to listen to her as she played. When the song was finished, he rose, saying, "That was lovely."

Startled by the voice behind her, Mary turned and smiled. "To what do we owe the pleasure of such illustrious company on this dreary evening?"

Alex chuckled and walked over to the pianoforte, taking the puppy in his hands as he sat down on the bench beside his intended, "Would you like to join me in a duet?"

***

Wednesday, June 30, 1812

It was decided the Darcys, along with Mary, would return to Pemberley for one week, then Alex would meet them there to ride with them to

Hertfordshire. Darcy was more worried about his wife than ever before, but she insisted she was well enough to travel, and that the babe would not be coming for several months still. So there was no need to stay here nor to make Mary and Alex marry here when clearly it was her desire to return home one last time before she moved away.

Though he was still not completely happy, he knew he could not change his wife's mind, so Darcy gave in to this newly hatched plan. One week. He would have one week to see to the details of their travel, and he was determined to stretch it out into as many days as he felt was necessary, even if that meant they only covered twenty miles in one day.

Darcy sat at his desk and sharpened and laid out his quills all in a row, then pulled paper from his drawer to write some letters of business, not noticing his wife who looked on from the doorway. His attention was drawn to her when she chuckled.

She walked over and sat in her chair on the other side of the desk. "I love watching you work."

"Really?" he tilted his head, "Why is that?"

Elizabeth giggled and pointed to his desk. "You are very precise with everything you do. First you sit in your chair and put your feet up," she indicated the scuff marks on his desk where his feet usually landed, "and you sharpen exactly ten quills."

"Ten?"

"Yes, always ten. Then you put your feet back down and lay the quills out in size order, going from largest to smallest," she nodded towards the quills lying on his desk. "Next you pull a stack of paper from your desk, leaving it on the corner," she pointed to the paper on the corner of his desk, "and you place one piece in front of you."

Darcy looked down to the layout of his desk and noticed she described everything exactly as it was. "So what will I do next?"

"You will lay out the letters you need to answer, putting them in order of importance." She reached across and picked up the stack of letters, going through them, and pulled one out. Handing it back to him as she set the rest back on his desk, she said, "I think you should answer this one first."

Darcy eyed his wife warily, "And just what should I say in this response?"

Elizabeth walked around the desk and kissed his cheek, "I think you know just what to say, but I wonder why you never mentioned it to me?"

Darcy looked up into her eyes, "Jane must have told you in her letter."

"Yes, she wrote me of what you said to Charles. Why did you not tell me?"

Darcy reached for her hand, "I did not want to get your hopes up until I heard from him that they were, indeed, interested in living closer to Pemberley."

"Well, now you can write your letter, and be sure to tell him of my excitement over the possibility."

He laughed, "I will. I have a feeling they will have an announcement to make when we get to Meryton. He hinted that he wants to be settled in their permanent home before having too large a family."

"Oh I hope so! How wonderful to have Aunt Maddie and Jane also with child at the same time as us. Jane has not mentioned anything to me, but that is not something she would say in a letter. She is too shy to put such words on paper." Elizabeth sighed, "I always hoped to grow up with cousins, but my only cousins are the Gardiners and they are much younger."

Darcy smirked, "I had cousins, but always wished for brothers and sisters instead. Georgiana was born when I was nearly twelve. While we played together some, we really were in two different worlds because of our ages."

"It is funny how we each wished for what the other had."

"Yes it is."

"So, what of these properties? How far are they? When are you going to view them?" Elizabeth asked.

"I need to write to the solicitor that is handling both properties and set up a time to go look at them. I thought of writing to Alex and see if he can come a few days early and go with me. He might see some things I overlook that would be a potential problem for Charles, or, better yet, something that would help him to negotiate a greater deal on the price."

"I hope one of the properties will be perfect for them." Elizabeth stood and walked over to her husband, kissing his cheek, "I will leave you to finish your business. I must go write to my sister and Mama—you can imagine just how she will take the news of Mary's engagement!"

"You can always share my desk to write your letter," Darcy offered.

She smiled, "Are you certain I will not be a distraction?"

"Of course you will be," he wrapped his arms around her waist, "but a pleasant distraction is one I think I could use today."

Within a few minutes they were both settled on either side of the desk, writing their own letters and eying each other, Darcy's foot lightly nudging hers under the cover of the large oak desk between them.

<hr />

He kept his distance as he followed the man through the crowd, the red coat and large size making it easy for his trained eye to keep him in view. When the red-cloaked man ducked down a familiar alley, he waited at the corner. Ten minutes later he walked down the same alley and knocked twice on the door at the end, entering the dark establishment when the small child answered the door. He addressed the father who stood behind the boy, "Is he in the same room?"

"Y'sir," he answered as he shooed his son away, accepting the coin the man tossed his way.

With a nod, he sauntered down the hall and entered the room, not at all surprised to see the colonel sitting in the same seat as before. "I see you are back in Town."

"Yes, I just returned this afternoon and was informed you needed to see me as soon as I could get away."

He sat down opposite the colonel, "From everything I can tell, George Wilson is just spying on the young misses that live at Longbourn. He follows them, especially the youngest, any time they leave home."

"Has he tried to make contact with them?"

"No, not that I have seen. He has stayed completely hidden from view." He pulled out his notebook and flipped through his notes. "I did trace him to a seedy establishment about four miles to the north of Longbourn. He has given the name of *George Wilson*, as you suspected, to the proprietor, but I was finally able to get another name from the young girl whom he frequently favors with his attentions."

"And what is that?" Fitz asked.

"It is a name I am certain you will recognize immediately," he eyed the much larger man across from him. "*George Wickham.*"

"Wickham! Are you certain?"

"Absolutely certain. The man is not very smart in covering his tracks."

"What does Wickham want with the Bennets?" Fitz asked himself aloud as he thought.

"That I have not been able to ascertain as of yet," the thin man looked back to his employer.

"My brother, my cousin, and I just found out information about Wickham, but I cannot piece together the details yet."

"What did you find out?"

"He and his twin brother are the bastard sons of our uncle, Lewis de Bourgh, and the wife of Pemberley's old steward. The steward would have nothing to do with the boys, but was paid off handsomely by my uncle for their use of his last name." Fitz looked up at the face across from him. "This information does not shock you."

"No, I cannot say it does."

"You already knew?"

"I knew some of the connection, though I did not know until just recently that *George Wickham* and *George Wilson* were the same man." He opened his notebook once again, flipping through a few pages.

"Why would he be interested in the Bennets?"

"He is a cheap, two bit thug who will do anything for a bit of change to gamble or drink away. Maybe he was hired by someone to ruin this girl?"

"But why? Who would be out to do such a thing to this family who is neither excessively rich nor titled? They have no enemies…"

"Except the mad sister, I can find no one as well," he looked back up to the colonel.

"What mad sister?" Fitz asked.

"Mrs Bennet's half-sister," he looked down at his notepad again, "a *Mrs Miranda Philips*." He looked up again, "She is certainly one that has caught my attention. I have not looked too deeply into her background, but if you wish it, I will do so now."

"You think she is dangerous?"

"She has that look to her eye; I do not trust her."

"Yes, look into that connection, and any other you think may have anything to do with George Wickham, including his twin brother, Geoffrey." Fitz rubbed his eyes wearily, "Do not discuss this with my cousin, only come through me with any information you find. For now, I wish to keep this from him."

"Is that because of the connection to his sister and her accident?"

Fitz looked at the man across from him and tossed a coin purse onto the table in front of him, "If you were not on the side of good, you would be a formidable enemy."

"Yes, I know." He stood, placing his notepad and the purse back in his pocket, "I will be in touch when I know something more." With that, he strode from the room.

Fitz stood and quickly made his way back through the streets and to the more familiar side of Town. He stopped by his office and pulled out his case files, trying to focus on his own investigation of the murder of his two soldiers, but he could not shake the feeling that these two cases were connected. *How? How are they linked?*

He rifled through the notes again, coming across some from two years ago with a slight description of a female accomplice to the man they were now trying to find – *slim features, high cheekbones, and piercing black eyes. Black eyes. Where have I heard that before?* He looked through his notes but did not see such a description written anywhere else. His head began to pound and he knew he would get no more work done today. He packed up his files and put them in his bag, intent on taking them back to Rosebery House with him where he could spread everything out and organize the notes, hoping he would come across something that would bring this investigation to a close soon.

He quickly wrote a note to his associate and sent it to be delivered, then rode home to take a bath and request some of Mrs Gibson's tonic for his headache. *Sleep will help,* he told himself, *and tomorrow Denny and I can go through everything we have. Maybe a fresh pair of eyes will help.*

CHAPTER

XX

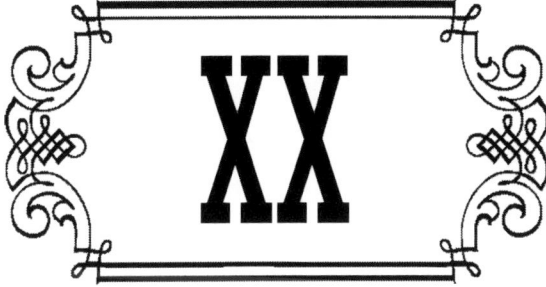

Thursday, July 2, 1812

Henry Bennet strode through the house, his limp barely perceptible on this nice summer day. What made this day even better was the news he had for his wife, contained in the three letters he held in his hand—one from Darcy, a second from Mary, and the third from Viscount Primrose. He entered the sitting room and only saw his youngest two daughters, Kitty and Lydia, as they sat together remaking some bonnets at the table.

"Has your mother not come downstairs yet?"

"She left for Netherfield just over an hour ago," Lydia said. "Jane sent her carriage, and she and Mama were to go to Meryton then back to Netherfield to begin plans for redoing some of the rooms before they are to fill up with visitors next month."

Kitty excitedly added, "Charles is to have a ball for Jane's birthday!"

"Yes, I have been informed," he said without as much enthusiasm as clearly his two youngest felt. "I am surprised neither of you wished to go with your mother."

"We were not invited," Lydia said in a slightly whiny voice.

"Come now, my dear," he said, lifting her chin with his finger, "we mustn't get down about such trivial things. As it happens, I can take you to Netherfield myself, as I have news that cannot wait. I will call for the carriage."

Both girls jumped up and rushed from the room, talking gaily about what the news could possibly be. They were soon donning their hats and gloves, ready to join their father in the carriage.

When they arrived, they were led to the sitting room where Jane and Mrs Bennet were sitting before many magazines laid out in front of them, discussing what was seen on the pages.

At the sight of her husband and other daughters, Mrs Bennet jumped up, "What has brought you here? OH, do not tell me it is bad news! I simply could not take such at this time."

Mr Bennet chuckled as he stepped his wife's side, kissed her cheek, and while pulling the letter from his jacket pocket, assured her it was of a good nature. He greeted his eldest daughter as well, and asked that the master of the house be called.

When Bingley arrived in the sitting room, he was glad to see the smiles everyone wore—assuaging his fear that it was bad news that had brought his father-in-law and sisters all the way over here unexpectedly.

"Ahhh, there you are," Mr Bennet said as he stood to greet his son-in-law.

"Not that I mind the visit, but what brings you here today?"

"Sit and I will tell you all at once." he said, giving Bingley time to take a seat beside his wife. He smiled at the tender way in which Bingley took Jane's hand in his own. All eyes were now turned towards him, so he cleared his throat, and began. "I received some news from Derbyshire today, and it contains some intelligence which I knew you would all be happy to hear. It seems, Mrs Bennet," he said, addressing his wife with a large grin, "that we are to lose yet another daughter to a fine, fine gentleman."

"He proposed! OH! What joy she must feel at such a match!" Mrs Bennet's hand immediately reached for the handkerchief her son-in-law held out for her as the tears began to fill her eyes.

Lydia spoke up, "Who has proposed? What am I missing?"

Seeing that her parents were in need of a few moments alone, Jane stood and wound her arm through Lydia's, urging her to join her in another room. When they were walking from the older couple, Jane leaned closer to Lydia's ear and said, "I have a feeling we are to have yet another even closer connection to the Fitzwilliam family."

"The Colonel has proposed? *To Mary?*"

Kitty chuckled, coming up beside them, "No, silly—the viscount!"

"The viscount! Why, I never imagined!"

"Did you not?" Bingley replied. "He has had eyes for Mary since the first day he arrived. I am surprised it has taken her so long to accept him, but I am glad to know it has finally happened. They will make quite the couple."

In shock still, Lydia followed the others out into the garden, "Viscount Primrose... and my sister Mary... I simple cannot fathom such a match! Why—that means Mary will one day be a countess!"

Mr and Mrs Bennet soon joined them in the garden and the family from Longbourn were all invited to stay for dinner at Netherfield, where they would have a small family celebration for the coming nuptials and where plans would be underway by the end of the evening for the visitors that were now to be arriving in the coming week instead of nearly a month away as originally planned. Though the bride and groom had not yet told their particular desires for the ceremony, this did not stop Mrs Bennet from forming ideas of her own for the festivities to come.

Friday, July 3, 1812

Alex quickly walked through the garden. Upon entering the dower house, he was informed his parents were in the dining room, so he went to find them.

"Good morning, dear. I see you are ready to leave for Pemberley bright and early," Helen tipped her cheek as he came over to give her a kiss.

"I do not wish to be out riding in the heat of the day."

"Oh, of course, because the heat is such a problem this year here in northern Derbyshire," Hugh said with a smirk, referring to the unusually cold and wet weather they were experiencing. "I suppose it could not possibly be the inducement of your intended who awaits you on the other end of your short journey. Help yourself to a plate, son."

"No thank you, I have already eaten. I just came to wish you farewell. I will let you know when the wedding is to be."

"Please do, and we will fix our plans accordingly," Hugh replied.

"I have not yet spoken with Mary about where she wishes to return after the ceremony, but we still have time to decide that." His cheeks blushed as he continued, "I do hope to take her on a wedding trip though."

Helen's hands drew up to her lips, the napkin she held being used now to tap the corner of her eye where the tears began to gather. "I am so happy for you!"

Alex smiled, but did not know what to say. Luckily his father spoke up.

"Now, now, we mustn't keep him all to ourselves forever. After all, we do wish to still be spritely enough to chase the grandchildren around, do we not?"

His teasing manner cheered her and she dried the last of the tears from her eyes. "I do so love the way you can turn things around for me so very quickly, my dear."

"Well, as touching as this scene is," Alex said as he watched his parents' hands embrace over the tabletop, "I must be on my way. Darcy and I are to look at a few local estates tomorrow. Bingley wishes to move further north, and we are hoping to find something nearby for him to consider." He reached over to firmly shake his father's hand, Goodbye Father; goodbye Mother," he was quickly embraced in a tight hug from his mother.

Alex was soon on his horse and riding towards Pemberley.

"ALEX!" Georgiana saw him coming from the stable and called to him.

"Hello Georgiana," he walked up to the bench where she sat and leaned down to kiss her cheek. Turning to Mary, he took her hand and lifted it to his lips, bestowing a kiss on the back, "I have missed you this last week at Dalmeny… and your little companion," He petted the puppy that eagerly barked at his feet.

Georgiana saw a spark between the two and the blush on Mary's cheeks, "You are here a few days early, I see."

He reluctantly turned his gaze back to Georgiana, "Yes, your brother has some properties to look over and he asked me to accompany him. I told him if I finished my business in time I would come today to join him," he looked back to Mary again. "I hope you do not mind my company?"

Mary smiled sweetly, "No, of course not, you are always welcome."

He cleared his throat, "So, have you come up with a name for your puppy yet?"

"No, nothing seems to fit. I was going through this book when you came upon us. I was hoping to find a suitable name, but so far have not found anything."

Alex reached for the book she held in her hands. When his fingers lightly brushed against hers he heard her take a deep breath, but her face did not change. He looked down to the tome they both held, "Hmmm, well, if this one does not have a suitable name, what better place than a library to find one that does?" He smiled and bowed, "I need to let my cousin know of my arrival and clean up from my ride, but would you like to join me in a perusal of the library shelves before a stroll around the garden?"

Mary smiled and stood, "I hope we are successful in finding a name; the poor thing has been without one for over a week now."

"I am certain with three minds on the topic, we are sure to come up with a name for this little one," he bent down to pat the puppy's head again.

Georgiana, deciding to give the betrothed couple a few minutes alone, replied, "I am actually a bit fatigued, Alex."

Alex looked back to his cousin and winked his thanks, receiving a small nod in response. "I am at your disposal for the rest of the day, so whatever you fancy I am willing to do."

"Maybe . . ." Georgiana bit her bottom lip as she thought, "no, never mind . . ."

"What is it Georgiana?" he asked.

"We were to practice a song together this afternoon, and I was going to invite you to join us, but my leg is feeling too sore today, so I may have to cancel our practice. I am sorry Mary," Georgiana looked to her friend.

"Do not fret," Alex replied with a smile, "I will see my intended is not left in the doldrums all alone while you rest." He reached down and picked Georgiana up in his arms, "I am going that direction now, so I will take you to your chambers."

"AHHHH!" she screeched when he picked her up unexpectedly. She hit his chest with her fist, a cloud of dust coming from his clothes, "Look at you. You will get me all dirty!"

"I will meet you in the library after I have had a chance to clean up, if that acceptable?" he said to Mary.

"Yes, of course," she tried not to laugh as Georgiana squirmed in his arms to no avail.

He turned and walked away, in a hushed voice saying, "As much as I appreciate your attempts to give me time with my intended, you should not be setting up such schemes, Sweetling."

"But you both have so much to talk about with the wedding plans," she started to say.

"While I might agree with you," he raised his eyebrow, "I do not need your brother, or Mary's father, thinking I have set up such private and compromising assignations with her. I wish to marry without such dramatics as that would cause."

She heaved a heavy sigh, "Oh, very well, I will stop trying so hard, but only if you promise to name your first child after *me*, your *favorite* cousin!"

He laughed and winked, "My son will surely be the talk of his class with a name like Georgiana, especially with a title such as Primrose."

She joined in the gaiety as they entered Pemberley. "That will simply not do! I will, however, promise to stop my scheming. Did you know my brother had absolutely no idea of your feelings for Mary before you proposed?" she asked.

"Well, that does explain why he has never questioned me about it."

"Questioned you about what?" they heard a familiar voice say from behind them as Alex started to go up the stairs.

Sarah Johnson

"Darcy! Good to see you"

"Yes, yes, it is good to see you too, and I appreciate your coming to help me with these properties, but do not think I will forget what I just heard. What is it I have no idea about?"

"Is it possible for me to take Georgiana upstairs and get cleaned up, then later I can meet with you in your study to begin going over these properties for Bingley." Alex knew from the look in Darcy's eye that he would have to tell him how long he had held this flame in his heart for Mary—but somehow even that prospect did not look so bleak with the knowledge that Mary would soon be his wife.

Darcy gave him a small nod, and when Alex turned around and started to walk away with Georgiana, he replied, "No need to search me out, I will be in your room in a few minutes for an explanation of just what it is I do not know."

Alex gave Georgiana a look of displeasure, and she tried to hold in her giggle as they went to her room.

"Was that your cousin I heard?" Elizabeth came up beside her husband.

"Yes, he just arrived. I overheard him say something about my never questioning him about something—and it sounded of much import. Just what is it I could have no idea about?"

"No idea? Hmmmm…" she thought for a few seconds. "Oh, right," she nodded, "I have a feeling I know what that is about."

Darcy wrapped his arms around her expanding waist and kissed her cheek, "I told Alex I would speak to him in a few minutes, but if you can enlighten me beforehand, that would be even better."

"It probably has something to do with his feelings for my sister," Elizabeth replied calmly.

"Of course he has feelings for your sister. He is going to marry her, is he not?"

"Georgiana and I were talking just the other day about how clueless you were to Alex's feelings *before* he proposed. Why he was smitten nearly from the first moment of their acquaintance."

"And you assume that is what they were talking of."

"Yes, Georgiana said she may have to start teasing you about how your lovely wife keeps most of your attention these days to the point that you are oblivious to everyone else around you."

"No, that is Charles; I am not like that. I can focus on more than one thing at a time. I think my cousin hid his feelings for your sister from me, knowing I would question him for details he did not wish to reveal."

Elizabeth kissed the frown on his lips, "I hate to contradict you," she saw his eyebrow rise at such a statement, "but I feel I must advise you of something, dear husband. There are certain times when even the house being on fire would garner no notice from you."

Darcy chuckled, "Oh, you think so, do you? If that were true, then I would not know *you* are sneaking outside for a walk without me."

Elizabeth closed her eyes and sighed, "You found me out. Well, if you are going to join me then come," she let go of him and turned to the door.

Darcy grabbed her hand to keep her from walking away, "Oh no, I must speak with my cousin in a few minutes, and then we can go for a stroll."

Elizabeth sauntered up to his side and kissed his cheek, "If he wanted you to know he would have told you. Let the man have his privacy, and let him woo his intended as he must. He does not need to have you on his back about what move he chooses to take or not take. My sister is having a hard time accepting that she is worthy enough to garner attention from someone like him, and he is in for quite the time of it when we arrive at

Longbourn. They will both need to gather their strength in order to face the coming weeks of my mother's full attention. *That*, I know you can understand."

Darcy stopped and turned to his wife, squeezing her hand in his, "You are a very understanding woman, Elizabeth Rose Darcy. I love you."

"I love you too," she looked into his green eyes. "I took that chance when you led me to my father's study and closed the door, and I am glad I did. I cannot imagine my life without you by my side."

"If we were not in view of every window on the front of the house and the gardening staff milling about I would kiss you right now."

"Maybe we need to find a quiet path and *get lost* for a few minutes, Mr Darcy," Elizabeth suggested.

"Me? Become lost on my own land? Never, madam; but I *can* show you a path we may not have fully explored yet," he led her around the bend and they disappeared.

Alex watched from his window above, grateful for the reprieve from having to talk to Darcy right now, though he knew he would get none when they were to go and view the two properties for Charles on the morrow. Quickly changing into fresh clothes, he left to find Mary in the Library intent on spending some time with her before the others returned. He found Mary, along with her puppy and her maid Claire, in the library.

"Miss Mary," he bowed when he entered the room, picking up the dog that came running to his feet. "I see you have your own protector, though I doubt he could do much damage."

She laughed, "Yes, William says he is the image of that old proverb that says *timid dogs bark worse than they bite.*" Mary walked over and took the puppy from Alex's arms, handing him to Claire, "It is time for him to go back to my room for a while, unless you are attached to having him around?"

"No, whatever you desire—it matters not to me whether he is with us or not when we decide on a name."

"I like having a companion, but I am not used to being followed all day long, so I have learned to put him in my chambers for a break." Mary nodded to Claire, who took the dog and left the room.

Once they were alone, Alex wrapped his arms around Mary's waist, pulling her closer, "Now may I greet you properly?"

She started to giggle, but her laugh was cut short when his lips found hers. Her arms came up to circle around his neck, and when he broke the kiss she could not help but laugh again.

"What has amused you so?"

She blushed, "It is nothing of consequence." She started to pull away.

"No, no…we cannot have our union starting with deceptions. Now," he held her tighter, "what is it?"

She could not look in his eyes when she admitted this, so instead she focused straight in front of her, on his expertly tied cravat. "Last year, when I was determined I would never find a husband, I decided to make a list of attributes for my perfect partner, should such a gentleman even exist. One of them stated that he had to be tall, but not too tall, as I did not wish to need a stool just to kiss him."

Alex leaned down and whispered, "And do I make the mark?"

"Oh, yes. You are perfect."

"Just what other attributes were you looking for?"

Mary giggled, "Come now, must I reveal all my secrets?"

"If you are not going to tell me at least one more, then I shall require a penance from you."

"And just what will I have to pay?"

"A kiss will do." Once again he pulled her closer, the two happy to spend the next few minutes lost in each other's embrace.

When they finally separated, Mary asked, "Do you wish to go for a walk first?"

"Actually, I saw my cousin and your lovely sister walking out, and they looked like they wanted to be alone, so I thought maybe we could do something different with our time."

Mary smiled, "They like to disappear on walks alone quite often. Perhaps we could just sit here in the library?"

"As you wish," Alex indicated the sofa and sat beside her. "So, are you excited about leaving on Monday?"

"A little; it will be good to see my family again."

"I cannot help but notice your lack of enthusiasm about going home," he stepped a little closer and reached for her hands, his voice dropping as he asked, "I hope it is not second guessing your decision?"

She blushed, "No, of that I am certain."

"Good—then nothing else need matter. It will work out in the end, and very soon I will be driving away from Longbourn with you beside me… for always."

Mary's heart beat wildly in her chest, and the desire within for him to kiss her again grew with every breath. Finally, just as she saw him growing closer, a noise in the hallway broke the moment, and he leaned back, bringing only her hands up to his lips instead.

Alex drew his arm up around her shoulders, urging her to rest her head on his shoulder. When she was finally relaxed, he asked, "So what has you so downtrodden about going home to Longbourn?"

She sighed. "My Mama. I know she means well, but she will simply be too much to handle for all these weeks we are to have to be there before we may marry. The banns must be called thrice, and that means the earliest we could marry is practically the end of the month. I just do not know how much I can take."

He gave a small smile as he leaned close to her ear. His lips touched her temple and left a tingling sensation on her skin and he quietly said, "In my letter to your father I asked that he please have mercy upon me and see that the banns are called starting this Sunday. However, if you feel you cannot endure for even that long, I shall gladly travel on to London and purchase a special license with which we can be married even sooner and anywhere you wish."

Mary's body tingled from his light touch, her mind beginning to swirl in a fog of delightful emotions emanating from without. *Oh, what this man would endure for her sake.* "I think I would rather not have you gone from my side for a few more days still after we arrive. I shall endure it… after all, I know it is only out of love that my mother acts so."

His voice was just a little lower as he replied, "Believe me, it is for purely selfish reasons on my part, as I would have you as my wife right now if it were possible."

The two remained in such intimate talk, and shared a few secretive kisses, until they knew Darcy and Elizabeth would be returning from their stroll. Finally, Alex suggested they remove to the music room, and they were happily playing, sitting side-by-side as close as the bench would allow, when Darcy and Elizabeth found them.

"Beautiful!" Elizabeth said as she entered, sitting down in a chair and clapping her hands as the two at the pianoforte turned around.

"Oh, you have returned," Mary blushed at her sister finding her in such an intimate situation with her intended.

"Yes, we have been back for a while, but thought we should give you two a few minutes alone, so we went to speak with Georgiana. She said you were on the search for a name for your puppy?"

"That was our intention, but have not yet thought of something fitting," Alex said.

"Perhaps," Elizabeth suggested, "since your cat is named Beatrice, then you should name your dog Benedick. It is fitting, do you not think?"

Both Alex and Mary looked at each other, smiling at the memory of when they discussed *Much Ado About Nothing* being a favorite for each of them.

"Yes, very fitting," Mary said.

The rest of the afternoon was spent talking of the nuptials and what plans the two had made so far. Alex pulled Elizabeth aside long enough to find out where she thought her sister would enjoy going for a wedding trip. Elizabeth assured him that Mary might not be enthusiastic about a long journey—just someplace simple where they could be together. She even had a suggestion of a hunting lodge that was not too far from Netherfield that would give them privacy, but keep them near the family. She assured him she would keep his confidence, and would get him the information so he could see if it was available. With it not being hunting season, it was a hopeful plan.

CHAPTER XXI

Thursday, July 9, 1812

"Come, come, my dear, we mustn't be late!"

"We are not late," he looked over at the clock, "actually we are nearly an hour early," Bennet tried to ignore his wife's excitement, but she was now pulling him up from his chair. "All right, all right, I can stand on my own."

"Oh, I am so excited! My Lizzy and Mary are finally returned… and Darcy and Georgiana. Did she say the viscount is traveling with them as well? All my girls back together again after all these months. Oh, Henry, it is too much," she started gasping for air and pulled out her handkerchief, waving it in front of her face.

Bennet stood in front of her and in a firm voice, he replied, "That is quite enough, Susannah. I will not have your nerves causing such a ruckus in my study."

"Yes… yes, of course," she calmed, but continued to wave the handkerchief around.

"Now, since you cannot leave if you are in such a state, I think I will read another chapter while you rest," he picked up his book and started to sit.

Susannah took a deep breath, "I am perfectly calm now, my dear; let us leave," she grabbed his arm and nearly pulled him from the room before he could sit again.

"Very well. I can walk on my own; there is no need to pull me." He protested all the way to the carriage, but she would not let go. Bennet helped his wife and daughters into the waiting equipage and listened as Susannah and Lydia excitedly chattered the three miles to Netherfield Park. Looking at the much quieter Kitty, he lifted his eyebrow and she giggled quietly. *It will be good to see all my girls again*, he thought. When they arrived, they were shown into the drawing room where Charles, Jane, Elizabeth, Darcy, and Mary sat waiting.

"Oh, look at you!" Susannah hugged her second daughter then stepped back to see the physical changes that had taken place in Elizabeth's growing mid-section over the last few months. She turned around with tears in her eyes, drawing Mary into a hug as well. "How I have missed my girls!"

When all the others had a chance to greet the newcomers and everyone was seated and talking amongst their small groups, Kitty leaned over towards Elizabeth, "I thought Georgiana was coming with you as well, Lizzy?"

"Yes, she and the viscount will be joining us later. They wanted to give us a few minutes alone to greet our family." At Kitty's acknowledgment, Elizabeth reached for her hand and squeezed her fingers, "You have changed just about as much as I have these last few months. Why, I hardly recognized you when you all came in the room."

Kitty smiled, then leaned closer and in her bubbly say, said to Elizabeth, "I will have to tell you everything that was left out of my letters—about Mr and Mrs Hurst and Amelia, and how much she has grown. The last letter indicated she is sitting up on her own now." She hardly took a breath before saying, "Although, I would rather hear more of how you are faring," she looked towards Elizabeth's expanding stomach.

Elizabeth rested her hand on her mid-section, letting out a sigh. When the baby inside kicked, she giggled and leaned near Kitty, "It is a very strange feeling to have someone on the inside of you. Maybe someday soon you too will experience this joyful condition."

"I hope so. I have always wanted to have children." Leaning a little closer, she whispered, "Do you think Jane is . . .?"

Both looked over to their eldest sister, and Elizabeth caught Jane's hand gently resting on her stomach. She turned back to Kitty, "I would say it is a good possibility."

"Lydia has wanted to question her several times, but Mama told her it is just not proper to do so and we must wait for the announcement to be made. Now that you are here, maybe they will make it known this evening."

Alex entered the sitting room and greeted the others before taking a seat next to his intended, explaining that Georgiana was extremely tired and would not be coming down this evening.

Bingley thought it best to give their announcement now, so he stood and, pulling his wife to her feet to stand beside him, he cleared his throat to garner the attention of all those in the room. When everyone was looking at the couple, he smiled at his wife and began, "We are so very thankful for many things throughout this last year, and for me personally, I am especially grateful for being drawn into the bosom of the family that now surrounds me, as if I were born to be a part of you all. I am not like Darcy here who tries to produce as many four syllable words as possible in his speech, so I will end by simply saying this – my wife and I wanted you all to be the first to know that we are expecting to add another member to our branch of this family tree early next year!"

"OH, I knew it! Oh Jane, Oh Charles," Susannah rose and went to hug the two, her effusions drowning out all the other family member's congratulations.

Eventually, sense returned to the room, and Elizabeth went to sit beside her eldest sister. Taking her hand, she leaned over and whispered, "I am so very happy for you and Charles. Our children will grow up with cousins around their age." With a raise of her eyebrow, she said with a smirk, "If only you lived closer to Pemberley."

Jane blushed, a small smile on her lips, "Charles said William found two properties, but he has not yet heard of their particulars."

"He would tell me nothing about them. He did not want me unduly influencing your decision." Elizabeth sighed, "Well, I do hope you choose something close to Pemberley so our children can grow up seeing each other more than just once a year, but if you choose another property further away I will understand." Elizabeth turned back to her sister, tears starting to gather in her eyes, "Oh Janie, I am so very happy for you!"

Jane squeezed her hand, tears forming in her own eyes as she replied, "So am I."

After so many days on the road, the travelers were tired, so the residents of Longbourn returned early to their home. Mary was glad to sleep in the familiar surroundings of her bedroom once again, though she felt odd that she would only call this her home for a few more weeks. Starting tomorrow, the wedding plans would begin in earnest, and she knew the whirlwind of events that would encompass the next few weeks would be very tiring, so she snuggled into the softness that surrounded her for a peaceful night of sleep.

***

Friday, July 10, 1812

At the knock, Bennet called for the person to enter and he was not surprised when the door opened to the viscount.

"I was waiting for you to come and speak with me." He nodded to the chair, "Would you like some tea or coffee this morning?"

"No thank you, sir." Alex sat down, trying to contain the nervous energy that pulsed through his body. "I came to talk with you about Miss Mary."

"Of course you did," he offered with a large grin. "I see your persistence has paid off, and she has finally accepted your hand—I trust for the right reasons?"

"Oh yes, of course, sir."

"Capital, capital—I would have it no other way for one of my girls." He leaned further back in his seat and asked with concern, "Your letter did not indicate whether you found it necessary to speak with Mary about the goings-on in Town. Is she still unaware of the scandal she very closely avoided?"

"It became necessary to tell her what we discussed, including the entirety of my past with Lady Elaine Stalwood." Alex looked down at his hands, "She was not happy with what we decided without her knowledge, but she has forgiven me for my part. I would guess she is willing to do the same for you when she has a chance to speak with you alone, sir."

Bennet sighed, "I was afraid of her being hurt when you came to me with your plan. I knew she needed to be told, but I chose to keep quiet because of my own fears for her reputation. It seems I owe her an apology of my own today."

"If she can forgive me for everything she held against me, I have no doubt of her forgiving you as well, sir. She is a very gracious person."

"I will speak with my daughter later today and clear everything between us. Is that all you wished to speak with me about?"

Alex took a deep breath, "No sir, I feel with our last meeting being what it was, it is best if I try again—for Mary's sake—with what must be asked." He sat forward in a nervous way, and continued, "Mr Bennet, I am here before you to request the honour of your daughter's hand in marriage."

Bennet chuckled, "I suppose if you must be official about it, then I can be as well." He stood and leaned over his desk, his hand outstretched to the viscount, "I will be glad to give her hand in marriage and welcome you, officially, into our family bosom."

Alex took the elder man's hand in his own and shook it, relief filling his heart and mind at having completed his mission. He did not doubt the result of what he came here to accomplish, but knowing Mr Bennet as he did, he expected a little more of a trial in achieving that end. The man was forever teasing those around him, and, according to Darcy, he especially loved to do so to the gentlemen who found their interests turned towards one of his daughters.

Bennet sat back down, "So, tell me, how it is you won my daughter's heart?"

Alex went on to tell of the many misunderstandings the two held, and of their clearing the air. Then he told of Mary's visit to Dalmeny and how it came about that the two were now to marry—though he did leave out a few private moments he would never speak of to anyone, but would forever hold so dearly in his heart.

When the story was told, and Mr Bennet's curiosity of the particulars assuaged, Alex asked if he could speak with Mary. He was given permission, and the father said she would probably be about the garden at this time, so Alex left to find his intended and tell her the news of the meeting with her father.

He entered the garden, winding his way along the path towards the bench on which Mary sat. Her back was to him and she held a white cat in her arms, speaking softly and running her fingers through the mass of fur.

Mary was telling Beatrice of all her adventures in Derbyshire when she felt someone come up behind her. She turned and noticed the viscount walking down the garden path in her direction. "Good morning!" She stood and gave a small curtsy when he stopped beside the bench.

He returned her curtsy with a bow, "It is, indeed, a good morning. I see you are quickly recovered from our arduous journey?"

"It was not too difficult for me, though I do worry about Georgiana."

He indicated the path that led to the back of the garden, "If I am not intruding upon your solitude, I will gladly tell you how she is faring."

Mary blushed, her voice low as she replied, "You are welcome to join me any time." Mary pulled Beatrice closer to her chest in nervousness as Alex walked beside her, his hands clasped behind his back. "Is Georgiana in much discomfort today?"

"Darcy has sent to Meryton to have Dr. Jones come and examine her. She insists she will be well after a few days of rest, but Darcy does so wish to take away her discomfort." Alex saw the look of concern on Mary's face, "I can assure you she will be well, Miss Mary. My cousin is just overly protective after all his sister has been through. Georgiana assures me she will just need a few days of rest before she is able to spend some time with your family again."

Mary looked into his eyes and knew he was telling her the truth. "Thank you for your assurances."

Wanting to change the subject, Alex looked down to the ball of white fur in her hands, "May I be introduced to your feline companion?"

Mary smiled and held the cat out for him to see, "This is Beatrice. She would have nothing to do with me last night when I returned home, but this morning she seems to have forgiven me for my extended traveling of late."

Alex reached over and ran his fingers through her thick fur, "I am pleased to meet you Beatrice."

Mary giggled, "I am surprised she did not bite your hand. That is a high compliment, indeed, as she is usually finicky about whom she allows to pet her."

"Well then, I take great pleasure in the compliment," he replied. His hand still running through the fur, he addressed the animal, "I am glad we have gotten off to such a start, Beatrice, and I hope in the future you do not hold it against me that we shall share your mistress. Perhaps we can find a common ground and become good friends as well."

Mary chuckled as the cat meowed and began to purr, pushing her head up against the viscount's hand as she insisted he continue the attention he gladly bestowed upon her. "She was not too happy to see me return with Benedick though."

Alex leaned closer, his voice dropping as he said to the cat, "I do hope you will not hold it against me. I promise you will have free rein of any of my homes—if you but promise to always like me."

Beatrice stretched out her paw, placing it on Alex's sleeve as she closed her eyes and purred louder.

"I think she has given in to your persuasive words," Mary giggled.

Alex's eyes came up to see the twinkle in hers, "Any pursuit that leads me to you is worth the cost, whether that be mud covered clothes, or furry pets running around my home." He looked up to see that they were alone, then turned back to his intended, "I mean that—every moment I have had to endure has been worth it to finally have your good opinion."

Mary felt her arms suddenly empty as Beatrice jumped down to go about her own pursuits.

Her hands now empty, Alex reached for them, lifting them in his own as he stood before her. "I know the next few weeks will be quite overwhelming at times, but please promise me that if you need my assistance, you will but ask."

She gave a small smile as she nodded. "I am certain I shall endure well enough. With the Banns having already been called once, there is not much time to suffer—only ten more days—and it seems the ceremony details are nearly already planned." She giggled, "I intend to let my mother do what she needs, as I have no particular ideas of my own."

"Well, there is one thing your mother cannot plan, as it is left in my hands, and that is the wedding trip. As much as I would like to stay here with you this morning, I must return to Netherfield and get on with the task at hand," Alex replied.

"Oh? And where are we to go?"

"That," he said, drawing her hand to his lips and depositing a simple kiss to the back, "is a surprise." He bowed and took his leave, promising to see her when he was to return to Longbourn to join the family for dinner.

Sarah Johnson

CHAPTER

XXII

Monday, July 13, 1812

Bennet walked along the well-worn path towards the girl who sat in the midst of the roses in one section of the garden. "Your brother said I would find you here," he replied when she looked up.

A small smile crossed her lips, "My mother loved roses, so I find them soothing at times."

"May I sit?" he indicated the bench beside her.

"Yes, of course."

"I accompanied my wife and daughters on their visit for tea, and when Darcy said you were out here I volunteered to come and retrieve you. I hope you do not mind?"

"No, not at all." She looked around to the roses that surrounded them and quietly said, "I was missing my mother and father today."

Bennet reached over and took her hand in his, squeezing her fingers in a loving manner, "There are times I miss mine as well."

Georgiana held onto his hand as if it were the lifeline to her parents, tears that before were easily forming in her eyes were now running full force down her cheeks. It was not until she felt a cloth wiping across them that she even realized she was crying. Bennet's arm surrounded her shoulders and she found it natural to rest her head against his chest, sobbing into his waistcoat as he tried to calm her with reassuring words.

Eventually she was able to take the handkerchief from him and dry her eyes, "I am sorry for ruining your waistcoat."

"If ruining it has helped sooth your soul, then it was worth the cost," he joked. "Are you all cried out now?"

"I thought so an hour ago, but I guess I was wrong. Thank you." Georgiana handed him back his now sodden handkerchief.

"Now, what is this all about? What has upset you so much today?"

She looked everywhere but at his face, trying to find the words to express what was wrong, but she knew no one could understand.

Bennet asked quietly "You are now coming to accept all the changes your life will have to make because of your accident?"

Georgiana's eyes finally met his, "Yes; yes that is it precisely. How did you know?"

"You sit here in your wheeled Bath chair, when just a few months ago you would not think of using it." When she looked down at her feet, he put his finger under her chin and drew her eyes back up to hers. "Your father is not here to tell you this, so I will say it in his stead. I am proud of you, Georgiana. You have had to face a situation which could have caused so much more hurt and bitterness in your life, and you have chosen not to let it change you. I know some people twice or even three times your age who could not endure what you have had to this last year and a half."

"How can anyone be proud of me when I have spent all this time ignoring the reality of my situation? I knew when I was lying underneath the carriage that I would never walk again, and yet I have refused to accept it until now. That is certainly not something of which anyone should be proud."

Bennet held out his hand and waited until she put her own in it, then he sat back and began. "When I was trapped under the carriage I knew my life would change. The pain was unbearable, but more than that, I did not want to put my family through the tremendous struggles I knew we would all face. So, I decided death would have to claim me, and I laid there accepting that it would. It was at that exact moment that I felt the coat of my friend being draped over me. In all my selfishness I did not even think of what others would go through if I were to die. My wife and daughters would have been practically destitute, left to the derision of a distant cousin who did not talk to us for twenty years because of my wife's status as the daughter of a solicitor. It was in that moment I realized I must make it through. Even if I had bad days to deal with, I would have good days as well. Even if I had to lose my leg, I would still have my wife and daughters by my side. Do you understand what I am saying to you?"

Georgiana closed her eyes and took a deep breath, "Yes, I do. I need to focus on the good days instead of the bad."

"Yes, exactly."

He sat waiting as the silence surrounded the two, comforting both in its embrace, until she quietly broke its hold with a whimper, "I thought... I thought I was... I was the only one to wish for death to take me."

As her shoulders started to shake, he drew her to his chest once again, calmly running his hands over her hair in a fatherly fashion as tears once again soaked his clothing.

Finally, when she was properly composed again, she drew back from his chest and wiped the tears from her eyes. "I was so alone, and so cold. I woke up several times, and every time I did it was later in the day, and yet no one found me. I thought I would die there, and I began to welcome death's embrace. I wanted to be reunited with my parents and did not even think of my brother and all he would go through if I died. Oh, how selfish I was."

"Yes, you were just as selfish as I was, but maybe it is normal for those in similar situations to feel that way? Whatever the reason, we both chose at some point to live, to not give in to the pressures around us, to rise above the situation and put it all behind us." Bennet smiled at her, "That is precisely why I am so exceptionally proud of you. You have chosen to go on living your life even though the path before you is a difficult one."

She sniffed, "Thank you."

Bennet noticed Darcy walked down the path towards them, "Your brother has come to see what is taking so long," he pointed out to her with a small smile.

Georgiana wiped the last of the tears from her eyes and smiled, "I do love him dearly."

When he was close enough to be heard, Darcy asked, "Is everything well?" Noticing his sister's swollen eyes, he hastened to her side, bending down on a knee and running his hand over the side of her face as he cupped her cheek, "What is wrong, Sweetling?"

Georgiana's eyes met his and she covered his hand with her own, "Nothing is wrong – nothing at all."

"Are you sure?"

"Yes, everything is just… perfect." She looked over to Mr Bennet and smiled.

Darcy stood, "Would you like me to carry you back inside?"

238

Georgiana sat up straighter, and with a new confidence replied, "That will not be necessary. Mr Bennet was just about to push me back in my chair."

Darcy leaned down and hugged his sister, smiling in appreciation at Henry as the older man stepped behind her chair.

When they were all three back inside, Darcy pulled Bennet aside, "I do not know what you said to her, but thank you. I was the one that insisted she try to use her chair today, but she was not very accepting of my idea."

"She just needed to be told she is not alone," Bennet replied. "We all need that sometimes."

"Yes we do. Thank you," Darcy patted the older man's shoulder then the two joined the others in the drawing room.

***

London

"Is he here yet?" George asked as he came into the small, dimly lit parlour.

"No he is not," Mrs Younge answered with irritation in her voice.

He sat down, nervously drumming his fingers on the table. When she stared at him, he stopped, switching to bouncing his foot instead.

Annoyed, she asked, "What brings you to my door anyway?"

He reached into his pocket, "I received this—thought it might be best if we open it together, as I am certain it contains our instructions."

She stood and walked over, taking the letter from his outstretched fingers. She turned it over, examining the seal—it was certainly from the great lady. "I thought we already had a plan determined?"

"Did we?" He stood, starting to pace. "I do not remember."

"You would not remember your name if it were not for your brother keeping watch over you," she mumbled.

"What was that?"

"Oh… nothing. Do you want a drink?"

"Why must you ask? Of course!"

"Yes… of course…" she mumbled again, grumbling under her breath as she poured the drink and put it on the table, hoping it would make him stop his incessant pacing.

"When did you say is G.W. to arrive?"

"I did not say… and I do not know when."

"Perhaps we should open this without him?"

She was saved from having to answer when the door opened and G.W. joined them.

"What brings you here," he asked George, shaking the rain from his coat and draping it over the screen in front of the fire.

"I received this…"

"Finally!" He snatched it out of his brother's hands. "Sit, we have some things to go over."

"I thought we already had a plan in place?" Mrs Younge replied.

He lifted the letter, "This is only the final piece to it. The Darcys are to return to Hertfordshire in a month, and we must have everything prepared."

The three sat talking of the details that were still left to work out long into the night.

Friday, July 17, 1812

The days passed with trips to the shops, talk of lace and fabrics, and visiting the neighborhood parlors for all manner of teas and calls, while the evenings were often spent at dinners and musicals, along with a card party hosted at Lucas Lodge, and even a special evening just for the family at Longbourn, with Alex included.

Only one incident caused Mrs Bennet some consternation. While in Meryton at the modiste's shop, her half-sister, Mrs Philips, came in. She did not exchange words with anyone, but it was clear by the glare she gave to Mrs Bennet that she had heard of the joyous occasion to happen with now the third of the Bennet's daughters, and was clearly not pleased. The others were behind the screen with the modiste, only Lady Lucas and Mrs Bennet awaiting the reveal of the dress. Susannah felt she must make a stand now, or her sister might cause a scene.

So, her chin raised and shoulder held stiffly, she glared back at Miranda, silently daring her to say something. Finally, knowing she was defeated, Miranda Philips turned and darter from the shop.

Lady Lucas leaned close to her friend and whispered encouragements of the silent dual, then the two ladies returned their full attention to attending to Mary, who was ready to show off the beautiful gown the modiste had been working on day and night since she arrived. What a gown it was! Nothing too extraordinary, but it did show the station of what Mary Bennet was soon to take on in marrying Viscount Primrose.

Other than Henry Bennet, no one else was told of the encounter, and Lady Lucas saw to it that the incident remained out of the ears of those who would spread it about all too easily.

The seven days on the calendar soon ran together so much that Mary was mentally exhausted. Today however was not the day to rest—in fact it would be far from rest, as the Earl and Countess of Rosebery, as well as Anne de Bourgh and Colonel Fitzwilliam, would be arriving at Netherfield, and the wedding ceremony was a mere three days away.

The morning was spent at the modiste's shop in Meryton where the final small details of Mary's wedding dress, as well as a few more items for her trousseau, were the focus of this last visit.

The sisters, as well as Mrs Bennet, then returned to Longbourn to complete the final preparations for the wedding breakfast, leaving the gentlemen to their own plans for the day, which, above all else for Alex, included seeing the hunting cabin he was able to procure for their retreat after the wedding. It was only a few miles north of Netherfield—just far enough that they would be left alone, but still close enough that the one last thing he insisted upon for the evening of his wedding could be seen.

The Longbourn party was hardly seated in the drawing room when the travelers were announced.

"My lord, it is always a pleasure to have you in my home," Bingley replied with a bow before he wound his arm through his wife, and looked upon her with love as she stepped into her role as hostess now, offering to show them to their rooms where they could change and rest.

He followed along, ensuring the guests were settled, then, when he and Jane were once again alone in the hallway, he pulled her close and leaned near her ear, whispering, "Do you know what it does to me to see your joy at such hospitality?"

Jane giggled a little and sighed as her body formed against her husband's in a familiar way, her cheek resting on his chest.

"I hope you do not mind having so many visitors so close to your birthday. This is not too much for you, is it?"

"Oh, Charles, I am perfectly happy to have a place large enough to have my extended family visit. And who could not be overjoyed with seeing Mary so happy? No, it is not too much."

"And this will not interfere with my plans to have a Ball for your birthday next week?"

"Really, Charles, it is truly not necessary," she started to say, but was cut off by his finger reaching up to silence her lips.

"I will have my Ball—it has been too long since I danced with my wife, and, with your condition, I doubt we will be able to dance together much longer. Now, in three days your sister is to marry, and then one week hence we will have a Ball. Alex has already assured me that they will return from their wedding trip in time, and the details will keep your mother from going into doldrums after the wedding is over. So I think, for the sake of all involved, it will be the perfect celebration of your birthday."

"I shall be happy with whatever you wish, my love," Jane said just before her husband's lips met hers.

When he pulled back from the kiss, he reached for her hand, "Come, we must not leave our guests for too long."

Sarah Johnson

CHAPTER

XXIII

Monday, July 20, 1812

Being unable to sleep the night before, Mary sat in her window, Beatrice curled up on her lap and Benedick at her feet, both asleep. She looked out across Longbourn's lands, and beyond, as the sun began to peek out from hiding, slowly filling the sky with hues that were not often seen. It was a gorgeous sight to behold, and Mary's trembling hands held her journal to her chest as the tears that gathered in her eyes finally found their way down her cheeks. Unlike in the past when she cried because of pain, this time they were tears of joy. Today, she was to marry!

When the sun was high enough to see the words on the pages, Mary turned to the familiar journal entry she had made so long ago, and began to read it with new understanding.

> October 31, 1812
>
> Today was the first day of Lizzy's engagement to Mr Darcy. Not to be outdone however, Mr Bingley asked to court Jane. These two brave gentlemen

will, I fear, soon find out of what mettle they are made. Mama was full of anxiety after they left this morning.

I wonder—will I ever marry? I know it is the duty of every good daughter to marry and not leave herself open to ridicule and mockery, but I am not certain anyone would want to marry me. I am not the most beautiful, my glasses are thick and awkward, I am short like Lizzy, but unlike her, I do not walk often enough to be as slender.

Papa says he will leave the decision of who we marry up to us, but what if I decide I do want to marry and yet no gentleman will have me? I know what torment Charlotte Lucas receives from the neighborhood for not marrying by her age, and I am not certain I could endure such ridicule. Yet it might be my fate with the country's lack of males due to the war.

My list of requirements in a husband, if such a gentleman should exist:

1. He must be tall, but not as tall as Mr Darcy. I do not want to have to use a ladder to kiss him.

The viscount was, indeed, tall, but not quite as tall as his cousin. As she had told him when she revealed this quality to him in the library at Pemberley— *he was perfect*. If only she had known so early on in their acquaintance just how perfect he was.

2. He must be in possession of strong eyesight; it would not do to have two people with poor eyesight marry—think of our poor children!

She chuckled at the remembrance of their first meeting, and how gallant he was to go back and find her missing spectacles. Yes, his green eyes were just perfect; not only in function, but also in that she could stare into them all day and never grow tired of their brightness.

> 3. A sense of humour is a must, otherwise my not-so-graceful nature may one day become a burden to his sensibilities.

After hearing the stories of Alex's misadventures, she was certain he would never look down upon her own clumsy nature.

> 4. He must be able to carry on intelligent conversations and be comfortable speaking. Two quiet individuals, such as Mr Jonathan Lucas and myself would make a very dull house indeed.

Mary now wondered if she had been describing Alex all along, even if she would not admit it to herself at the time.

> 5. While I am certain Mr Bingley is the perfect person for Jane, I cannot imagine being married to someone who is so fidgety. A calm individual would do nicely.

Once again she thought of her intended—yes, calm and yet determined. Once his eyes were fixed upon winning her good opinion, he did not lose heart, even though she had

> 6. Unlike Mr James Lucas, he must be humble enough to admit faults, and yet amiable enough to not point them out in others.

Remembering the harsh words spoken about her by their neighbor at the party so long ago, she felt a tinge of pain in her heart still. And yet there was something about the way in which the viscount had proudly held her arm as they walked through the crowds at the theatre that impressed upon her the depth of love he felt. He would never embarrass her like Mr James Lucas had done.

Beatrice complained as she reached for the pencil on her desk, but when she was settled again, the cat began to purr in her sleep once more.

Mary went to the bottom of the list and wrote,

> Added July 20, 2812

> Today I marry the man who not only possesses all these attributes, but who, above all, loves me beyond what I could ever imagine!

She lifted the book to read the words aloud, running her hand through Beatrice's fur as she addressed her feline friend, "…beyond what I could ever imagine, Beatrice."

The cat lifted her head to push against Mary's hand.

"Yes, we will both be very content with our life."

The chiming of the clock in the hall meant the household would soon be alive with activity. Mary closed her journal, and, carefully pulling her feet out from under Benedick, she stood and placed Beatrice on the window seat, then went to the trunk that was left opened for the few items she had left to pack, and placed the journal inside, right next to the new one she had received for her birthday just a few weeks before. So much had changed, and yet it was all so familiar. Alex had pursued her heart and her hand, and when all was said and done, they had both found a place of contentment and love that could not be found with any other.

Just as Mary was closing the trunk, she heard a knock on the door, and Kitty and Lydia both entered, giggling about the events of the day and excitedly talking of all they had to accomplish before they were to meet the others at the church.

It was a whirl of activity already when Mrs Bennet joined her girls in Mary's room a few minutes later.

Rosings Park, Kent

Lady Catherine de Bourgh awoke with a start, She reached her frail hand up to her chest and felt her heart pounding frantically.

A knock at the door drew her attention. That must be what startled her so. "Enter," she called out.

"A letter has arrived," the servant declared, holding out a silver tray with the missive in the center.

She reached for it, dismissing the servant as she stood from her place on the sofa to retrieve her letter opener. She carefully heated the metal and slid it underneath the familiar wax seal of her brother's, then opened the pages, expecting to read an update on Anne and how she fared in Derbyshire.

It was a shock to see that, instead of being written from Dalmeny, the letter was addressed from Netherfield Park in Hertfordshire. *Now why would he have traveled such a distance without first telling me*, she thought as she returned to her seat.

> Saturday, July 18, 1812
> Netherfield Park, Hertfordshire
> Dear Catherine,
>
> I am certain you are quite taken aback at my writing this letter from Hertfordshire instead of from Derbyshire, so while you are in such a state, I shall assuage your curiosity quickly.
>
> My wife and I, along with Anne, have traveled here over this last week to join our other family

members in celebration of my son finally finding his heart's desire. As you can imagine it is quite the triumph for us to accept his soon-to-be-wife into the bosom of our family. It is quite an easy task, as she is already a particular part of our family through our connection to Darcy, for it is his wife's sister, Miss Mary Bennet, who, by the time you receive this letter, will be standing before the rector and taking vows to forever be connected in life to my eldest son.

I must apologize for keeping this from you for so long, but as you can imagine we have been quite busy with the preparations, and I knew you were not feeling up to the traveling it would entail to invite you anyway. I also know you would not withhold your felicitations, so I gladly accept them with all joy, and will pass them on to Alex and his wife on your behalf.

Anne is doing well and wishes me to include a letter from her. When know not how long we will remain in Hertfordshire yet. Perhaps it will be until I am needed back in Town for my position with Parliament. When our plans are made, I will write again.

Until then, your loving brother,
Hugh Fitzwilliam

Catherine stood, seething from the obvious plot her brother had devised to keep her from interrupting the wedding. She looked to the clock—it read half past two. If the two were to marry today, the ceremony was sure to be well over with by now. There was no way for her to stop it now.

Not only was her nephew Darcy dumb enough to connect himself to such a worthless family, but now Mrs Darcy's sister was to one day take over a position even she could never achieve—that of a countess. All she would ever be was the daughter of an earl, and the widow of a knight.

She sat down at her desk, pulling a piece of paper out and writing her instructions to have her band of insipid cohorts brought to Rosings immediately. She would not stand for this Bennet family to encroach upon her family any longer. It was time they learned just what she was capable of doing to ruin them forever.

The Earl of Rosebery stood beside his youngest son in the midst of the crowd gathered for the wedding breakfast. His eyes kept darting over to look at the clock.

"What has your attention so closely bound to that clock?" Fitz asked his father.

"I sent my sister a letter telling of the wedding, and it is to be delivered to her right now."

"Ahhh, I see you were intelligent enough to not give her time to interrupt the ceremony."

"Yes, I would not have her disrupt such an occasion with her vitriol." He sighed, "She has become such a bitter person—I hardly recognize her any longer."

Fitz said a little quieter, "Anne too is concerned with the changes she has seen in her mother, especially over the last year."

"If I could force my physician upon her, I would—if only to assure Anne of her health. But you know such plans will never come to fruition with my sister as part of the equation." He looked across the crowd and saw his eldest son standing with his new wife at his side, and could not help but smile at the sight. "It is a day to celebrate, and here I stand thinking of my sister. Come, we will convince someone to play a lively tune, as I wish to dance with my new daughter." They were both in step with each other walking towards the couple, when he asked, "So when will you marry? Or will you forever be a confirmed bachelor?"

Fitz did not expect such a question, and nearly tripped over his own feet.

Hugh turned back and smiled at his youngest son, then went to ask for a dance from Mary, whisking her away from her husband for a turn about the room. Halfway through, Mr Bennet stepped in to finish the steps with his daughter, then before she knew it, Mary was being led back to her husband's side, as everyone gathered around to wish the couple felicitations on their wedding trip.

Alex was glad they were not going far, but he could not voice his joy with anyone for fear of their destination being found out, so he stepped up into the carriage that looked like they would be traveling far and wide over this next week.

As the couple waved to the family and friends, Alex took Mary's hand in his own. When they were finally out of sight, he scooted closer and lifted her gloved hand to his lips. "Are you happy Lady Primrose?"

"Oh yes, Mr Fitzwilliam," her eye twinkled at the joke between the two about the first day they met and how he introduced himself to her. Alex drew his arm around her shoulder and Mary snuggled into his embrace.

"No need to get too comfortable, as well will arrive at our destination very shortly," he said.

"Oh? Where are we to go?"

"Not far at all—to a hunting lodge just north of Netherfield that Elizabeth let me know about. I spoke to the owner and he has allowed us use of it for the next week."

Mary smiled, "As long as I am with you, my joy will abound."

Very soon they arrived at the small hunting cottage, and when their trunks were unpacked and both changed into more comfortable clothes, Alex led Mary outside where a feast was prepared for them under the light of the setting sun.

As the darkness slowly encroached upon the light, pulling colors, once again, from the spectrum surrounding them, Alex stood and held his hand out to his wife. She took it and stood as well, squealing when he pulled her into his embrace and began to sway to the music Mary now heard coming from somewhere. She was too entranced to even care about how he had performed such a feat.

The two were lost to the sensations around them until finally Alex stepped back, "It is about time."

"Time for what?"

Alex stepped behind his wife, his arms drawn around her, as he turned them towards the south, where, off in the far distance, the party at Netherfield still gathered for the last of the celebrations of the day.

The dark sky suddenly illuminated with a bright explosion, and Mary's face showed awe as time and again the fireworks lit up the expanse above them.

Mary remembered well the night of Elizabeth and William's wedding, when she had seen fireworks for the first time. What had been trepidation at his touch then, was now an acceptance that he would forever be by her side. She drew his arms tighter, hugging them to her chest as she snuggled into his chest—the chest she had been drawn to since the first day of their acquaintance.

Alex watched the sky above, with his wife in his arms, as the day came to an end. And yet, there was something about it that symbolized a wonderful beginning as well.

Sarah Johnson

TO BE CONTINUED...

ABOUT THE AUTHOR

Sarah Johnson is a professional juggler in the circus of life! Married to her own Mr Darcy for sixteen years, they traveled the world thanks to the US Army. Now back in the civilian life and settled in Texas, where she grew up, they focus on homeschooling their six children and participating in church and community activities. She can often be found writing a manuscript between spills, science labs, and pencil wars, or late into the night when the house is finally still enough for her imagination to run wild! When she has a few spare moments, she enjoys just about anything crafty — scrapbooking, painting, sewing, quilting, crocheting — basically anything except knitting, a craft she swears few left—handers truly ever pick up well.

A devotee of all things Jane Austen, she enjoys exploring the story lines Jane never lived long enough to give the world. She is often found discussing with her online friends the intricacies of the novels we do have from our dearest author. It is these discussions that often lead to the plot bunnies that have now become many stories over the last few years, and hopefully further into the future as well.

CONNECT WITH SARAH JOHNSON

E-Mail:
sarah.johnson.jaff@gmail.com

Twitter:
@SarahJohnsonPL

Facebook:
https://www.facebook.com/SarahJohnsonAuthor
https://www.facebook.com/sarah.johnson.jaff

Website & Blog:
http://sarahjohnsonbooks.com

Goodreads:
https://www.goodreads.com/author/show/8118710.Sarah_Johnson

Printed in Great Britain
by Amazon